Ohio Writers' Association
Presents

Metamorphosis: An Anthology

Table of Contents

Introduction

Change is natural—it's beautiful, it's cathartic, it's necessary. But change is also painful, and ugly, and destructive. It's one of life's only constants. You can either embrace it or struggle against it but it's unlikely you could ever stop it.

Inside this anthology you will find many different forms of transformation. Some lift the spirit, some crush the soul, and some show the pathway to the future.

It's difficult to capture the essence of a true metamorphosis, but like the chrysalis, this collection contains the "goo of change," so to speak. These 27 Ohio writers have provided touching and ephemeral poems, intelligent and hilarious nonfiction, and fiction that spans from the distant past to the distant future all while being somehow grounded in the present.

We hope this collection of stories, poems, and essays manages to take your breath away, break your heart, and even inspire change in your own life—because there's no time like the present to break out of your cocoon, spread your wings, and embrace your own metamorphosis.

Wild Animals

James Siegel

We have lost so much, but in Istanbul
the dolphins are braving the Bosphorus.

From the coast you can see them surfacing
where the freighters once cut their paths through the waves.

And in Thailand the endangered dugongs
are returning. Rarely seen by human eyes,

their girthy hides glide along the channels,
grazing on sea grass, no fishnets to fear.

Even here in San Francisco we've lost
the trolley car rumble of Market Street,

but last week a coyote was spotted
walking like an exonerated man

in the shadows of the vacant buildings.
A rat in his mouth, a spring in his step,

he owned the empty Embarcadero,
and I am falling in love with his kind,

falling in love with the Kashmiri goats
breeding until they have formed an army

then invading the streets of southern Wales,
devouring hedges and flowerbeds.

Let their kind take over and multiply
like the flamingos in Albania,

the lagoons overflowing with pink wings,
pelicans and herons, creatures of flight

unapologetic in their return,
feathering the beaches we've left behind.

Even the hummingbirds in my backyard
have descended on the Angel's Trumpets,

the branches bustling with their vibrations,
they have decreed the end of winter.

The long-lost honeybees, reborn again,
drunk on snapdragons, the absence of man.

And when day fades, four-legged invaders,
families of raccoons scale the garden walls.

You can hear them digging up the rock paths,
overturning the outdoor furniture,

but who could bear to stop them when they splash
in the pond like children out past curfew.

The night alive with nocturnal creatures
refusing to mourn what we have misplaced.

Everything we're searching for is out there
where the coyotes gather on the streets

of North Beach and howl at the midnight sky,
signing out songs for a world that has died.

I am desperate to sing along, to touch
the feral animal tethered inside.

James J. Siegel is the author of the poetry collection, "The God of San Francisco,"
published by Sibling Rivalry Press. He is the host and curator of the monthly Literary
Speakeasy show at Martuni's piano bar is San Francisco. Originally from Toledo,
Ohio, his first poetry collection, "How Ghosts Travel," was a finalist for an Ohioana
Book Award. His poems have been featured in a number of journals including The
Cortland Review, Borderlands: Texas Poetry Review, HIV Here & Now, The Good
Men Project, and more.

Upon the Zinnia Petal

Curtis A. Deeter

The needles used to feel so good. The drag of CJ's scalpel across the nape of my neck sent chills down my spine. They reminded me that I was alive, that pain and healing were still possible, still real. Now, lounging in the dimly lit workshop surrounded by gearheads, spare parts, and the gummy bear stench of mod grease, I'm not convinced any of it's real. How can it be?

CJ started this place when he got bored with hotrods and PCs. Something about the intricacies of the human brain, he says. A sharp edge between life and death, between unparalleled metamorphosis and irreversible vegetable state. We all have our thrills. Mine, for a time, was mods. CJ's, a surgical obsession with slicing the "has beens" and stitching the "could bes."

He's a G at mods, too. The best there's ever been. I wouldn't trust my body to anyone else.

"Yo, you sure this is gonna fix my headaches?" CJ's current client: a tweaker turned gearhead.

These dudes stumble into the workshop, mistaking it for some kind of tech-age Mecca because they heard about his lifesaving hands, and swap one addiction for another. If the cash talks, CJ obliges. He's no Messiah, but he'll accept new Faithful guilt free if it pays the rent for another month.

"Connects all good, brother. Whatever aches and pains you've got, ain't from the tech."

"How do you explain it then? It's like a tire's burnin' rubber behind my eyes." The gearhead sniffs and clears his throat. "I get nauseous easy, too. Ever since I started comin' in here."

I can hear CJ typing away, making a show of reviewing specs, no doubt. With CJ, it's an upgrade and a show. "Yeah, I don't know what to tell you. Your diagnostics are green across the board. I gotta ask, you back on that other stuff?"

"Serious?" The gearhead's voice is high-pitched, accusatory. "Are you callin' me a liar? You know I quit that stuff way back, man."

I zone out. I've heard this conversation before. Tweaker turned gearhead drops the dope for the mods, the mods take the edge off for a while, make the dope withdrawals easier to deal with, then it's no longer enough. Why just one or the other? Why not both? When CJ's in your head, redirecting the pathways of your brain, there can be serious side effects. We sign waivers for this kind of stuff. We watch "informational materials" to truly understand the potential harm that came come from rewiring the human psyche, no matter how skilled the technician. Add dope to the mixture and there can be complications.

Time moves in funny ways when you're on the verge of changing your life forever. Minutes melt off the clock, while the hours remain frozen in place, only to spring forward when your time has come.

I run my fingers on the palm of my opposite hand, along the smooth, almost sensationless skin of my forearm, and up my bicep towards my chest. I see the scars between my knuckles where CJ once wove a million nanofilaments, and follow the dim, blue-green glow of my most recent lumivascular injection all the way back to my fingertips. I should find the swirling patterns that make me uniquely human, but even those are gone, replaced by biometric codes that allow me access to a world beyond the natural world, a place of fiber optics and data-polluted airwaves.

All of it will be gone soon, as if it were never there. I'll be gone soon, too, vanished with the most delicate of traces. It's damn near sentimental. If I had tear ducts, I'd cry.

"Tasha?" I hear my name, far off in the distance, echoing in the void between my ears. "Hey, Tasha!" CJ's on one knee, leaned in close, his hand on my shoulder. His eyes are wide with concern as he shakes me gently. "Everything okay?"

What does okay even mean? I've been a lot of things lately, but okay isn't on the list.

"Yeah," I say. My voice is unfamiliar, now. Not like when you hear yourself recorded for the first time, but like when you overhear a friend turned stranger in a public place. It's a layer, buried beneath innumerable other layers. It's a foreign language, spoken too fast in the heat of a moment. "Yeah, I'm all good. Is it time?"

CJ nods and rises to his full height. With the extenders he had fused to his femurs, he stands nearly nine feet tall. He moves with such grace now, and he's larger than life, a mechanical god among us empty flesh sacks.

I follow him back to his bay, waving at his receptionist, Machelle. As we get closer, I'm overwhelmed by the smell of bleach and synthetic air freshener. My nostrils flare, and it's not lost on me that this might be the last thing I smell. There's a drain beneath a single chair, and the ground around it is stained rust-red. No matter how much you scrub, some things never come fully clean.

On a small, rolling table beside the chair, CJ's laid out tools you would expect to see at the optometrist or the dentist, but these tools are much more sophisticated than your run-of-the-board ophthalmoscopes or scalers. They're all hard-wired to the workshop's mainframe, programmed to carry out their plethora of individual functions to an insane margin of error, all the while communicating real-time client status updates throughout the entire procedure.

"If I come within even a nanometer of cutting wrong," CJ once explained, waving his scalpel in my face, "this baby will shut right down. Takes a bit of the fun outta the job but saves me a fortune in malpractice."

CJ indicates for me to take a seat. I don't hesitate. I trust him implicitly, and there are a lot of pre-procedure questions he no longer has to ask. For us, what is usually a thirty to forty- minute interview is an exchange of knowing glances and a quick signature. Once I've signed, he disappears behind his computer for a few moments. When he reappears, he's snapping on surgical gloves and fitting a mask over his face.

"This is it," he says. "Ready, kid? Or are you startin' to feel the last-minute flutters?"

"Yeah, I'm all good," I repeat. Part of me knows I should be feeling otherwise, feeling something, but I'm completely calm. I've never been surer of anything in my life. "Let's do this."

"I started to dial down your emotional center last visit, to prepare you for the transition. You should have been feeling pretty apathetic lately, out of touch, with some minor stress responses to extreme highs and lows. Sound familiar?" I nod. That's been most of my adult life, even before we got started. "Great. Today's our last session together, before I let you free in the wild. You'll be under for about eight hours. Any drugs or alcohol over the last two days?"

"Nope." I shake my head. Mods have always been my drug of choice. "Nothing."

CJ swivels to the opposite side, grabs one of a dozen or so tubes protruding from the ceiling, and flips his surg-op goggles over his eyes. With all his gear and PPE, he looks insectile, almost alien. I envy him, his ability to change faces, to change the very nature of who he is, and to be satisfied with every competing version. I envy him, the way he never judges, never makes his clients ashamed of who they know themselves to truly be. A clear liquid travels through the tube, which ends in a needle. He finds a vein, and the cold fluid begins to course into my bloodstream.

The holoprojection of his workstation caught me off guard the first time I sat in his chair. Now, it's reassuring, and I deeply appreciate his transparency. The keys appear in the blank airspace above me, and I can read all the charts and sequences he enters. It's all meaningless, of course, but I watch transfixed as he makes all the necessary last-second adjustments.

Tiles slide apart, and a domed, plastic structure appears from underneath the floor. It's a cocoon-like apparatus that I've only ever seen from a distance. Up close, it looks more like a synthetic coffin for robots when they die.

CJ notices my apprehension and smiles. "Don't worry. The cocoon will monitor your vitals throughout. I'm dialed in, so if anything goes wrong while I'm workin', I'll know it before your body even knows." A pneumatic slot opens on the cocoon, and CJ reorients my chair so that my head is suspended just at its threshold. "What about physical sensations?" he asks. "Specifically, in your extremities. Are those subsiding?"

My vision wobbles and blurs. Everything seems suddenly far away and surreal, tinted with a golden-red hue, like I'm seeing it through a drop of nectar.

"Uh huh," is all I can manage. I can't move my jaw, and the lexicon I've built over my nearly four decades of life is slipping away.

"Goodbye, Tasha," CJ says. "See you on the other side. The new you, at least."

He slides me into the cocoon, and it closes with a hiss of air. Everything begins to fade as the anesthesia sets in. Words…I'm running out of words…to say. I…I…am finally becoming me, after all these years. With my first real smile in a long, long time, I drift off into the threshold between one life and the next.

***

CJ finishes screwing in this latest gearhead's new optical array, slides the second lens into place, then works his fingers nimbly to attach all the microscopic threads. The lens extends and retracts, calibrating itself based on his meticulous programming. Then, the procedure is done. The gearhead can now zoom in and out, capture ultra-res images, record and stream real-time video, identify a massive database of objects with a bat of an eyelash, and blah, blah, blah.

He rolls away from the chair, rips off his gloves and mask, and tosses them to the floor. "We're done here."

"Can I test it out—"

"We're done here," he repeats, rubbing the bridge of his nose. "Give Machelle a call if you have any technical difficulties, but you're all set."

The gearhead's mouth drops open. She can't believe she's getting pushed out so quickly, but CJ is too tired to care.

Everyone always wants to see more, know more, be more. But nobody wants to live more. Except Tasha, CJ reminds himself. Tasha saw what she needed to see, knew who she wanted to be, and understood that what fundamentally made her human was also making her miserable. Increments weren't enough for Tasha. Quick fixes only dulled the pain.

He opens the channel to the front desk. "Machelle?"

"Wassup, boss?"

"Any more clients on the schedule?"

"Couple walk-ins." Their profiles appear before him. Familiar faces. Gearheads chasing the quick fixes, trying to dull their pain. "Ready for your next procedure?"

"Nah." He shuts down his tools and swipes his workstation out of sight. "Send 'em home. I'm done for the day."

The city streets are quiet. A hot breeze snakes through the buildings. CJ slides the panel on his forearm open and adjusts his internal temperature. Inside, a series of cooling fans whir to life. He sighs. Is this why he started modding? To keep cool on hot summer nights, to turn his body into a glorified HVAC system?

At first, he ambles without a destination. His strides take the solarescent sidewalk squares three at a time, and familiar scenery passes in a blur. He hardly notices any of it anymore. What's the point? It'll all be gone, in the end.

Then, he realizes where he's going. He's headed for an old part of the city, an all-but-abandoned block that was once home to vagrants and tweakers, tech hotshots before them, and even more vagrants before the techies. A warzone, for a time, featured on every news brief and every forum for weeks on end. It was a place that broke itself down in the most violent of ways, only to be born anew once the cameras dispersed and the spotlights flicked off. A gray place, filled with hollow dreams and rusted metal.

CJ disables his internal coolant system and keys a factory reset protocol, something he programmed into his personal CPU in case the wrong kind of people ever got their hands on his tech. But he hesitates, unsure if he's really ready to throw it all away.

He turns a corner and gasps. Zinnia Boulevard, they call it. Where skyscrapers have been replaced by mile-high, vibrant purple, yellow, and pink stalks of bio-synthetic flowers. Beyond the city's bright lights, the flowers practically glow. They're like individual suns, each radiating heat and life and hope. It's unlike anything he's ever seen. It takes his breath away, and he makes his decision. CJ backs out of the reset protocol, but he leaves his fans dormant. There's something about the hot, sticky air on his face that reminds him he's still alive, that pain and healing are still possible, still real.

Large, humanoid butterflies flutter from bud to bud. They're golden and radiant, so carefree in choosing where to land next. Occasionally stopping to kiss antennae or to share nectar, these beautiful, amazing creatures are the very definition of dreams made reality. These people might have deleted all physical characteristics of their humanity, but in doing so, they've become more human than anyone else in the history of humankind. They've realized what it truly means to be alive, to them.

He watches the spectacle for a long time. The sun's first rays are peeking over the skyline when she alights besides him. Her face is the only part of her he recognizes from the woman who first came to him. It's the only natural born human aspect left. She had been shy, broken, and lost. She had been beautiful, but by someone else's standard. Because of that, she had been unhappy.

"Look at you." CJ smiles and reaches a hand towards Tasha. Her antennae tickle the tips of his fingers, and she makes a sound like a chime. Seeing her here, where she belongs, brings tears to his eyes. "You're exactly where you're meant to be, aren't you?"

She doesn't respond verbally. She can't anymore. Instead, Tasha flutters her wings in a splendid display of color and pattern. Above them, a dozen other butterflies appear, each displaying their own chosen patterns. Together, they cocoon CJ in a kaleidoscope of color and joy.

"You're incredible." He wipes tears from his cheeks. "I'm so proud of you."

Tasha's wings flutter once more before she takes off, joining her new family. They all disappear into dawn's horizon, and CJ leaves Zinnia Boulevard, knowing that even if all he ever does from that moment on is enhance a bunch of gearheads' sensory systems, he's accomplished one truly real thing in his life.

.

Curtis A. Deeter is an author of fantasy, science fiction, and horror. He is also the editor of arts and lit publisher *Of Rust and Glass*. When he is not writing, he enjoys spending time with his family, discovering new music, and taste-testing craft beer at local breweries.

The Hidden

Ellen Austin-Li

I know if I pulled too close
you would use your ink
to hide yourself in a cloud
and jet away.
We are more alike than not
in this sea   you and me
blush crimson when excited
and camouflage ourselves
when threatened.   I draw close
to the thick glass and watch your limbs twirl
like ribbons in a rhythmic dance
your body glistening like a raw wound—
sometimes I also feel as if my skin
has been peeled away.
We float   through our atmospheres   water & air
sensing everything   hyperaware.
Scientists say your brain
has five times the number of neurons as mine—
then tell me why humans believe
in their superior mind?
A gold-rimmed eye winks wise
in the aquarium light and you shrink
down as if you sense my scrutiny.
A crowd gathers at my side
and you retreat to your cave   in an instant
flush brown and gray like the faux coral skeleton
in the corner   nearby I overhear
school children complain they *can't see
any octopus in the tank*   I nod
and whisper *well done* to your stony shape
now part of the seascape.

Ellen Austin-Li's poetry has appeared in Artemis, Thimble Literary Magazine, The Maine Review, Rust +Moth, & elsewhere. Her chapbooks, *Firefly* (2019) and *Lockdown: Scenes from Early in the Pandemic* (2021) were published by Finishing Line Press. Ellen earned an MFA in Poetry from the Solstice Low-Residency Program. She lives in Cincinnati, Ohio.

The Sisters

Jamie E. Galioto

They passed through the graveyard each morning to get to the glade, the sisters skipping hand in hand. They each held their own little basket full of goodies and freshly picked flowers if the season allowed it. It was a ritual of theirs; the girls would picnic in front of a gravestone, talking and laughing until noon, and when they were done, they would leave an offering—one of the cakes they had brought or a pretty trinket they had picked up from somewhere. Then they would climb the wrought iron fence and play in the glade where I could watch them, unnoticed, in the form of whichever creature I took a fancy to that day.

I've never crossed the fence into the graveyard. Despite the daylight it was always dark and unsettling, and I feared it would consume me if I entered. But the girls loved the shade the trees offered, and when they were tired and sweaty from playing their games, they would return to the gravestone of their dearly departed for respite.

They fascinated me, not because they were human, a form I had never taken, but because of their seemingly unbreakable bond. They always came together; I have never seen one without the other. On days when I was feeling bold, I'd find them in the village side by side skipping down the lanes or dancing to the street fiddler's tune. At times when they did not appear in the graveyard, I would find them in their home, and I would watch them through the paned windows. They did not come when they were both sick, or worse, only one had fallen ill. This rarely happened, though when it did the healthy sister was always in a state of despair; crying by her sister's bedside or moping in a chair by the fireplace, watching as her sister breathed heavily in her fitful sleep.

I always waited nearby until they were well.

Ever since I first saw the sisters I had been struck with envy. It wouldn't be right to call them mirror images of each other. Everything was the same on both sides, their features identical down to every minuscule detail; the slanted noses, the unevenness of their curved jaws, how one ear was a little higher than the other, the tiny mole below their thin lips, and the way they stood a little lopsided because one leg, the same leg, was slightly shorter than the other. I could never be an exact replica of another being like them.

Be it a small finch or a hulking hawk, I always got something wrong; the shape of the beak or the color of the feathers being slightly off. It's not just birds, any creature be it fish, mammal, or even a flower was a form I could not replicate in its entirety. If you took one moment to look hard enough you could tell I was fake, that I didn't belong among the flock of birds perched in the tree or that the color of my petals didn't match hues—details you would think imperceptible.

People are frightened of me. Once I had pretended to be a sheep, though upon realizing something wasn't right the sheepherder tried to drag me to the slaughterhouse. Another time I had mimicked a monarch, and without thinking I fluttered onto a pretty flower in the hand of a young woman. She marveled at me for some time while I drank the sweet nectar, though slowly her expression became puzzled; her brows drawn and her face pale, then she dropped the flower and ran to the priest to have her hand blessed, screaming about a demon having touched her.

I wouldn't make the same mistake again. This time I wouldn't approach until I was sure I had gotten the form right. I studied the sisters carefully each day watching how they moved, studying their habits, and paying close attention to their voices; the sweet murmurs when they talked low, the melodiousness when they sang, and how they'd become more high-pitched when they laughed or deep when they were upset. The more I studied them the more I began to notice slight differences between them, not in how they looked, but in how they acted.

Millie would always decide the game and Molly would appoint the characters. If Millie wanted to play a knight and princess game, then Molly would assign the parts—taking the better roles for herself—but Millie never complained. Molly liked to make her characters loud and bold, while Millie made her characters sweet and charming, unless she was playing the villain, then she was ruthless and frightening. They always decided the villain by throwing a stone and seeing who could be the first to catch it before it hit the ground.

Watching them I had grown a preference for which one played the villain. Millie was more calculating with her devious plans to trap the knight, while Molly would try to outright attack him with magic. I knew their games weren't real, but when Millie was the villain and plotted her evil schemes, I couldn't help but become wrapped up in the story wishing I could play a role myself. I'd transformed myself into a stone once, and when Molly tossed me up, I shifted for only a moment so that I would fall closer to Millie and into her soft hands. That was the first time I had touched the sisters.

I'm not sure what came over me. One touch awakened a desire; I wanted to talk and laugh with them, hold their gentle hands in mine, and spin them around in the streets as the fiddler played. I wanted to partake in their picnic by the gravestone, even if it meant going into the darkness I feared and leaving offerings for their dearly departed. I wanted to become a part of their bond. I thought they would be delighted to have another sister, that they would accept me immediately as one of their own so they would no longer have to throw stones to decide the villain. I would gladly take the role if it meant I could take part in their delightful games.

When sunset came one evening and the sisters had gone home, I practiced changing. It had been some time since I took a large form. Since meeting the sisters, I only became small creatures like ladybugs and crickets; the less noticeable the better. I started with a monarch, observing my reflection in a puddle of muddied water. Satisfied I tried a kingsnake, then a mockingbird, gradually growing bigger until I became a horse. Horses were always tricky, I had to pay careful attention to their graceful and delicate, yet strong and powerful legs. Then I finally tried a human.

Humans have always looked complicated, with their dangling forearms ending in spindly appendages and their oddly curved backs that somehow held them upright on their legs. It made no sense to me how they could walk on two feet with those backs of theirs. Regardless, if I could master a horse, then a human should be no trouble. Breathing in and out slowly I morphed, my coat tearing apart and fading to skin, my body becoming smaller as my forelegs shrunk inwards and stretched out again, hooves cracking apart into fingers and toes, my back snapping as it shifted upright stumbling on new legs, head tingling as black curls grew from my scalp, and my face burned as my muzzle shrank and shifted into place as a human jaw. I finished with a gasp and fell backwards into the mud breathing heavily. When I had gotten my bearings, I checked my reflection in the puddle. I was almost there, but not quite. My reflection did not match the sisters. I tried again, this time using my fingers to mold my face like clay. At first, I had gotten the shape of their eyes wrong and made their jaw too wide, then I had forgotten about the ears and had to pull one down, ignoring the tears that prickled in my eyes, and as I moved the ear, I realized the shape of their lips was off; too thin compared to their full cupid bows. I kneeled at the puddle for hours trying to get it right until finally I was convinced I looked identical to them. Though the longer I admired my transformation, the more I felt the feeling that something was off. I felt like an obvious forgery to a work of art, though my untrained eyes couldn't spot the differences.

But I brushed my worries aside and practiced how I would introduce myself to them. I would call myself Martha, for I needed a name, and Martha was always the name of their made-up protagonists. Speaking took some effort, I had never spoken before, and my voice cracked and splintered as I practiced my words, constantly changing the pitch of my voice until I became an exact recording of theirs.

Fully confident in my looks and words, I anxiously waited for the sisters' return to the graveyard. When they appeared the next morning hand in hand as usual, I watched from behind the wrought iron gate in the form of a squirrel. Having been possessed with the idea to introduce myself, I had worked up the nerve to cross the gate, and not knowing how to climb as they did in my new form, I scampered up only to freeze at the top, balancing on the curlicues, and staring at them with quivering eyes.

They began their ritual, removing a blanket and pastries from their baskets and dusting leaves away from the gravestone. One of them carried an umbrella, for the darkened sky was promising rain—bad weather never deterred them—and she propped it against the gravestone. A sudden gust of wind pushed me forward, and before I knew it, I had tumbled down to the other side into the graveyard, hitting a pile of leaves with a soft crunch. I darted behind a tree. My heart beat faster than a hummingbird could flap its wings. I couldn't move, my ears filling with the sound of my rapid heartbeat. A giggle broke through the drumming, and my heart began to slow. Drawn by the sound of their sweet laughter, I began my transformation, for there was no turning back once I had crossed the gate.

I tiptoed around the tree remaining out of sight behind the bushes, ducking behind gravestones as I made my way closer to them and avoiding stepping on the dead leaves and sticks littering the ground. Finally, hidden behind the nearest gravestone, if I just reached out my hand, I could touch them. I could smell the lavender tea cakes they had brought with them, and a sweet scent emanating from their skin.

I thought I was being quiet, and the girls didn't indicate that they had heard me with their body language. They continued their pleasant conversation, yet gradually their voices began to drift until they became silent and still.

"Millie…" Molly whispered, biting her lip.

"Hush!" Millie surveyed the graveyard nervously. They sensed I was there.

My chance had come. "Millie…Molly…" I rasped, rising from behind the grave. Their eyes widened. They clung to one another, nails biting into each other's arms. "Hello." They screamed. I recoiled, stumbling backwards until I was pressed against the gravestone, as the girls held each other and burst into tears.

"Do not be afraid," I stammered, "I'm Martha." Sobbing, the twins shook their heads, their cries becoming shriller, and all I could do was watch them as if I'd become a statue. When they realized I wasn't moving, they hitched up their skirts and fled, knocking over their picnic baskets. For quite some time I remained there unable to accept their reaction. I had done my transformation perfectly, I looked no different from them, but just like the sheepherder they had seen something inherently wrong with me.

As the sky darkened, I moved, stepping towards their gravestone. My shock had morphed into rage, and all I wanted to do was defile their precious place, yank the flowers from the ground and trample them, spit on the stone, and kick it until it cracked. Then I read the words inscribed: *Martha Marisol, beloved sister.* My heart splintered. Pinned beneath a rock was a faded photograph of three smiling girls, hand in hand, each of them an exact copy of the other.

Jamie Galioto is a recent graduate of the University of Cincinnati. She wrote the first draft of *The Sisters* during her fall writing class, inspired by Tana French's *The Likeness*.

Chaoyangia[*]

Dong Isbister

<pre>
                              My
                         very first cry
                    awakes the morning sun
                     and it rises from
              the *chaoyangia's* Phoenix Mountain
              making young dreams shine.
           Its matutinal lights crawl on my sleepy eyes,
                     tickle my Mesozoic bird bathed in dew.
      I blink   I fledge   a reincarnated *chaoyangia*
       flapping young wings against the gale   soaring across the Pacific Ocean
perusing shoreline after shoreline   perching under a brighter morning sun,
where new dreams rise for me and those to come.   *Emituofo* glory!
</pre>

---

[*] Chaoyangia is an extinct ornithurine bird genus from the Early Cretaceous near the City of Chaoyang in western Liaoning Province, China. The city is known as the place where the first flower on earth bloomed and the first bird on earth started to fly. Phoenix Mountain in the area is known for the earliest Buddhist temple in Northeast China. Chaoyang (朝阳), meaning "the morning sun" or "facing the sun" in Chinese, depending on the intonation, symbolizes hope, joy, luck, and prosperity.

Dong Isbister found her new home in Ohio when she was a graduate student at the Ohio State University over two decades ago. She has a deep interest in writing about immigration, cultural identities, location, and environment. She has published creative and scholarly works in English and Chinese.

A Place for My Brother

Susan Oelbracht

In May when it rains, the garden smells of sweet promise, but this spot in the woods is not like that. Not like that at all. The dirt smells of decaying leaves and mold, and the unturned Ohio clay is hard, not like the garden dirt Daddy plows each spring while I throw compost ahead of the rototiller. This day I pull the shovel and half-empty bag of peat moss from the shed and drag it to a flat spot behind the house among the hickory trees. I'm ten, and barely as tall as the shovel itself. I punch the blade into the ground and jump on the top of it like my pogo stick, but I keep falling backward only to have the handle conk me in the head, making my ponytail all lopsided. I need more tools, so I hurry back to the metal shed, making sure to take the blue shoe box from K-Mart with me. It says *Trax* on the side, size 5, and contains the remains of my infant brother.

In the shed, I find a trowel and a crowbar under the work bench, making note of exactly where I found them. The trowel is on the bottom shelf, handle pointing toward the door, at a perfect right angle to the edge of the bench. My hands continue to shake as I place a leaf to mark the spot. Daddy is very particular about his tools.

Kneeling in the dirt, hickory nuts digging into my knees, I grab the trowel with both hands and stab at the ground like a murderer in the horror movies on television. When the muscles in my arms burn too much, I scoop the clods out of the hole with my hands. I should have brought some gloves, the brown ones with the pink and blue flowers Mom bought at the garden center on Saturday. They're really pretty. She hid them from Daddy in her underwear drawer. He would call them "frivolous". He thinks everything pretty is frivolous, especially her. But there isn't time to go back for the gloves. It's already late afternoon, and I have to be done by dinner. Daddy would say I'm resourceful to bring the crowbar to loosen rocks and chop through roots. More stabbing, stabbing, scooping. Sweat drips off my face into the earth and disappears without a sound.

The sun is setting. I've heard the term "six feet under" but I don't know if that means six shoes piled on top of each other or stacked heel to toe. The hole doesn't look deep enough, but it will have to do. I open the box's lid and pack peat moss all around my brother. Daddy says it helps things grow, and even though I know my brother's dead, I do it anyway. I close my swollen eyes as I replace the lid. I slide the shoe box into a white plastic trash bag and nestle it into its home. I pack peat and dirt around it, breaking up the heavy clods with my hands as I say a hurried Hail Mary. An earthworm tries to wiggle its way deeper into the moist, dark lump of earth that I hold in my hands. At first, the thought of worms crawling around my brother makes me anxious, but then I remember that boys like slimy things, and I finish my work, putting a big flat river rock on top of the spot. I clean and polish the trowel and put it back in its place, handle pointing toward the door.

It's late when I get back to the house, and Mom can't seem to talk very well, and her skin is the color of dough. Mom told me earlier not to call an ambulance, but I run to the neighbor's house, and Mrs. Campbell calls them. They take her away, and I tell Mrs. Campbell that I'm okay to stay by myself since Dad will be home soon. It's not really a fib, because "soon" could mean anything. She looks relieved and scurries away. She doesn't ask questions. Adults never do.

I lie down in Mom's bed but can't sleep. Maybe if she comes home tomorrow, we can make bread. I'll warm the water and she'll test it with her pinky finger to make sure the temperature is right, and then she'll let me stir in the sugar and yeast so it can come back to life. She'll mix in the flour and tap some onto my nose, and then give me my own ball of dough to knead and shape. While the bread is rising, we'll talk like we always do. This is the best part. This time we'll talk about the baby. Maybe she'll say she's sorry that I had to work so hard, and that I did a good thing, and not to worry about the mud and blood stains on my pants because she'll scrub them herself before Daddy sees them.

Mrs. Campbell brings Mom home two days later and puts her right to bed. She sleeps a lot, though sometimes when I go to check on her, I think she's only pretending to sleep. She doesn't want to talk anymore.

I scrub my own jeans, but the stains don't come out. I'm glad they still show.

***

That was forty years ago, and yet I still smell those decaying leaves as I sit in the police station waiting for the detective. I'm nervous, not about being arrested or anything, but about discussing something so intimate. These words have never been exposed to the light of day, but then neither has my brother until now.

"So, you have information about the article in the paper?" Detective Kennedy's curly hair is graying at his temples. He leans forward, bark-brown hands relaxed on the table. Behind him a crack in the drywall runs from the top of the door jaggedly toward the floor, a scar barely covered in bone white paint.

"Yes. I read in the paper that the remains of a baby were found on Antioch. That's my brother. What do I have to do to get him back?"

The detective looks at me, evaluating. He stands and reaches up toward a black box on the wall behind him. "You don't mind if I record this, do you?"

"Of course not."

He sits back down and pulls a silver pen from his shirt pocket. This is a quality pen, I notice, thick and weighty, with his initials engraved in the side. I'm glad he's not using some cheap plastic pen to take notes. He asks me again to state my name, date of birth, social security number. "Now tell me again why you're here."

"To claim the remains of my brother. Apparently, they were found by the utility company digging over on Antioch Drive."

"And how did your brother come to be there?"

"I put him there."

The officer alerts, like the English Pointer my father used for hunting, still and focused.

I take a deep breath. "In 1970, my mother had a miscarriage at home after falling down the steps. She made me promise not to call an ambulance, so I thought the best thing to do was to bury him. I was ten."

"Did your mother tell you to bury the baby?"

Already he is looking to fit this neatly into a chapter of the Ohio Revised Code. "No. She was too weak to say much other than *'Don't tell your father.'* I knew I had to clean up the mess, so I did the best I could."

"Was anyone else home? Where was your father?"

"No. My older brother Charlie spent the night at a friend's house. My father was off drinking. Besides, it would have just caused him to go into another rage. He did that a lot when he was alive." I didn't figure the detective needed to know about the fight they'd had that morning. The name calling. *Whore!* The sound of a slap, someone falling on the oak floor, and the closet door being thrown open, the knob splintering the drywall where it hit. Daddy kept his hunting rifle in that closet.

"So, she fell down the stairs. Then what?"

"I ran down the steps and told her I was going to call an ambulance because she was holding her stomach and sweating. She told me not to call, and just to get her a bag of ice. Listen, it was a long time ago and I don't remember much of the details."

I remember everything. The desperation, like an electric current under my skin when I heard the Buick's tires on the gravel as my father left me. The uncontrollable shaking of my legs as I tried to make them run to the freezer for the ice. The smell of blood and sour vomit. First hers, then mine.

"Well, it doesn't seem like something you would forget."

"What's the point, Detective? My mother lost a baby, and I did the only thing I knew to do at the age of ten."

"Why didn't she want an ambulance? Your father didn't know about the pregnancy?"

"I don't know, Detective."

I had often wondered myself. Though I never heard them talk about it, her oversized sweatshirts didn't quite hide her half-moon belly, not that he ever really looked at her. Did he see it? Was I supposed to keep the baby himself a secret from Daddy, or the way the baby looked?

No matter. It's easy to keep secrets when no one asks questions.

"How far along was your mother in her pregnancy?"

"It was forty years ago, and I'm not an obstetrician. Tee was tiny—probably weighted less than two pounds, but he had hair. Brown, curly hair."

Detective Kennedy studies me for a moment. "Your mother named the baby?"

"No, of course not. I told you—she was weak. I named him Tee." The detective gives me the cop look—the one that says I'm pretending to believe you, but I don't. "The baby had dark hair—not like my father."

Tee's hair reminded me of Mr. Jameson's, my teacher at St. Mary's. When the school hired him, their first black teacher, the town buzzed like a hive. Daddy threatened to pull me out of school, but I lied and said I didn't have any classes with Mr. Jameson, so I got to stay at St. Mary's. Mother knew it wasn't true, but she went along with the lie. She never said so, but I think she liked keeping a secret from Daddy, and she liked Mr. Jameson. I liked him too because he would look me in the eye, nod and call me by name, "Miss Kathleen". When I told him that I couldn't go to college because only rich people did that, he loaned me a book about Booker T. Washington and that's who I named my brother after.

I wanted Tee to be smart and courageous and clever. I wanted him to be different than Daddy. Daddy hated anyone who wasn't like us—chinks, spics, kikes. And I wanted to have some ammunition in case I needed it. His wife giving birth to a Black child? It would have caused Daddy to lose his mind. This secret was powerful, and I liked that it was mine.

When Mother was late picking me up from school, which was often, Mr. Jameson would sit on the steps with me to wait, and he taught me how to play chess. He asked me questions—even my opinion—on all kind of things. When Mother would finally arrive, he would call out, "Be well, Miss Kathleen."

We grew up together, Tee and I. It was him and me against the world. At first.

Sometimes I would go out in the woods and sit by his grave and read him stories. Of course, the first one was about Booker T. I wanted him to know just how smart and strong a boy could be. "You'll need to be clever and brave like that," I would tell him, "I don't know what it's like where you are, but here lots of folk don't like Black people. Daddy said Blacks are stupid and lazy, but he doesn't know Mr. Jameson."

I smile at the memory, but when I look up, the detective is not smiling.

"What else do you need to know, Officer?"

"Did you bury anything with the body?"

"A pacifier, my heart-shaped lucky stone—white with shiny gray flecks. And I wrapped him in a baby blanket. My blanket actually. I kept it from when I was little. Mother threw it away, but I found it in the trash and hid it. It had rocking horses on it—red, white, and blue rocking horses. It was edged in that soft, silky material I liked to rub between my fingers when I sucked my thumb."

The detective shifts in his chair and looks down at his note pad.

"Sorry, that was more information than you were looking for. I was told not to call an ambulance or tell anyone." I shrug. "I knew I had to clean up the mess before Dad got home—he was very particular. I knew Tee was dead. I couldn't just throw him in the garbage, so I did what I thought was right."

The detective nods.

"Look, I know you're going to have to check all this out. How long will that take? When can I have my brother back?" For the first time in my life, I don't know where he is. My heart races, and the air is stuffy. I look at the clock on the wall.

"We can't release evidence…" He catches himself. "We can't release your brother's remains until we do some forensic work, and of course your mother would be his legal next of kin, and we'll need to talk to her."

"Forensic work? What are they going to do to my brother?" I picture some lab-coat-wearing milquetoast of a man scraping Tee's little bones. I feel lightheaded. "Do you have some water? I think I need a glass of water."

"We want to be sure of the baby's identity and verify your story. Where does your mother live now?"

"She lives on Franklin, but she won't admit this is her child." I stand and pace between the door and the desk. "In forty years, she hasn't talked about this baby, never even acknowledged his existence, even after my father died. I've been the one that took care of him, that kept him safe until the utility company started digging the place up."

"Let me get you that water." Detective Kennedy leaves the room, shutting the door behind him.

Okay, he's letting me calm down, watching me in that two-way mirror no doubt. I can do this. I take two deep breaths and sit back down. What if she did want to claim him? What would she even do with him? She doesn't know him. I do.

As a kid, I had done my best to get the bloodstain off the wood at the bottom of the stairs where Mother had landed. The blood had soaked into the oak floor, so there was a big dark spot where she laid until I could take care of things. A few days later I saw that she put a hook rug over top of it, but I kept moving the rug. She kept putting it back. Every day her stomach got flatter.

When Mother felt better, we started having dinners in the dining room again and it was my job to set the table. I always set a place for Tee. The first time I pulled the high chair out of the storage closet and set it up at the table, she was startled, like she had seen a ghost. I hoped she had.

"What are you doing?" Her voice trembled.

"I'm setting a place for my brother."

She turned and scrambled around in the utensil drawer, her back to me. "Well, I highly doubt your big brother's going to fit in that chair. Charlie must have grown half a foot in the last month alone."

"My other brother."

Mother said nothing.

"I heard my name. What's for dinner, and what's up with the high chair?" Charlie sauntered into the kitchen and plopped down onto a seat across the table, hands behind his head.

Mother turned, her eyes that of a drowning woman. She looked at me as she spoke.

"Your sister is playing a game. Put the chair away, Kathleen."

I saw Tee in that highchair, curly brown hair and little fists pounding the tray. He smiled and squealed. I held my mother's gaze. The air was thick like the blood I had wiped on my jeans just a week or two ago.

"No."

Charlie laughed. "You are so grounded! Little Miss Goody Two Shoes talking back."

Mother whirled. Her voice crackled like cellophane. "Charlie! Get your damned feet off the table."

Charlie sat up slowly and glared at me. Mother never swore.

"Why am I getting yelled at? She's the one talking back."

I gripped the top of the highchair. "The chair is for Tee."

"Who the heck is Tee?" Charlie looked confused. This was not unusual.

"Must be your sister's imaginary friend." My mother's eyes were gray steel, fixed on mine. I started to speak, and she interrupted me, her voice low now, like an animal. "The place setting can stay, but you will put that chair away. Your father will be home soon. We will not discuss this nonsense at the dinner table."

Or anywhere else, as it turned out. I was trying to give birth to a conversation that was as dead as my brother.

My father showed up, pink tea roses in hand. My mother's favorite. He never acknowledged the extra plate at the table. Even in his ignorance, he knew when to let sleeping dogs lie.

But every day, I set a place for Tee. Every day.

***

The detective returns, water bottle in hand. He sinks into the chair behind the desk. Taking a breath, he squares his shoulders and asks for my mother's name, address, phone. He doesn't look up. He records the data. "Do you remember the date your brother...the date when all this happened?"

"Of course. My brother was born May 15, 1970." I want to tell him that it was a cool May day, the kind that hasn't quite made up its mind what to be, and the dogwoods were blooming. I want to tell him that my brother's tiny, spindly body was reddish brown—an alien really. I want to tell him that I was glad my brother's eyelids were shut tight, because there was so much blood. So much. It would have scared Tee to see it. I want to tell him that when I tried to wipe my tears with the back of my hand, I spread my mother's blood across my face, and sometimes I still see it in the mirror. I want to tell Detective Kennedy all of those things, but there isn't space on the form, and he doesn't ask.

"So, what do I have to do here, Detective? My brother deserves a proper burial this time."

"We'll have to talk to your mother, of course, and your brother Charlie. I don't know how much time the forensics will take…could be months before we get the tests back. And we'll need to get a DNA sample from you too." He looks at me out of the corner of his eye.

"So where do I have to go to do that? I'll do that today. Months? Really? Do you have brothers or sisters, Detective?"

My question seems to anger him. Shoulders back, he lays his hands flat on the table and looks at me. Hard.

"How long would be an acceptable time for anyone to keep your family away from you, Detective?" I hate that my voice sounds small and thin, like the communion host at St. Mary's. "Please."

I hold the officer's gaze. I hold my breath. I hold my dead brother's hand.

Detective Kennedy's jaw unclenches, and he stands slowly. I reach out my hand to shake his, and as he responds, I look down, breathing in the sight of his brown skin against the alabaster of my own. My left hand reaches up and, for a moment, cups the back of his. I don't mean to do this. I spin away then, grab my purse, and move toward the exit.

His voice, behind me, is softer than before. "I'll do what I can to speed the process along."

I don't stop long enough to say thank you.

***

I drive to the Lake Erie beach that Tee and I escaped to so many times growing up. The water is bluer than it was back then. The sun warms the bitter January air, and I sit on a piece of bleached driftwood.

"So, what do I do now, Tee?" In my mind, he smiles and puts his arm around my shoulder. In my mind, he is forty years old, tall and lanky, and likes to play chess and listen to jazz. He is smart and clever.

You'll figure it out. Remember, you're the resourceful one.

I laugh. That's what the old man used to say. *My little problem solver.* He said it when I fixed the handlebars on my bike after Charlie wrecked it, and when I figured out how to keep the squirrels out of the bird feeder. He also said it when I learned how to unjam my 12-gauge. I had convinced Charlie to teach me to shoot, even before I was allowed to get my own gun. I'd practice shooting into the hill down in the quarry. I got really good and won first prize in the 15-18 age division in the Mason Turkey Shoot, which made the boys really mad. I put the trophy on the nightstand in my father's bedroom, on top of a white crocheted doily. Mother moved it to my room. I put it back, told her Dad was proud of me, and I wanted my own gun for Christmas. She said no, but the old man got it for me anyway since Charlie didn't like to get up early during hunting season. Charlie was lazy and stupid, which were the worst things a person could be.

I never did go hunting. All my parents' fights ended the same, with my father reaching for his shotgun to point it at my mother, or himself. One day I got to my gun first. He looked down the barrel, and then at me like he only just noticed I was there, his eyes wide like a doe. He moved out after that. Problem solved.

Tee would have been five or so at that time. For Christmas I got him a yellow dump truck, and I wrapped the box in silver paper and tied red ribbon in a bow on top. We opened it in the woods on Christmas morning before anybody else got up. The leaves, hardened by frost, crunched beneath my boots, and my breath hung in the air before disappearing like a whisper. I brushed the snow from the top of a tree stump, plopped down, and crossed my ankles in front of me. I imagined the look in his brown eyes when he pulled it from the box, delighting in the levers that moved the bucket up and down, picking up nuts and dirt, and depositing them in another pile. I watched him play until my toes went numb from the cold, and it was time to make breakfast for Mom and Charlie.

Mother and Charlie. I picture their horrified faces when a police officer tells them he wants to talk about a dead baby. My laughter is drowned out by the sea gulls squawking overhead. Tee chastises me. *You've got to call them before the detective does.*

"I suppose you're right."

This is going to be hard on Mom.

"I hate it when you call her that."

The reality is—she's my mother too.

"Only in name. She never cared about you."

Call Mom.

"I'll call Charlie first."

Tee stomps away. He seldom gets pissed with me. My chest feels hollow.

"Tee, wait." I brush the sand from my jeans and follow him to the car.

***

A good daughter would drive out to tell her in person, but I lost that title years ago. I remember the day, in fact. It was spring break at the university, and as I drove back to Mother's house my mind grappled with a pervasive sense of homelessness. I thought I would find my nest at college. I had anticipated immersing Tee and me into the diversity that the school touted in their literature. But there were parties only Tee was welcome at, and conversations only Tee could be part of. My voice felt as irrelevant in this new world as it had been in my old one, a decaying leaf in the woods.

When we arrived at my mother's house, she was baking. The familiar, musty smell of yeast hung in the air, and in the middle of the flour-dusted counter a pregnant mound of dough waited to be turned into braided Easter bread. "It's good to have you home." Mother wiped her hands on her yellow floral apron and reached her arms out, pulling me into an embrace.

"This isn't my home anymore, Mother." She was remarried, and my old room has been turned into an office—a reminder that I was an orphan.

"Shush. You know what I mean. You're just in time to punch down the dough. You always loved doing that as a little girl."

She was right about that. Yeast bread rises twice. The first time, the bone-colored ball of dough rests in a warm kitchen until it doubles in size, the surface stretching, effacing. At the peak of fermentation, I would punch it down to release the air that had built up. There was something deeply satisfying about landing a punch and feeling the dough collapse around my fist.

"So, how's school going? Have you decided on a major?"

I sifted flour onto my hands so the dough wouldn't stick. "Political Science—in prep for law school—with a minor in African Studies."

"Why in the world would you be interested in that?" Mother busied herself polishing the spotless dining room table.

"Apparently, it's a family propensity, isn't it?"

She sunk into a high-backed chair just as the dough shrunk around my clenched fist.

***

As I said, a good daughter would drive out to see her mother to let her know about the visit she was going to get from the Police Department. I call on the phone instead.

"It's me. I wanted to give you a heads-up."

"Kath. It's so nice to hear from you. It's been so long."

"Yeah, well the phone works both ways." I refuse to allow her to pull that absent daughter crap on me. "You're going to be getting a call from the police department."

"Oh God, what's Charlie done now?"

"It's not Charlie. I don't know if you saw it, but there was an article in the paper recently about the remains of a baby being dug up at the old house. The baby is Tee. It's the baby you lost." I wait. I expect a '*What are you talking about?*' or for her to hang up or something. I wait for the sound of a weak cry, or some kind of desperate plea. I picture her imploding.

"Okay." Her voice sounds like mine—I never noticed that it had the same timbre. I hear her breathing. "Okay. You and I need to talk. I'll come over tonight."

"Little late, don't you think?"

"Yes, I do. But we can start now."

"Tell it to the detective." I hang up the phone.

"Happy now, Tee?" Tee says nothing.

"You know how many years I spent aching for a conversation. Now it's her turn."

***

It takes forty weeks to get the call. The tests are done, Detective Kennedy told me on the phone. Could I come in?

The creases in the detective's forehead make him look old and wilting.

"I trust that everything's in order. What's the process from here? Is there a release form or something I have to take to the coroner's office?"

"The coroner confirmed that the child was likely stillborn. DNA tests also corroborated your story."

I think about asking about the DNA test, but I don't. In my mind my brother is tall and brown skinned, and there is no red clay under his fingernails, and no sunburn on his neck. He is a man who stays and takes care of his family. He is brilliant, and the source of my courage. Our stories are intertwined like braids of Easter bread.

"So where do I have to go?"

"Sit down, please."

"What? More questions? I thought we were done with all this." I perch on the edge of the chair. The scar on the wall behind him has silently lengthened in the months since I first sat in the room, or perhaps the walls are closing in.

"We're releasing your brother's remains to your mother."

"Oh, hell no! No." I am standing again, pointing my finger at him. Detective Kennedy is still as stone, his chair pushed against the back wall. "What the hell is she going to do with him, put him out with the trash on Monday? Now she wants to be the responsible one? I'm the one who buried him and cried over his dead body. I'm the one who baked a cake every year on his birthday, kept his place at the table, read him Langston Hughes by the lake." I can't catch my breath or control the sobs that sputter like a garden hose from my chest as I slide down the scarred wall, my hands over my face, any more than I could control them at age 10. "I'm the one that taught him how to be a man of substance." My voice was high, floating near the florescent lights. "A man worth a conversation."

I feel Tee's arms around me. *You were always worth a conversation, Kath, even if those around you were mute.*

***

I find myself back at the beach, not entirely sure how I got there. Maybe Tee drove. I smile at the thought. What car would he drive? A German make probably, given his practical nature, but candy apple red—he has always been more adventurous than me.

The icy gusts off the lake serve to blow away most of the thoughts ricocheting in my head. Most, but not all. November is a good time to walk the beach. Children and gulls have fled, and gray snow clouds roll low in the sky. I turn up the collar of my trench coat, button it at the neck, and walk with Tee down the beach, arms crossed in front of me to keep the wind at bay.

Tee is the first to speak. *Call her.*

"So, she can explain why she's stealing you from me? That conversation can't end well. Besides, she should have called me."

You haven't answered your phone in weeks. The voicemail box is full. Who's avoiding the conversation now?

"She wants to talk after all this time? She didn't want to talk to me when I was ten, and where was she when I was sixteen? You were the only one I could talk to about boys. It wasn't sage advice from her that kept me from 'going all the way' with Bobby Timms. That was you. She was doing plenty of talking all right, but mostly to drunks at that dive bar in town."

She worked there. What did you see in Bobby anyway?

I respond without thinking. "A way not to be alone." I shiver and pull my coat tighter around my body. "But then I remembered I had you."

A dead brother's a poor substitute for a real relationship.

"Oh, like Bobby Timms wanted a real relationship! The only thing Bobby wanted was a handful of my 34 C's and whatever else he could get. It was the fear of getting pregnant and disappointing you that kept me from going down that path."

You sure it wasn't Mom you didn't want to disappoint?

"You can't let down somebody that has no expectations of you. I was as invisible to her as you were."

Why didn't you introduce her to Roger? He was no Bobby Timms.

"What are you bringing Roger up for? I told you at the time—it just wasn't going to work."

Roger was perfect. We met in our thirties. He was smart, curious, took me to New Orleans so I could hear blues done right, and made me laugh with his dry sense of humor. I knew his interest in me was romantic, but I viewed him as a dear friend. The romantic thing never felt right. He asked more questions than any person I had ever met, but when he asked to marry me, it was one too many.

Why couldn't it have worked with Roger? He loved you, you know.

"He drove a red Mercedes. I could never marry a man that drove a red Mercedes." Tee doesn't laugh.

Good job of deflecting the subject, by the way. You still need to talk to Mom if only to find out where I'll end up—she's in control of that now.

"We'll see about that."

Are you afraid of what you'll say, or what she's going to say?

"I'm not afraid of anything." I yank at the collar of my coat, pulling it tight to my neck.

Still, I got your back, like you always had mine.

***

She picks up the phone on the first ring. I don't waste time on pleasantries.

"What right do you have to take Tee away from me, Mother?"

"No one's trying to take him from you. We can decide together what happens from here. With Tee and otherwise."

"One big happy family—the dead and the dying." As soon as the words leave me, I feel Tee's disappointment. I hold the phone against my ear listening for the sound of her breath.

Moments pass. "I was not the mother you needed. I may not be now."

"I don't need mothering. Not anymore. How could you leave me alone to clean up after you? I buried my brother. You never once asked about him."

"This isn't about Tee. It's never been about Tee. It's okay to say it—I wasn't there for you."

"No, you weren't. I buried your son, protected you from the old man, but who protected me?" I slapped tears off my cheeks. "Don't tell me you didn't hear me crying in my bed."

"I heard. Your anger scared me even then. When you fell asleep, I would crawl into bed next to you."

"I doubt that."

I hear her say quietly, "Unless you have issue, I'll have Tee cremated and we'll have a service. You can choose where he's buried. I'll be in touch. It will be okay, Kathleen." The voice is firm and warm and comforting. It must be Tee's.

I wait for Tee to say something else. Anything. I hear nothing but a relationship being reduced to ash.

***

"This is so ridiculous, Tee. She's having a service at a funeral home? For what?"

I had decided to go, but also decided that I would leave with my brother. Who would stop me? Those pasty guys at the front door in bad suits and worse cologne? She may have stopped me legally before, but she was too weak physically and emotionally to stand up to me now, just as she could never stand up to the old man. Maybe next Christmas I'll buy her a backbone. I'll wrap it up in silver paper with a big red bow on top.

The Funeral Director opens the door, smiles and sweeps his arm in the direction of the room on the right. The combined smell of gardenias, formaldehyde and air freshener makes my stomach turn. I make note of the proximity of the door, the fact that it opens outward. I hesitate, take a step into the room, prepared to walk past her and go directly to Tee.

24

At the front of the room is a full-sized coffin, the lid open. I must be in the wrong room and turn to leave. Then I see my mother standing off to the side, leaning on her husband. She looks tired and frail, and her makeup fails to cover the lines that run jaggedly across her face. Mother wears a black shift dress. It is not her color, and for a moment I wish she had worn the gardening gloves with the pink and blue flowers.

I look again across the room at the gaping wooden box, angry that she had allowed herself to be talked into buying a full-sized coffin in addition to an urn. She had always been frivolous with money.

"What the hell, Tee? Do they have the urn in the coffin, like a Russian nesting-doll thing?"

Tee laughs. *Quit bitching and check it out.*

I will my legs to walk across the room, but my knees begin to buckle, and I feel someone slip an arm around my waist, supporting me. I turn, half expecting to see Tee in the flesh, but it is her. She is stronger than she appears.

She looks me in the eye. "I'm so sorry, Kath. You deserved better. I was as empty as a promise, but I gave you what I could."

"You gave me nothing."

Tee's voice is a distant whisper. *She gave you me.*

My chest feels as though it's collapsing in on itself. My charge, my brother, my confidant, my friend. My Tee. My Tee had come from her.

Her arm tightens around my waist, and we cross the room together. The brown marble urn is sitting in the middle of the coffin and tucked in the corner is the yellow dump truck. The stuffed tiger I bought when he was three is in the other corner, as well as the soccer ball from Tee's tenth birthday, and the poster of Janet Jackson from his fifteenth. Every gift I had ever left for him in that spot in the woods is here. Albums, books I had forgotten about, photographs, all in perfect condition. I'd assumed the neighborhood kids had taken the gifts, which was okay by me. But they had been kept safe and cared for. My lucky stone laid on top of the urn. White with gray flecks, smaller than I remembered. And there were letters, in my mother's handwriting.

Hundreds of them, some yellowed and brittle, but others fresh as dogwood in May. I hear her say, "When I lost the baby, I lost you both." The scent of decaying leaves blows through the room.

I see my hand reach out and pick up a letter written on stationary with lavender roses around the edges. It begins, *"Dearest son: You would be so proud. Today your sister graduated with honors…"*

I drop the letter as I drop to my knees and lean my head against the softness of my mother's belly. I let her stroke my hair. I call out to Tee, but he doesn't answer.

"Tomorrow," she says, "We will bake bread."

Susan Oelbracht is the former President and current board member of Literary Cleveland. She writes poetry and literary fiction and is a life-long Ohio resident. *A Place for My Brother* is her first short story to be published.

Spring Forward

Elizabeth Barrickman

In Ohio, the first days of spring
are more like the last days of winter.
One charcoal smudge blurs into the next.
It's easy to ignore the promise
of a sweet breeze from the south
and the vague scent of darling buds.

I want to bust out like a new green sprig
daring the last frost
to freeze my limbs dead.
I want to wake up like animals
driven by forces they don't understand
and challenge a road with speeding cars.

Elizabeth (Betsy) Barrickman lives a quiet life in Warren, Ohio. She's spent most of her working years as a designer in the memorial industry and is perpetually rewriting her own epitaph. Currently, it reads, "She made good pie."

Experiments in Living Chemistry

Kelly K. Ferguson

The first morning after my last day of fifth grade, Mom informed me that my summer vacation and girlhood were over. I was reading *A Wrinkle in Time*, hoping to pull a tesseract to another planet, when she knocked while opening the door.

"Great news! You get to attend those Summer Enrichment Seminars you enjoyed so much last year. And you can wear" —she pointed with her thin, well-manicured finger at the second drawer of my white dresser— "*your little bra.*"

That was how she pronounced those words, *italicized*, the final "ahhh" birthing in slow motion as it burrowed like a parasite. I ignored her. She smiled and shut the door, knowing I didn't think this news was great at all; I was going to be shuttled off to a glorified babysitting venue against my will, and the two pink pop-up tents on my chest could no longer be ignored.

I stared with great intent at my book, praying that Mrs. Who, Mrs. Which, and Mrs. Whatsit would come for me, after which Calvin O'Keefe would remove my glasses, see past my frizzy hair and braces to the real, beautiful me, where my oddball quirks increased my charm.

I pointedly avoided the drawer where the dreaded white-eyelet garment lurked. Inside, straps crisscrossed over a tiny pink rose, cups padded with wisps of cotton to puff the nipple buds into a shape. A video at school had warned me that I might need one of these someday, a training bra. The word conjured images of Wheaties box champions, teams of preteen girls racing, arms outstretched, as they competed for Olympic breasts.

The pink rose didn't fool me.

Sure, I was in training. Training for hell.

***

The first day of the Summer Enrichment Seminars I lucked out. Mom enrolled in summer school, so Dad would be driving me. No way would Dad confront me about anything to do with undergarments. That morning I insisted on wearing my yellow rain slicker to cover myself, even though it was July in Alabama.

"I'll *freeze* in there," I insisted. I had a point. Southerners, in retaliation against the heat, generally keep their interiors at meat locker temperature.

Dad gave me a sideways glance, but he didn't argue. We drove in silence. I didn't even whine about why I had to attend more school right after regular school was out. I hated the constant shuttling about, and many of these so-called educational events were suspect. One time, my mother enrolled me in a baton twirling class—held inside a trailer. And all the coach did was yell at us while she ate McDonald's. After that, I begged my father to let me stay at home. But then he dropped this on me: "Boy, when I was a kid, I sure wish I could have done all this great stuff."

Dad had grown up in a cold, grimy Catholic orphanage in Buffalo, New York, and there was just no arguing with that. He had scrounged and strived so I could live the pampered life of a middle-class ingrate. Still, I'm guessing Dad never had to Fancy Strut in front of a former soybean queen who yelled, "Glimmer, little glo worm! Glimmer!" between bites of her Big Mac.

All I am saying is this: if you are going to eat, you should bring enough for everyone.

I was plunked on the curb of Holt Elementary with a bologna sandwich in a rumpled paper bag and a Chronicle of Narnia stashed in my shorts. I filtered inside with the other nerds of Tuscaloosa County. We were handed a regimen ranging from Life Sciences to Macramé, and dutifully marched to our classrooms so we could become enriched, like flour. The seminars were for "gifted" children, those of us who had passed some third grade Mensa quiz that made sure we never got to spend our summers hanging out at the pool or skipping rocks.

Our first activity of the day was Dramatic Arts, which was held in the gym. When I put on my slicker that morning, I had counted on the usual Alabama indoor arctic blast. The gym was a sauna. Within a minute I had mortifying armpit stains and removing the slicker wasn't an option. Soon, sweat began to drip down my back. I waited in dread for one of the odd looks directed at my slicker to become an outright accusation. At some point I knew some loudmouthed girl (there was always a loud-mouthed girl) would shout, "Why are you wearing that stupid jacket?" while everyone stared, and I stammered through some lie. I carefully shifted around to keep myself a moving target. To my relief, this teacher was the bossy kind who left no room for chitchat or humiliation.

The woman's hair was albino blonde drawn back in a severe bun. She wasn't old or young. She didn't wear makeup or speak with a Southern accent. Her thin lips like a slash said there was *a special treat* in store for all of us. We would get to perform *Macbeth*. She informed us she was *a real live* director from the Alabama Shakespeare Festival who was going to help us perform a modified version of the play. We came to understand this woman was no ordinary educator and we were *very fortunate* to have her. This opportunity would be an *experience*.

We tried to look impressed even though we had no idea what she was talking about.

"Shakespeare was a great playwright!" shouted Norvin Richards, a scrawny dweeblet who came up to my neck. Norvin was a tow-headed philosophy professor's son with glasses held around his head by an elastic band.

The director dutifully acknowledged Norvin's superior knowledge, which fired the geek cadre into life. We were all used to being number one in our classrooms, but now all the number ones were gathered together. Who was number one now? We didn't know anything about the Great Bard, but we were familiar enough with school plays to know that someone would get to be the star. The director furrowed her brows for a minute before she arranged us in groups. Then she stood back, hand on hip, scrutinized, frowned, and rearranged us again. This second grouping appeased her. I was moved to the back. The slicker stuck to my skin where her hand cinched my forearm.

With a heavy sigh (*Oh! Woe! Why had she agreed to this?*) the director handed out scripts and explained how things would be: there wasn't much time, and this wasn't how a theatre was usually run, but she would make do. We were not to *roughhouse* around the stage props, which were *very generously* on loan. Auditions would be held at our next meeting. The performance would be held in two weeks.

It wasn't too hard to figure out that if the name of the play was *Macbeth*, then the female lead was Lady Macbeth. While the director paced and lectured, I took inventory of the competition. These girls with bony limbs and terrycloth onesies weren't of the sleek blow-dryer tribe from public school. One girl with a freckle-smeared face adjusted her scoliosis brace. Another bent to scratch her scabs. No gleaming, tanned, tube-topped cheerleaders here. I had a shot. The Norvin kid poked my arm. A shot of panic ran through me. I had almost made it through the day unnoticed.

"Hey, lemme tell you a secret," he said.

I bent down. He cupped his hand over his mouth, leaned into me, and belched.

***

Our last enrichment of the day was Living Chemistry. Within a minute we were all in the thrall of Miss Bussian, a college chemistry student with honey-blonde hair, tan skin, and a mesmerizing Aztec skirt. The despair of our lost summer vacation melted in a desire to merge with her orange-blossom scent. She loved us each the best, we could tell.

Miss Bussian gave us each a Petri dish and a sterile cotton swab. We were instructed to lightly touch a surface, and then lightly touch the agar, and see what grew on the special medium. Just like real scientists!

Being the enriched child I was, I gripped my swab and overanalyzed the situation. I had already bombed Life Science earlier that day. While everyone else *oohed* and *ahhed* over the paramecium flagella in their microscopes, I had faked fascination over a water bubble. The pressure of redemption weighed heavy. This was my chance to make visible the microscopic, to reveal an object's true nature. Everyone else seemed confident as they ran around the room, dabbing the aquarium or the pencil sharpener, but every time I started to make a move, I froze. I mean, who really cared to reveal the inner spirit of a crayon?

Then I thought of something I wanted to know more about.

I snuck the swab into the bathroom, locked the door, pulled down my shorts, and performed a preteen version of a pap smear. I slipped back in the classroom, stealthily lifted the glass lid, touched the cotton end the exact way I was instructed, and sealed the dish.

***

"Out, damn spot! Out, I say!" I practiced in my closet to escape parental scrutiny. If I tried to add intensity, I only sounded shrill. Mostly I sounded drab, put to shame by the dramatic skills of the housewife who mourned "those dirty rings" on her husband's shirts, before she discovered the delights of Spray 'n Wash. For the sake of High Art, the word "damn" had been approved for minors, but it stuck in my craw. Raised in the Bible Belt, I just couldn't shout a curse word. As I tried to project "How tender 'tis to love the babe that milks me," I knew the word "milks" was gross somehow, causing me to fumble.

Yet I persevered. My desire for the female lead was rooted in a long history of frustration. As an early puberizer who had always been tall for her age, I had always been assigned male parts in school plays.

In first grade all the girls were sunflowers, except me—the tree.

In the play about a cavity, I was the dentist.

In *Charlotte's Web* I played Fern's father, Mr. Arable. For my big moment I got to waddle on stage in overalls, slop Wilber, and shout, "That's one terrific pig!

In our fifth-grade production of *Broadway Musicals* I lip-synced "Go Greased Lighting" in a mechanic's suit.

29

I was determined to break my long string of roles performed in drag, so in my closet I persisted. I knew my voice was wrong. I didn't sound like a Scottish queen driven to psychosis, but the *blah blah* of a *Peanuts* character with a southern twang. But I had experienced transformation again and again in my piles of books, so technically, I knew the experience was possible. Everyone knew it took the pressure of a real challenge to forge greatness.

***

That next day the director shouted our roles while we squirmed. My heart thudded as the bit parts were doled out. Eventually, there were no female parts left except Lady Macbeth, and I allowed myself a giddy whiff of hope until— "Kelly Ferguson! Macduff, loyal Thane of Fife."

I didn't even get to be a Weird Sister, and worse, I had a *wife*. Lady Macduff and I avoided eye contact. Ashley Phelps, a willowy girl with blond hair, freckles, and a soft voice was awarded the prize role. She squealed for joy, and we all hated her.

One look at the director, already back to grabbing people by the elbow, made me realize it was no use complaining. For our first read-through I wandered Birnam Wood (potted banana trees) with Macbeth, Norvin Richards. As the director went to work on the Weird Sisters we giggled and roughhoused with the props. That we were not supposed to touch anything made wearing the helmets and scurrying around all the more awesome.

***

In Living Chemistry, Ms. Bussian told us to check on our Petri dishes.

"Don't be disappointed if you don't see much," she said. "It can take up to a few weeks."

We had labeled our dishes so everyone could keep them straight. Needless to say, I had no intention of writing "My Vagina" with black marker on a piece of masking tape, so I wrote "Inside Desk" instead.

Despite everyone's excited swabbing, most kids only had a few dark specks, while most had nothing at all—Special Class once again specializing in the mundane. But in the back, one disc emerged from the wash of spotted beige. Encased in glass, a black furry caterpillar crawled across its dish.

"Wow," said Miss Bussian. "That's really something."

She checked the label and looked at me askance, but no way was I telling. Everyone gathered around the dish and gawked. I worried that Ms. Bussian, a science expert, would know vagina growth when she saw it, and that I would be outed somehow for cheating. Given the creature coming to life in the Petri dish, perhaps I should have been more worried about personal hygiene. God knows what that swab picked up from the Holt Elementary bathroom. But health was a small sacrifice to pay for glory. I found myself pleased as Miss Bussian examined the dish in the fluorescent light.

My macramé bracelet was crooked. I still only saw water bubbles in Life Science. The more I tried to project in Shakespeare, the more my atonal voice matched my limp cardboard sword. But in Living Chemistry, I was a star. As the weeks passed, other kids had blotches, smatterings, maybe a little gray fuzz. An unfortunate few, like Lady Macbeth, still had nothing (ha!), her surface blank.

Miss Bussian tried to interest us in the periodic table, and she brought in some liquid nitrogen, which was pretty cool, but really, we all just wanted to see what was

30

growing in our Petri dishes, or, more to the point, what was growing in *my* Petri dish. By the end of the week the caterpillar had morphed into a baby hamster surrounded by tornado funnels dervishing in the air.

"Dude!" said Norvin Richards in admiration, whose beige slab sported only an unimpressive smudge.

***

The day of the play it was time once more for me to don male drag. My mother slicked back my long hair with Dep gel. I was allowed to wear makeup, but only base and extra eyebrow pencil, not eye shadow or lipstick. The true horror of my situation emerged when I put on my costume—tights with a man's white shirt (my father's) worn over the top and belted. The shirt, though, came up too short for comfort and was transparent. With my mother involved, there was no avoiding another debut— *the little bra.*

Today girls can opt for a training bra that is more like a little tank top—the Velcro version of shoelaces. In the seventies, bra training was more serious. We were thrown into the deep end of adjusting straps that dug into our shoulders. We trained for discomfort, for how to adopt a constant half-smile when in fact we were freaking out over the elastic strangling our torsos. We trained for the telltale straps that everyone could see through our blouses, and how to maneuver our arms so we could hook and unhook the back. The "wiggle in" technique worked for the novices, where we assembled the gear, stepped in, and shimmied up. All this training supposedly existed for the purposes of modesty, but these bras only seemed to highlight the two chest beacons that would forever define a part of how we would be perceived as women.

When I shuffled out of my room in my Scottish warrior garb, my parents' hands slapped over their mouths, trying to disguise their mirth. My overall look was completed by a pair of old moccasins, making me a dead ringer for the last pirate Mohican. My parents had just pulled it together when I reached for my sword wrapped in aluminum foil.

"Lead—on—Macduff," Dad sputtered, and they fell over again, wheezing and gasping with tears glittering cruelly on their cheeks. I ran back to my room and slammed the door. No way was I going to be in that damn play. Although eventually my Catholic heritage of guilt and duty kicked in as my parents reminded me of my responsibilities. When they wanted pictures, however, I balked. No gruff voices, guilt trips, or sighs from Dad could make me budge on this point. I didn't care what sort of selfish, ungrateful wretch I was.

"She's feeling *sensitive*, Patrick," Mom said, the corners of her mouth twitching, and all I can say is it's a good thing that sword was fake.

At the auditorium, Lady Macbeth was in full regalia. She wore an empire-waist lavender gown with floating gauzy layers, her blonde hair piled in a medieval topknot with ribbons. We thanes and witches choked with envy. I looked around to discover that all the other Scottish warriors at least had a real tunic and real tights. My tights were not tights but support hose—I looked as though I had forgotten my pants. Now I was angry. Not only had I been miscast, I had parents who would rather be thrifty than make sure their daughter didn't look like a complete idiot. Perhaps some of my own Scottish ancestry kicked in; I was ready to go onstage and kick some serious Elizabethan ass.

While internal pep talks and personal belief are the cornerstones of children's literature, they're best left to those with the ability to tesseract across outer space, a skill I would soon pray for. Once I had been given the part of Macduff, I had lost interest in the play, goofing around with Norvin Richards during rehearsals and reading Madeleine L'Engle books at home. I hadn't learned my lines. When it was time to take the stage, I had absolutely no idea what to say.

Terrified my shirt would fly up, I minced across the stage as I kept my sword clutched by my side, shoulders hunched to hide my *little* bra. I patched together pieces of dialogue, hoping to mask my botched lines, but the hot white lights and auditorium of staring parents did nothing to help. My tepid storming of Dunsinane Castle had the texture of Velveeta. The bird-chested Norvin Macbeth could barely lift his sword. My brawny guns, strong from after-school activities and fueled by resentment, made the outcome of the duel a gimme, my execution perfunctory as I splatted the corrupt king to the ground in one swat, thereby killing whatever there might have been of a crush as well.

Tomorrow?

Nobody thought so, not three times, not even once.

My one consolation was that all the enriched kids bombed. Lady Macbeth wailed through her soliloquy with wretched melodrama. The Weird Sisters were depressingly normal, hunched, and giggling through all the best lines. As thanes flung fake mutton at one another, I wondered if anyone had really ever seen a paramecium in Life Science. The director spent the performance running around and hissing lines. Her hair pulled tighter and tighter, causing her expression to resemble a botched face-lift. Banquo's ghost was the only success. His comedic interpretation, a brilliant improv in which he "did the Hustle" around the banquet table, brought the performance to life. At curtain call we shuffled out hangdog to take our bows, but Banquo sprang to the front, arms outstretched as the applause meter surged from golf clap to the real thing.

Afterwards I hid backstage pretending to fuss with my props. I didn't want to face my parents, who would tell me I had been good while their amused smiles told me otherwise. I was in pantyhose. All the parents would chat with other parents, who would all say how great it had been. I would have to congratulate Lady Macbeth and have my picture taken with Lady Macduff—my *wife*—all of us squirming while the adults suggested we get together and play sometime.

I was too old to play.

I made my escape. The heavy door clicked, erasing the small-talk echoes of the auditorium. I ran down the hallway, my hose sliding on the glossy linoleum. I checked both ways before entering the Living Chemistry classroom. It was dark and silent except for the gurgle of the aquarium. I tiptoed to the back of the room, where the rows of tiny, quiet moons gestated on the counter. The growth in my Petri dish was now a long-haired guinea pig smooshed between two clear Frisbees. I put a brown paper towel in my hand to keep from leaving fingerprints. I formed a tiny teardrop of drool, and just when it was about to drop, lifted the lid and gently spat on the fuzz of my genius.

Kelly K Ferguson is the author of *My Life as Laura: How I Searched for Laura Ingalls Wilder and Found Myself.* Her work has appeared in McSweeney's Internet Tendency, The Cincinnati Review, South Writ Large, Storysouth, The Gettysburg Review, and other publications. She lives in Athens, Ohio.

I Am Gilgamesh

John Y. Graham

Memories from my early years are odd, rhomboidal things I have trouble fitting into a context as if I've borrowed them from someone else's life. I remember with clarity stacking cans from the pantry into towers higher than my head and feeling it was my purpose. I ate ashes from the fireplace and banged my head against things. How could I ever have been that boy?

I recall less clearly either of my parents in those years. They seemed benign intrusions from a too-large world into my space. I had erected walls I considered obvious boundaries, but they ignored them. When they brought their faces too near, I turned away and barred the gates.

What I do remember with great vividness from the time of the Other Me was the dream. It's my oldest memory. As far as I know, it started the day I was born.

Doctors still theorize about the sleep state of autistic children. If they'd ask me, I'd tell them: it's a world of order and chaos in equal parts. Sleep came to me as either a welcome cushion of nothingness or a dizzying swirl of partial images and half-thought ideas as if fed through a blender into my brain. I luxuriated in the nothing. I often awoke screaming from the blender. When I did, the dream saved me. I would awake with a cry, cower at the crack where mattress met wall, melt back into sleep, and, as the broken things began to rise again on their dark, limbic wind, a voice would speak.

It sounded like a giant standing behind me, proclaiming, calmly and hugely, "I am Gilgamesh, ruler of all I see."

Every night, the marauding fractals in my mind jumped at his eminence and marched like soldiers away, one by one, to leave me in peace. The words continued, deep and kingly, over and over.

"I am Gilgamesh, ruler of all I see."

***

I wasn't around other children much, sometimes at the supermarket or while at the doctor. I ignored them. Mother invited another boy of my age to our house when I was four. I screamed and hit him. He cried. His mother came to get him and called me cruel.

How so? Is a rock cruel? Or a stump?

I don't know how my parents put up with me. I rarely looked into their eyes or responded to their voices. To do so could cause a breach. I pushed my mother's face away with a screech many times. I struggled from my father's arms when he held me. What a wound I must have been.

I can recall a few images of joy: my toys ranked and filed and the universe in order; and a few of jaggedness: a piece of furniture moved, a new food at the table, a stranger at the door. As hard as I fought to maintain my walls, the barbarians got through and taught me time and again, I was not armed to survive "out there." But I had Gilgamesh and I faced "out there" the best I could.

His voice persisted in my dreams for years and often followed me into my waking hours. Curiosity had never been a driving part of me, and I had no facility with words, but I had to know. I stood in front of the chair where my father sat, slapped my little hands on my thighs and blurted, not so much a question as an utterance.

"Giggamesh."

I didn't understand the concept of happy, but I felt goodness radiate from Father's face. He stooped to catch my eye but ended up addressing the back of my head.

"Giggamesh?"

"Giggamesh," I repeated to the floor next to my feet.

"Do you mean Gilgamesh?"

He opened to an illustration in my Tales of Heroes showing a warrior with a helmet and spear standing astride a mountaintop. "Gilgamesh was a Sumerian hero who feared nothing. Remember when I read you the story?"

I didn't, but I felt the hero in the painting had to be my Gilgamesh.

***

The most traumatic day of my life came the following year, my sixth. My father died in a bicycling accident. You'd think nothing could be worse for a boy, but his death didn't register until years later. The scathing event was school.

The doctor put me in a class at a special needs academy. Mother walked me into the school and left me with a squat brown woman with a thin red smile. I watched the floor, counting the tiles as The Smile guided me down the hall to a door. I looked up into eight round faces and a seat for me waiting among them. I screamed and hurtled away, veering from the hands of a man in brown lace-ups, through the front door and to my mother's car.

I cowered in the space beneath the glove box. Mother knew not to touch me, so she spoke, letting the drip of warm words calm me. Back at the door of the class, she knelt and, as my panic began rising, whispered into my ear.

"Be my brave boy."

Gilgamesh would be brave. He ruled over all he saw. "I am Gilgamesh," I whispered to my shoes—and that was enough to propel a first step toward my seat among the barbarians.

***

That Christmas seemed lopsided with Father gone from the side of Mother, but I kept my eyes down and my walls up. I rearranged low-hanging ornaments, opened presents, and stopped when one revealed a toy helmet similar to the one Gilgamesh wore. I placed it on my head and instantly felt mighty. An uncommon urge to connect with my mother turned me around, beaming in my new helmet. She was weeping, something I'd seen before but had never stopped to consider. This time, I sensed crying was bad, and bad things sent quakes through the land and cracks up my walls.

I touched her face and shared my power. "I am Gilgamesh."

Her tears didn't stop, but they seemed to turn from cold to warm, bad to good. I had achieved.

***

At almost seven, "I am Gilgamesh" was the longest phrase I'd spoken. Maybe it excited my synapses because new words came faster to me. Not all of them pleasant.

One, in particular, stands out.

I had never been motivated to exercise, but I decided I wanted to swim. The community pool, with its fluid aquamarine contained neatly within its bowl of concrete, lured me. Mother read under an umbrella as my teacher gave me lessons.

In my first summer, all I could do was flail and sputter happily. In my second, I learned to move forward.

A big, cold-eyed nine-year-old with broom bristle hair and two leering minions showed up that second summer. I never realized their laughter was directed at me. I swam-splashed for half an hour and then climbed out to let Mother towel me. The trio watched from several chaise lounges away.

"Look at the retard."

They all laughed. Mother shepherded me away. She didn't tell me what a retard was, but I knew.

Two sessions later, I slopped up the ladder from the pool to find myself face to face with the boy. He had a wicked grin mirrored by his minions. My walls protected me from their looks but not his words.

"I hear your dad killed himself so he wouldn't have to live with a retard."

Whatever strength had developed in my right arm from two summers of breaststrokes and American crawls drove my little fist into his cheek. I can't imagine it hurt him, but it scared him enough to send him wide-eyed and screaming through the gate, drawing the others along with him. Maybe it was the surprise of being attacked. Maybe it was the horror of being touched by a retard.

Gilgamesh prevailed that day, but there were more bullies and years of beatings. I fought back sometimes, but mostly I endured.

***

The doctor said it was a good sign when I told him I liked a girl. Thirteen-year-olds should begin recognizing the differences in genders. I don't know that gender came to mind when Sara first approached me. She had quick brown eyes and reminded me of the squirrel in a cartoon I liked.

I met her—or I should say, she met me—in the cafeteria of the public junior high school in which Mother and the doctor placed me. My language and social skills had improved enough to make me eligible for its "guided learning class." I read at an elementary level and no longer hit the kids around me. My concept of others being barbarians had mellowed to others simply being others. I had developed a fascination for history, and it served as a path into learning.

I was eating with two other "special" kids when Sara breezed over, set her tray down opposite me, and said, "It's too quiet over here." The other two shriveled. I stared at her for a good five seconds before dropping my eyes to the table. I detected no threat, and I didn't feel like a retard in her presence. She ate and chattered about her dog Roscoe and how I should have a dog because dogs get along with everyone.

She never came to my table again, and that made me unhappy—an emotion I'd only begun to quantify. She ate with four other cute girls who had boys around them all the time, and she might as well have been a magical bird on a high pole for all the chance I had of being near her again.

Gilgamesh had faded from my dreams as if he couldn't keep pace as I grew up. I didn't think to call upon him to help me reach Sara. I had become like normal kids struggling through the trials of adolescence without a hero.

One morning, our English tutor taught us about the first alphabets and the birth of writing. She mentioned the Sumerian cuneiform script, and I did something I hadn't done in a while: I looked at the floor and blurted.

"Gilgamesh!"

In that class, blurting was not only accepted it was expected. Our tutors rejoiced when a student showed enthusiasm. This one stood up, as if to salute the flag and said, "Excellent, Justin, excellent."

During the rest of the class, I tried to recall the sound of the voice in my dream. The absence of Gilgamesh was heavy on my mind as I walked the hallway between classes and saw Sara coming the other way. One of her popular girlfriends walked on her right. A ninth-grade boy with dark eyes and a lip stud stalked menacingly on her left.

I had no notion of what I was about to do. I veered across the hall and halted in front of her. I stared into her neck—my bravery hadn't the power to take on her eyes—and I began to invoke my champion.

"I am—"

The ninth grader interrupted. "A fucktard."

The popular girl looked aghast.

Sara smiled. "Justin."

From then until I graduated high school, Sara and I were friends. I wasn't emotionally advanced enough to consider romance at first, and by the time I understood such things, we were solidly friends, and that was that. She said she liked me because I was different, and she believed I had something deep and interesting about me. That, also, was a notion I'd never considered. Could I be interesting?

We went for walks, rode bikes, hung out at my house with my mom. She invited me to parties, taught me to dance, and instructed me how to kiss in an awkwardly platonic session that more resembled CPR training than kissing. My social advancement went supersonic. Neural pathways that used to wander lined up for Sara.

Her family moved the summer after graduation, and I've never seen her again, except on Facebook.

Something else notable happened that summer. My doctor dropped the ASD from my diagnosis. I remained a bit socially awkward and had obsessive-compulsive periods, but people began viewing me as normal.

My doctor cited the medications and therapies. I credit my mother's patience, Sara's inspiration, and Gilgamesh. In any case, he pronounced me a "minor miracle, one of the fewer than twenty-five percent to recover to such an extent."

***

At twenty, I went to the community college to study history and English with the intention of teaching special needs kids. At twenty-four, a state-sponsored program allowed me to attend an out-of-town college for a Master's in education.

I write this now because, as I pack to leave Mom's house, I feel the need to examine the man I am now vis-à-vis the stranger I was. I also need to document a discovery of something long unknown.

Mom surprised me with a box of DVDs, transfers, it turned out, of videos she and my father made in the nineties. She wanted me to have a visual record of our lives when I moved. Most of the home movies I'd never seen. In the years before Mom stored them away in a closet, I wasn't receptive to them.

I'm glad she remembered them and glad my curiosity had developed enough to drive me immediately into the box and to fire up my laptop. I relived Christmases and Thanksgivings I'd barely been present for the first time around. I saw how beautiful my parents were together and how vacant looked the little boy in their arms.

Mom watched over my shoulder and selected one disc in particular. I placed it in the laptop. The image was wobbly and shadowy, shot by the nightlight of a four-year-old boy's bedroom. I could barely see myself asleep at the crack where mattress met wall. Mom must have been behind the camera because my father lay in bed spooning me, one hand on my hip, the other under his head. He looked up at the camera and put a finger to his lips, warning my mother to silence.

The camera pushed closer, framing my father as he rested his head, mouth next to my ear. The microphone only picked up certain frequencies well, and my father's whispering wasn't one of them.

Mother turned the volume up and said, "Listen."

I watched myself, a broken boy unequipped for the real world, in the arms of a father I barely remember who, in gentle repetition, armed me the only way he knew. I made out two words, and I understood.

"I am…" he whispered.

John Y. Graham has been writing ever since the doctor held him up by his ankles and burped him. Being an ad copywriter and producer for 40 years honed his discipline as a writer, but fiction has been his passion. *I Am Gilgamesh* was inspired by his experiences with two young men on the spectrum and the tantalizing thought that there was a 25 percent chance they could grow to higher functionality and socialization.

On Seeing My Great Granddaughter in the Womb
Robin Mullet

In the peachy glow of the amniotic fluid, you float,
tiny upturned nose, juicy lips, barely seen as you hold up
your hands and feet, hiding from the world a little longer,
wanting to keep that weightlessness, that warm safety,
the muffled song of your mother's heartbeat.

You are still consciousness, still wise
in the ways of the universe—until that jarring moment
of birth, of light and sound, when your first cry will erase all
you have known before and you come into the world
empty, a clean slate, waiting to be filled.

I want to fill you up with the magic of this world.
The plaintive cry of the first phoebe of spring,
the sound of wood frogs, their translucent egg cases
in ephemeral vernal pools, the buzz of bees on blooms.
I want to take you deer-counting in summer's dusk

as we did your father, to teach you
the names of birds, of trees, of wildflowers.
I want you to know, even though this world can be dark,
that tears will be shed, there is also this earth that holds you,
grounds you, a womb like the womb of your mother,

made green and alive by seed, like the seed of your father.
You are the child of the child of my child, and although
I will not see you grow to womanhood, I will be there in
the stardust that is in all of us. In the cool dirt beneath your feet
you will feel me, a woman who loved the earth and who loved you.

It is in stories that we learn what it means to be human. That is why Robin Mullet writes narrative poetry, most often about ordinary people—their lives, their loves, their heartbreaks, their triumphs. She has been published in several journals and has a collaborative chapbook with haiku poet, Holli Rainwater, called *The Curve of Her Arm.* (Nightballet Press, 2019)

Lump

Devon Ortega

Pony decided to sell her baby as soon as she knew it existed. She told us she was pregnant before but this time, it was real. She laid down on the living room carpet and pulled up her shirt, showing us the slight curve of her belly blooming from her unbuttoned jeans and a knob of a belly button; her pregnancy already far enough along to turn it inside out.

"Touch it," she said. "it's hard."

We did, and it was. Pony squished her protruding belly button down then allowed it to immediately pop back up.

"Maybe it's cancer" Fran chewed at a hang nail while trying not to look at Pony's exposed, deformed stomach, failing.

"It's not cancer, you twat," Pony kicked at Fran's ankles and missed, Fran dancing back from Pony's swinging leg. "I can feel it moving in there. It's a baby, dumbass."

Fran and I didn't know what to think—Pony of the many boyfriends, Pony of the late nights and needed alibis. Our Pony, big sister, knocked up with a creature big enough to pop out her belly button like a periscope on a submarine, watching our reaction, judging. Mom and Dad were going to be pissed.

"What are you going to do?" Fran said, keeping her distance from any of Pony's potentially swinging limbs.

Pony was only 16, still in high school, but she was both the smartest and the dumbest person we knew. Pony could manipulate any person to do anything she wanted, she was smart like that, but I was still doing all of her schoolwork even though I was only in middle school.

Pony patted her stomach and pulled her shirt back down. "Think I could get a thousand dollars for him?" She looked at me like I had some mathematical insight to the value of unborn babies.

"How do you know it's a him?" Fran said, eyes wide at the mystery of it all.

"Because I can feel his tiny baby dick pressing up against me inside. Jesus, Fran, I don't know, okay? I just know."

"You going to tell Mom and Dad?" I asked, fully aware that they would have to find out eventually.

"Hell, no!" She said, grunting up off the ground and tugging at the zipper on her jeans—the metal teeth straining to hold her pants around her slim hips since the button no longer buttoned. "Dad would have a shit fit. You better not say anything neither."

We swore we wouldn't, but it wasn't much of a promise. Fran and I might be young and dumb but we both knew babies had to eventually come out somehow and when they did, moms and dads tended to find out.

***

We only had a few days to keep Pony's secret; Pony was going around town asking anyone from the lady working at the post office to the secretary at the elementary school whether they knew anyone who would like to buy a baby. The secretary sent a letter to the house for "The Parents of Penelope Hale" after calling several times and being told by Pony herself that her parents were "most definitely not home and certainly wouldn't be back anytime soon." Pony never got the mail, Daddy did. Boys never wrote her letters, so why would she?

Daddy didn't make her kneel on the heater grates like he usually did when he was mad at us. He didn't bring out the belt or lock Pony out of the house. He just quietly folded the letter back up and waited for Mom to get home. He didn't even yell. Mom, on the other hand, yelled. She called Pony a whore. She said, "I'm not raising another God damn baby!" Fran and I hid in our bedroom playing board games until the storm passed.

Down the hall, Pony raged back, at first saying she loved the baby and she was keeping it then yelling that she was going to throw herself and the shitting kid inside her over the bridge into the Little Wolf River. She said she hated everyone in the house and she would burn the whole fucking shack to the ground. I never thought our house was a shack. She even got her own room, so I didn't know what she was complaining about.

After it had gone quiet for a while and Fran and I became bored with sending our pieces around and around the Monopoly board in a useless attempt to buy Park Place, we went down the hall to the living room. Mom was sitting on the couch, facing the TV but it looked like she was staring at the lenses in her glasses instead of watching anything that was happening on the screen. Her face was engraved with, maybe not hate, but at least 40 pounds of anger. Daddy was asleep in the chair, his big, bald head drooping, chin dug into his chest. A snore escaped his mouth, and it was like you could see sparks coming off of Mom. It was an oddly tense scene and Pony was nowhere to be found.

***

She talked about naming the baby Jonah but spelling it different, like Joena, but then decided that whoever she found to take the baby would want to name it themselves, so she just called it Lump or Lumpy.

"Outta my way! Lumpy keeps kicking me in my pee hole!" she would yell as she pushed past us to use the bathroom. "Lump must be blocking up my blood flow because look at how swollen my ankles are!"

Mom wanted Pony to keep the baby after all so that pretty much confirmed for Pony that she would get rid of it.

There were plenty of "that's your blood" arguments and "take care of your responsibilities" lectures. Mom never stopped badgering Pony about who the daddy was, but Pony refused to give a straight answer.

"I'm not giving some asshole the chance to have a say about what I do with this thing," Pony told us while painting her nails an awful taupe brown color she stole from the pharmacy.

"That's ugly," I said.

"You're ugly, scab face." She groaned a bit as she attempted to get up off the floor and stomp away, but she was getting pretty big, so she just settled for adjusting her position angrily.

"Are you really going to sell the baby?" Fran said, chewing on a spit soaked lock of her baby-fine hair.

Pony sighed, swiped her pinkie with another brush of color, and capped the polish bottle. "I don't know, Frannie. It seemed like something people did all the time in that movie. I mean, what's in it for me if I just give it away?"

"Uh, not having to raise a kid for the rest of your stupid life?" I said, fully expecting her to hit me but hoping she was too tired from growing people inside of her to get to me.

"Fuck you, Mags. You don't know shit." She slowly got herself up off the floor without another word. She didn't hit me. She didn't even slam the door as she left. I wished she had slammed it. It made me feel more terrible that she didn't.

***

Pony had the baby on the first Thursday after school let out for summer vacation. I felt sorry for her only getting less than a week of freedom from school before she had to have her vacation come to a screeching halt. But Pony had been incessantly complaining about the heat, the discomfort, the swelling, and how she had gotten fat for so long we were surprised she didn't just punch the baby out of herself months ago. She was ready. Past ready to be done with it all and had said so herself.

Mom and Daddy drove her to the hospital after she spent a full day in bed with what she said was "poop cramps." Fran and I stayed home. Played Monopoly. Drank as much Mountain Dew as we wanted. Ate all the cheese slices in the fridge.

Mom came home the next day and took a shower. She fixed her hair and put on makeup and went right back. She didn't ask us to come with her to the hospital to see the baby. She didn't even say whether Pony had given birth to a baby or a goat or a giant mosquito until Frannie asked and Mom only gave a clipped "yep" as a response, told us to eat Spaghetti Os for dinner and she would be back later. We ate "dinner" at 3:30 because we were bored and then ate crackers spread with margarine after because we were still bored.

We had the same conversation about fifty times: Do you think she had the baby yet? Do you think she kept it? Along with all of the other baby related questions people ask while waiting for a child to arrive into the world. We could only speculate about all of it. We became convinced that Pony had the baby and then sold it to a kindly nurse while Mom's back was turned. Or that she snuck the baby into the bathroom and flushed it away before anyone could stop her. We didn't allow ourselves to consider what would happen if she decided to keep it. Mom had set up a crib in Pony's bedroom that she had gotten from a girl at work, but Pony had filled it up with her dirty laundry. We didn't even have a single diaper.

***

Fran and I fell asleep on the couch but woke up when we heard the Chrysler pull into the drive. Pony came in first and went directly to her room.

"Pony?" Fran said, sleepy voiced yet expectant.

Pony responded by slamming her bedroom door.

Mom and Dad came in a few minutes later, Dad grinning and Mom's face as blank as a Moon Pie. The baby was swaddled in Daddy's arms, as pink and snub-nosed as a piglet.

We both leapt from the couch and across the laminate floor to see this creature, this thing that once lived inside our sister but now was sleeping in our kitchen.

"We named him John," Mom said matter-of-factly as she unloaded supplies onto the counters from plastic hospital bags.

"Does Pony hate him or something?" Fran asked. I rolled my eyes at her question. She knew damn well Pony hated the baby.

Mom said nothing. Dad asked if we wanted to hold him. We did. One at a time we were allowed to hold the baby for the first time. His face was covered in tiny scratches from his sharp fingernails, and he simply was not as cute as even my ugliest baby dolls but there was something charming about the heft of him and sweet warmth of a real live tiny thing in my arms.

"Okay, I've had enough." I handed the baby back to Daddy. I couldn't decide how to feel about it all. I wanted to talk to Pony, but she had to be in a mean and angry mood, so I didn't. Mom was on the phone with Grandma as she noisily put away baby stuff in the kitchen, the phone cord strung across the room, swinging dangerously as she moved from one cabinet to the next. She was faking being happy as she talked.

"Ralph's over the moon about that child already! Always wanted a boy!"

Daddy sat in his chair, letting the baby curl his tiny hand around his fat, rough finger, cooing into John's ruddy little face. I could see why Pony didn't like the baby. Something about the whole situation didn't sit right with me but I couldn't put my finger on it at the time. I felt guilty for feeling jealous even though there was no way in hell I wanted Daddy to sit me on his lap and gaze at me with that weird look on his face. It was likely a mix of awe and pride but all I knew was it made me mad for some reason.

I wished I could be more like Pony in that moment, go to my room and slam the door, wait for another boy to call. But boys held no more interest to me than doing Pony's homework. Instead, I just sat there with Fran and Daddy in the dark living room with this tiny stranger that seemed to take up all the leftover room.

***

Pony was sitting on the frozen ice pack Daddy used in his lunches to keep the ham salad cool while he was at work.

"Makes me feel better," she said.

I didn't know if she meant her lady parts or if it made her feel better emotionally to do something gross one of Daddy's things.

Fran sat on the floor, the collar of her shirt damp from being chewed on.

"Damn it, Fran, you always have to have something in your mouth!" Pony sneered as Fran made a wet sound, chewing on the fabric. "How do you ever think you'll get a boyfriend when you always gotta be sucking on something?" Then Pony laughed for reasons we didn't understand, "But what do I know, huh? Guess I should have taken a page from your book and…" she sighed and let the smile drift from her face back into the sour look she favored.

Pony looked around the messy room, the crib still full of dirty laundry and additional piles of random clothes and used plates scattered across the floor. The baby John either slept on Daddy's chest or snuggled in the crack between the couch cushions if anyone ever decided they needed to put him down, which wasn't often.

"I've got to get out of here," she said, finally looking at me. "How much money you got?"

I thought about the card in my sock drawer from "Down South" grandma that I got for my birthday that had twenty dollars in it and the tootsie roll can that contained maybe another fifteen. "Not much," I said.

"Can I borrow it?"

I shrugged. Borrow meant have and I didn't want her to have it, but I knew Pony never really asked for things. She was being kind by asking. She was taking it regardless of my answer.

"I have money," Fran said, crawling over to a pile of crap in the corner of the room and digging out her buried Miss Piggy coin bank. She shook it to prove it contained more than just a few nickels.

"Tommy says I can live with him and his grandma until we figure out what we are going to do, but I need a little cash to get by, for gas and stuff." She raised her hand to swipe her bangs out of her face and winced, looking down at her chest. "These things are huge but they're hard as rocks and they hurt like hell." She poked her right breast with her pointer finger.

Then Pony started to cry, awkwardly positioning her arms as she covered her face with her hands, trying to delicately avoid hitting her swollen breasts with her forearms. "I'm so ugly now," she said between sobs. "I hate that fucking kid, Mom and Dad, everything. I've got to get the fuck out of here!"

"You're not ugly," Fran said, her voice barely above a whisper.

"You wanna fucking bet?" Pony practically leapt off the bed, pulling her shirt up to show her stomach, the skin wrinkled and sagging, flashed through with silvery stretch marks. Pony wiggled the sad flesh of her stomach with her fingers for effect. "And look at this!" She pulled her shirt up further to reveal one of Mom's bras, wet from the milk leaking from her full chest.

I looked away, uncomfortable. I didn't know who this was, this Pony—weak and emotional, leaking from places I had never seen her leak. I had never even seen her cry once that I could remember and now even her boobs were weeping. I couldn't stand to look.

Pony noticed my discomfort and crumbed further, another sob escaping as she retreated back to the bed, burying her head under her flat, yellowed pillow.

Fran and I looked at each other unsure of what to do. It was Fran who made the first move, rising from the floor and walking to the bed. She placed the half-full Miss Piggy bank next to Pony on the bed. She petted Pony's back, stroking the stringy blonde hairs poking out from underneath the pillow covering Pony's head.

I went to me and Fran's room then and gathered up my life savings. Thirty-eight dollars, total, and brought it to Pony, too. I shoved the crinkled bills into the slot in Miss Piggy's head and dropped in what coins I had as well.

I didn't hug her or give her any kind of physical comfort. I just stood there awkwardly as she continued to sniffle under the pillow. I motioned for Fran to follow me out of the room, to leave her alone for a while but she ignored me, instead crawling up onto the bed and snuggling in next to Pony.

I just rolled my eyes and walked away. I didn't want to give Pony my money, but I did it. That was all she was getting from me, I reasoned.

I walked down to the creek. I tried skipping rocks for a while but realized I sucked at it. I sat in the shade and read the graffiti on the bridge. "Fuck U" and "Hore" and "Heathers a slut" scrawled in faded spray paint from illiterate boys trying to impress each other or get back at some equally illiterate girl.

I gave up trying to entertain myself after a few hours and the mosquitos started getting too bad. I wasn't really hungry, but it felt like it was getting about that time, so I headed home for dinner, the sinking sun hitting me hard in the face on the way back, causing me to squint. I tried to stare back into it, in defiance, feeling very tired of always having to look away from things too bright and powerful for my eyes to handle.

∗∗∗

Fran was alone on the bed when I got back. Mom and Dad had taken John to visit family and we could "do what we wanted for dinner" per the note on the table.

"Where's Pony?" The room didn't look any different, stuff still scattered everywhere, but there was a distinctly different feel to it that made me uneasy. It was brighter, I realized, the curtains pulled back from the window and the sun illuminating the mess in a way that seemed to mock the depressive state of the room.

Fran shrugged, not looking up from the Miss Piggy on her lap. She picked at a bit of peeling paint on the edge of the plastic pig's nose. "Gone," was all she said.

I didn't bother asking where. I knew Fran wouldn't know. Pony had said "Tommy's grandma's" but neither of us knew high school boys and their grandmas. Tommy could have been anybody.

I sat down next to Fran on the bed. I tried to comfort her, the way that she had tried to comfort Pony, but when I touched her hair, it was wet with slobber so I pulled my hand back and wiped it on my shirt. "Mom and Dad know?"

Fran shrugged, still refusing to look up from Miss Piggy's pocked face.

"Want something to eat?" I said, hoping at least having or mouths full would keep me from feeling like I had to say anything else.

Fran nodded and I went to the kitchen. I brought back crackers and some sliced up hot dogs and some mayo.

We had a picnic in Fran's bed. We didn't care about the crumbs or pissing anyone off. No one was sleeping here anymore anyway, we reasoned, without saying it, so why shouldn't it be a shrine of sad crumbs, dirty laundry, and a hand-me-down crib that no one wanted?

<hr>

Devon Ortega obtained a bachelor's degree from The Ohio State University and a master's degree in creative writing at Ohio University. She was the recipient of the 2011 Gertrude Lucille Robinson Award for poetry. Her poetry and short fiction have appeared in *Barren Magazine*, *Azure Magazine*, *Door is a Jar*, among others. She is currently the fantasy editor for *The Worlds Within* magazine and lives in Pickerington, Ohio with her husband and four children.

Transparent
Heidi Durig Heiby

> *Age has no reality except in the physical world. The essence of a human
> being is resistant to the passage of time.*

> *Gabriel García Márquez*

It all started two Fridays ago in this very grocery store, the Dollar Save. I was
waiting to check out, fitting my things onto the conveyer belt in my usual measured
way, when I overheard two young cashiers.

"Perms and Polyester," one whispered. They stifled a combined, breathy giggle
tinged with condescension. I don't know how I heard, as my hearing is not the best
these days, but I paid only partial attention, letting the comment tip and roll in my
head, like the contemplation of a good glass of wine.

"P and P," my cashier turned and mouthed to the second behind her as I paid.
They shook their heads, amused. Suddenly I felt transparent, like I was being looked
through. I glanced down to my nondescript polyester pants, and lay my hand against
the fine, permed hair that I had been dying a soft blonde, its former color. Since it
was a cool spring day, I was still wearing pants instead of my equally ill-fitting warm
weather housedresses. I looked around and there were two others about my age
checking out, alone, scooping groceries from cart to belt, slow and methodic. Old
women. To these youngsters, we were one pathetic thing, a conjugate of diminished
humanity. I stood, numb, as my cashier looked back, not realizing that I had heard
and understood their comedic code. She smiled and thanked me for my purchase.

"Don't forget, dear, I used to *be* you," I said, stuffing the receipt into my purse,
surprising myself as much as anyone with my sudden pluck. My cashier didn't say
anything, but looked at the other, and then back to me, the shock in her eyes
screaming, *I will never become you.* I felt angry, but not at these twenty-somethings, who
understand so very little about who I am, and I rolled my cart quickly out to my car.
I couldn't blame them. I was certainly one of hundreds of older women they had
seen that week, going through the motions, wash-and-wear polyester, wash-and-wear
perms, looking as if there was not a bit of life left in them.

On the drive home, I replayed every scenario in my life: the library, shopping,
church, eating out with friends, and spending time with my family. I had never
thought of my own disappearance as such. I had been adjusting slowly to life on my
own, but I always assumed that isolation and a feeling of nonexistence was my choice.
Then I saw flashes of attempted interaction with people, especially young people,
and the thwarted conversations and a brushing-off that I had missed. My kids love
me, but even they talk about me sometimes as if I'm not there. I realized that I was
becoming invisible. A ghost. Someone who *used* to be.

I am still here, I whispered to the inside of my car.

***

"I want a makeover." With my cell phone on speaker, my voice rang with resolve
as I put my groceries away.

"Fantastic!" my neighbor, Lora, exclaimed. She had been trying to get me to the
spa where she works as a hairdresser for years, but I had resisted, continuing to go

to Velma Rasmussen's home to get my hair re-permed, colored, and trimmed each month for $40. Lora is my age but highly polished and so surgically altered that she looks like a severely stretched version of her younger self. Nevertheless, she's a sweetheart, and I was glad at that moment to have someone to advise me.

"I don't want a peel or Botox," I warned Lora. I did not want anything drastic for the soft lines in my face nor the gentle sag of my throat, all of which I had earned. I just wanted to peel away the years of indifference and look like me again. At some indefinable moment, I had accepted the idea that effort on the part of oneself is for the young, but I was seeing that it is actually for the self-possessed. I decided it was time to reclaim myself.

"Oh, a haircut and color and facial will be perfect. Then we can do mani-pedis," Lora gushed. "A spa day for us girls!" Lora was thrilled. I had made the effort to have coffee with her often. She had been divorced for years and had no children. The parade of men in and out of her house and life was just that. A passing parade. I might have been the only steady in her world. She called ten minutes later to inform me to be at her house by 9:30 AM the following Saturday so that we could drive together. We would be there all day.

That afternoon I called my optometrist's office to ask about getting new glasses, even though I had just had an exam six months before. They squeezed me in at the end of the day. He came out while one of the sweet techs was helping me try on frames. He stopped in his tracks.

"Well, well, what do we have here?" I looked up at his face, squarish and perfect like Clark Kent, feeling my own face warm.

"Beth thinks these are the right ones," I murmured, touching the slim black rectangles that framed my eyes. He stood still looking at me, seeming to use some special optometrist's vision to check the exact fit without touching me.

"I'm getting my hair cut next Saturday," I tried to explain. "I plan to go short and totally natural." He didn't say anything but continued to stare, adjusting his head slightly on his neck to picture it, I supposed.

"They'll look good," he said. He seemed as surprised as Beth at this impromptu visit, and he squeezed my shoulder as he walked away.

That weekend I went on, as if spring was not blooming secretly inside me like a crocus shoot waiting under a thick blanket of snow. On Saturday, I quietly gathered garbage bags of my old clothes and sorted them with relish, the nicer ones put aside for the Salvation Army store. I went walking with my friend, Gloria, in the afternoon. My daughter, Danielle, and her family picked me up for Sunday dinner at my son, Ben's.

On Monday, I drove to the only small boutique left in town, Monica's, and walked in tentatively. There sat Monica at the front, as she had for over forty years, glasses down her nose, looking at a catalogue.

"Hi, Monica," I began. "I'm Adeline Needler. Do you remember me?" Monica and I had gone to school together and I had frequented her boutique in the years after she had first opened.

"Addie!" she said, standing, pushing her glasses up so that she could see me. She walked over and hugged me. "How have you been?"

"I lost John," I said frankly, "but I'm actually doing very well."

"I heard. I'm so sorry." She smiled sadly and I thought I saw her looking me up and down as nonchalantly as possible. "I'm glad you came in!" I was wearing a pair of jeans that I had kept. They were pleated in front and quite baggy. I wore a blue sweatshirt that my son had given me, stating, *My son and my money go to Duke.* I shrugged.

"I need help," I said. "I want all new things." I looked around and saw racks full of everything from jeans to full-length gowns. None of it was cheap, but Monica had always handpicked the best quality and even many one-of-a-kinds. I felt different already. She didn't question my sudden and unexplainable reemergence after thirty years; she just went to work.

Tuesday morning, I worked my four hours at the library, and no one suspected a thing when I snuck off during my break and looked for the first time, maybe ever, at *Vogue* and *In Style*. I called my daughter as soon as I got home.

"Take me shoe shopping," I begged. I knew that she had some time after her shift at the hospital and before Kate and Derrick, my grandchildren, would be home. She was happy to oblige.

"I want fashionable shoes like yours, Dani," I said over hot tea at Brewer's coffee shop.

"Really, Mom?" she asked, eyebrows raising. She had probably counted on the same sensible slip-ons and white canvas tennis shoes I had been wearing forever. "What's going on?"

"I just want a change," I said simply. She must have sensed something, because she didn't question, either. Three new pairs of shoes and a pair of boots later I went home. Dani and I hadn't had that much fun in a long time.

That week I worked two more mornings at the library and made several more shopping trips to get brand new undergarments and a few casual outfits. The warm, dry weather allowed me to begin gardening. I wore a set of old clothes that I had kept, digging my knees into the dirt, and letting tree branches tear at my sleeves. I washed them for rags when I was done. I felt like a snake shedding an old skin. I needed groceries again on Friday, and the Dollar Save felt like purgatory. I went to a different cashier and my girls didn't even notice me. My son, Ben, called Friday night.

"Mom, how are you?"

"Well, I'm doing just fine. How are Jill and the kids?"

"Great. Anna got an 'A' on that science paper she was telling you about last week."

"Oh, that's wonderful." And on we chatted. Of course, as his mother, I could sense his restraint, and finally, as I was about to hang up, he asked.

"Mom, I have to ask you… are you seeing someone?"

"What? What on earth gave you that idea?"

"Well, I talked to Dani Wednesday after your shoe shopping trip…" I wondered how long it would take Dani to tell Ben her suspicions. I loved it.

"I'm not seeing anyone, dear," I said honestly. "But I am getting a makeover tomorrow."

"A makeover? Mom, are you sure you know what you want?" Again, as Ben's mom, I knew how he would react. Anyway, men don't like change.

"I think you'll like it," I said to reassure him. Ten minutes later, Danielle called. My kids call each other about me as if I am some project they must work on together.

"A makeover? What will you do?" Dani sounded excited, as I knew she would.

"Everything," I answered cryptically. I refused to give details. She had no idea.

"You deserve it," she said, and then, "I can't wait to see you, Mom."

Lora almost jumped out her door when I rang the next morning. She cut the artificial curls completely out of my hair and rinsed the color out, leaving it cropped and silver white. She showed me how to style it to frame my face. After we each got facials, lunch was served to us on little parlor tables. I had never felt so pampered. In the afternoon, we sat side-by-side for manicures and pedicures, and then she took me back to her chair to do my make-up and show me how to apply it. I blinked at myself in the mirror, not because I looked so different, but because I looked so familiar.

There you are, I thought.

Sunday, I did some more light gardening, skipping church and Sunday dinner with the kids at Dani's, with the excuse that I was nursing a migraine. Monday, I called in sick to the library with the same excuse and cleaned the house top to bottom. I did not intend to unveil myself until the last piece was in place, my new glasses. Luckily, the optometrist's office called Monday afternoon. The next morning, I was ready for my debut. I donned the most daring of my new outfits, the black slacks and beige blouse with the black studded vest.

"Mrs. Needler!" Beth gasped when I walked in. "What a change!" She laughed in delight. I handed her my old, round, too-large plastic frames and took the new ones out of their sleek faux leather case. She sat me down in front of the mirrors and ran to get the doctor. I looked at myself with tears pooling at the corners of my eyes, only noticing him behind my reflection.

"Gorgeous!" he said. He watched me through the mirror patiently, as I could not tear myself away from my own image. Finally, I turned so that he could make slight adjustments. "You look like a whole new person!" he said, standing back.

"Actually," I said, "this is the old me." He smiled. Such a handsome man. I couldn't help but think that if I were only a few years younger, I would want to ask him out. I blushed. No thought even close to that had occurred to me since losing my John.

"Well, welcome back, Addie!" he said, and rushed off to see his next patient.

And so it went all week. Lunch with friends Diane and Sarah, coffee with Lora, the walking trail with Gloria, and back to Monica's, everyone pleasantly alarmed at my transformation. The pharmacy tech, who knows me well thanks to my arthritis and high blood pressure, stared at me for what seemed like several minutes before he recognized me at all. The bank teller did a double take and scrutinized my ID. Strangers started seeing me again. One young woman at the dry cleaner even asked me where I got my shoes, and the car wash attendant raved over my glasses.

On Thursday, after two fake sick days away, I walked past the front desk at the library wearing a long skirt, leather knee boots, and a deep V-neck. I walked directly behind circulation and Ellen asked shortly, "What can I do to help you?"

"Ellen!" I said, "If you don't need me up here just say and I'll go shelve." Ellen's hand flew up to her mouth.

"Oh, my!" She hugged me, giggling. "Look at you!" She held me at arm's length while the rest gathered, hearing the hubbub, and made over me like I had just come back from a long absence.

When I got home, I sat with my tea and began to really think about what I had done. I mean, looking different doesn't make you different. I had perhaps proven how shallow people truly are. But then it hit me that I needed to feel taken care of by me to be happy again. One needs to feel that her best foot is being put forward every day. To feel joy in order to foster it. That was really it.

So here I am again. It's my turn to have the kids over for Sunday dinner, and I am at the Dollar Save for my usual Friday shopping. I know that my children and grandchildren will be a little taken aback, but, ultimately, thrilled for me.

The man who has told me his name is Jim is engaging. He wants to know everything. We started talking when we reached for the same roast. I tell him that even though I live alone, I am having my children and grandchildren over for the first time since my big makeover, so he had better get his hands off my rump. He laughs. His eyes sparkle. He needs a smaller roast anyway, he says, being that it will just be him and his son and daughter-in-law. We chat, going up and down the aisles together. He files behind me in the checkout line, even though there are shorter ones available. I have told him the whole story, which started exactly where we are now standing.

"All week I've been having to reintroduce myself to everyone," I tell him, grinning. He nods, smiling back, and I look into his eyes and see something that I haven't seen in a long time: interest. The cashier is asking for my Dollar Saver card. This is the same cashier from two weeks ago, and her friend is right next to her, just as before. She is friendlier this time. She compliments me on the necklace I bought at Monica's when I went back. I look down at it. It does look nice, the large amber pendant and copper beads against my cream top. When she hands me the receipt, I hold onto her hand.

"P and P," I say softly. Recognition widens her eyes, and she pulls her hand back slowly. Her friend looks over, too. I smile. I laugh. I laugh until I cry. They laugh with me.

"You look great!" they say in a repeated cacophony.

"Thank you," I say. I'm thanking them for everything, these unlikely architects of my rebirth. The insensitivity of others can be a powerful, painful teacher. I am not transparent anymore.

Jim looks on, the only other one in the store understanding this odd scene, and there is a soft panic in his voice when he calls after me. I'm emboldened and I hand him a coupon with my name and number written on the back of it before I leave.

See you next Friday? it reads.

Heidi Durig Heiby is a former teacher, tutor, and Green Beret Language Lady living in small town Ohio. She most enjoys being a wife, mom and homebody who loves to cook, read, and write. Heidi has been previously published in *Chicken Soup for the Soul*, "Thanks, Dad," *THEMA Literary Journal*, the Columbus Creative Cooperative's anthology *Columbus, Past, Present, and Future*, and in a few local anthologies. Find Heidi, her blogs, and her varied writing at heididurigheiby.com.

Miracle of the Mass

Charlene Fix

Because I sometimes find myself in churches,
I look around, wondering who else might be a Jew.
Usually I pick the very old, for we steep
into shapes universally human. Muslim visitors
might imagine female congregants in veils,
for dressing others like ourselves helps us love them.
Once I saw a confused Protestant at a Mass
walk down the aisle to take communion.
She slipped the host into her purse. I smiled,
nudging my friend who was both Catholic
and not amused. "Now," she said, the Body
of Christ is trapped in that purse." But for me,
in that instant, the Miracle of the Mass came alive:
God, in humble transport, goes out into the world.

Charlene Fix, mother of three, grandmother of two and Emeritus English Professor at Columbus College of Art and Design, has written four poetry collections: *Taking a Walk in My Animal Hat* (Bottom Dog 2018), *Frankenstein's Flowers* (CW Books 2014), *Flowering Bruno* (XOXOX 2006), and *Jewgirl* (Eyewear, forthcoming 2023), as well as a prose homage/film analysis, *Harpo Marx as Trickster* (McFarland 2013). She is an activist for social justice and co-coordinates Hospital Poets at Ohio State University and Nationwide Children's Hospital. Her website is charlenefix.com

My Patient, My Aunt

Nadia Ibrashi

I bent over my aunt, dabbing her ankle with salt solution. Purple veins traversed her leg like an exotic species of vines.

Zeinat, whose name means "virtues," was the youngest of my mom's six siblings. Except for my mom, each of her siblings took turns at an early death, like a deck of cards being shuffled. I closed my ears when our phone rang, dreading sad news, another parting.

My aunt was a favorite playmate of my youth. She was a teenager when I was a child, and stood much taller than I. We sang of maidens sashaying to the well, as they filled jugs under Egypt's sun. We stomped our feet, danced, clacking cymbals and tambourines.

Slowly, I outgrew Zeinat and her games. My math skills superseded hers, I learned and spoke French fluently, while her Arabic, our native tongue, was hesitant; my curiosity about the world grew, while hers cocooned in a protective layer. My mom explained that my aunt was a "blue baby." The umbilical cord had entangled around her neck at birth, asphyxiating her as physicians worked to resuscitate her. She suffered from cerebral palsy and mental delays.

Zeinat was initially enrolled in a private French school "The Franciscaine," like my mom before her. She couldn't cope with learning two languages, Arabic and French, and she was sent to an Arabic school. She completed the sixth grade, then received private tutoring at home.

In 1980, the final year of my medical school studies, my aunt developed an ulcer in her lower leg. I knew enough by then to diagnose a venous ulcer.

She was in her early thirties, and she became my constant patient throughout my surgical residency and fellowship.

When I visited my aunt from the residents' quarters where I lived, it became my job to dress that ulcer. It was about two inches, though its size would ebb and flow, sometimes healing for stretches of times. I worried about the chronic ulcer developing a malignancy, and I checked for excessive hardening, a failure to heal, an outturning or beading of the edges. The cancerous Marjolin ulcers are extremely rare, but with the zeal of the newly initiated, I was constantly on the look-out.

Zeinat would sit on a couch in front of the TV. She placed her foot on a stool where I had arranged the sterile gauze, ointment, disinfectant, scissors, a curette, dressing forceps and the pressure bandage. Zeinat showered as I arrived, changed her clothes, and wore *eau de cologne*. It became a festive occasion.

I disinfected the area, applied the dressing and a pressure bandage. I checked the pulse on her foot, asked how she felt. If she was hesitant in her reply, I would undo the bandage and loosen it.

"May God protect and bless you, Nadia," Zeinat said. Her words were like poetry to my ears, her blessings and prayers a prized reward for my work.

Time has shown me that my love for my aunt has a purity that can only be felt towards a person who is mentally delayed. This love has a qualitative difference from the love you feel for an independent, typically functioning person. It is a love devoid of conflict or any of the complicated emotions that occur with "normal" relationships. It is a love that lives in its own rarefied dimension, an indescribable feeling that is akin to describing a rainbow to someone who never had the faculty of sight.

When my grandmother died, my mom lived in Buffalo, New York with my dad. Zeinat was left alone in a huge apartment, the kind of dwelling that was so big it boasted a winter side that was warmer, and a summer side that was cooler.

I moved in with her for two years. A housekeeper cleaned and cooked for us every day. My aunt "checked" on me when I studied and provided me with endless cups of coffee during my medical school years.

We lived in "The Gardens of the Cupola," a suburb edged by elaborate gardens and fountains, and a castle with a large cupola. Years later, the Shah of Iran would spend his last days of exile in the castle at the end of our street.

My aunt listened to Egyptian ballads and carried her portable radio with her at all times. She learned to cook beef stew, rice, and vegetables. She dipped her tea with biscuits, her only vice, and shopped the stalls at the vegetable market. She was clever with her money; no one could cheat her out of even a few piasters.

I assigned her math homework every day, simple addition and subtraction, and took her to the movies, tea gardens, and disco dancing. My friends liked her.

I remember looking up from her legs to her deflated face. Due to weak gums, my aunt had lost all her teeth. When she wasn't wearing her dentures, her face fell like a collapsed accordion, yet she was forever young, not a wrinkle on her fair skin.

Her legs were a confluence of shades, blue, purple, and yellow, her toes slightly curved with ridged nails. I was grateful for her ulcer for it gave me endless chances to spend time with her.

When I finally left for the United States, I was reassured that she lived with my mom, who had retired to Egypt a few years back. Across the Atlantic, we chitchatted on the phone. When my daughter was born, I thought that Zeinat would be a perfect companion and hoped to bring her to live with us.

One day my mom called.

"May you live a long life. As for Zeinat…"

My aunt was in her mid-forties. She had complained of stomach pains earlier that day. By the time my mom called an ambulance, her sister expired in her arms. A sudden, unexplained event. We never got an autopsy.

As people say in Egypt, Zeinat died of "death." In a deeply spiritual culture, regardless of the cause, death is believed to unveil everlasting life.

Zeinat possessed an innate spirituality. Regarding her parents and brothers' early deaths, she'd say, "They now reside in Paradise." Finally, she has joined them, in bliss.

Mystery School
Nadia Ibrashi

I clutch my untold stories
      enter a space ruled by secrets.
The surgeons could build
      a tower of Babel, their accents
might write the world,
      but tonight, they speak medicine,
they speak the human body.
Surrounded by scalpels, cautery, scissors,
      they cut and staple the mere mortal,
observe my inner colors,
      orange pancreas, russet liver,
      pink intestines
except for the withered parts.
They conduct their work of beautifying me,
      remove the lost
      from my community of organs,
      let the mystery of healing begin,
let it teach that the body is not just a body,
      but a chronicle of days,
and how to let go
      of what has died inside me,
as I awaken to a world
      full of noise
            in a new corner
                  of my life.

Negala Clouds

Felicia Cameron

There once was a young boy who lived in a village by the sea. He shared a comfortable hut with his mother, father, and two older sisters, and they all worked together to make a life for themselves. The boy's father was a fisherman, and every morning at sunrise he set out for the shore, carrying his nets over one shoulder and a woven sack of food over the other. The boy would watch his father from his small bed, dreaming of the day when he, too, would be big enough to make the journey to the sea. He spent his days helping his mother and sisters with their work in the garden, but when dusk fell, he would be waiting in front of their hut, listening for the sound of his father making his way up the path from the beach.

"I caught you a mermaid today, Tuturro," his father would call to him from a distance down the path, "but she slipped from my hands as I was lifting her into the boat." Then the boy would run to meet him with arms in the air, waiting to be scooped up and carried into the hut with the day's catch.

Every evening after their meal, the family gathered around the supper table where the boy's mother sketched pictures and his sisters combed and braided each other's hair. His father smoked a pipe and told them stories of the sea. The women shared secret smiles at his tales of riding the backs of dolphins and of the mystical creatures that escaped his net, but the boy believed every word, and could not wait to see these wonders for himself.

"Soon you will be big enough to catch your own mermaid, Tuturro." The boy's father ruffled his hair and pulled him onto his big lap. The boy leaned into him, pushing his face against his father's chest and breathing the sea smell on his clothes. These times after supper were the best for the boy, and he knew he would remember them always.

The seasons passed quickly, and soon it was time for the boy to make his first journey out to sea. He followed behind his father with their sack of food, watching the groove their little boat made in the wet sand as his father pulled it toward the waves. The sea and sky still clung to one another in their sleep, and the boy was unable to tell where one ended and the other began. He feared that if he met with that dark horizon, it would swallow him forever. The boy's father looked down at his face and put his arm around him. "Do not be afraid, Tuturro," he said. "In time you will come to know the sea as your friend."

As the boy's father rowed them out past the waves, the sun worked to separate the sea and sky, warming the air and breathing blue into the water. The boy helped his father drop nets over the side, listening carefully as he explained the rules of being a fisherman. By the time the sun reached the middle of the sky, the sea was flat and the air gentle. The boy pulled grilled fish and corn cakes from their woven sack and ate it with his legs hanging over the side of the boat. His father cupped his hands behind his head and closed his eyes, and the boy watched the sun touch different places on his face as it bounced off the water. The little boat swayed back and forth, coaxing him toward sleep, and the boy knew he would remember this day always.

Many days later the boy was fishing with his father when he looked up to see a bundle of gray clouds moving toward them. The sky was growing dark and, although there was not yet a wind, water began to slap the sides of the boat.

"Papa," the boy asked, "Will there be a storm?"

"No, Tuturro. The clouds are too high. They are Negala clouds." The boy's father called them Negala clouds because they were like a big dog with no teeth. The boy laughed and settled back into the boat. An hour later the clouds had passed, and the sky was blue again. By the time the sun met with the pink horizon, the belly of their little boat was filled with fish.

The next morning the clouds had already taken their place in the sky when the boy and his father arrived at the beach. They were thick and angry, quarreling with the sun as it tried to push itself out of the east. Again, the boy was fearful and turned to his father. "Will it storm, Papa?"

"Negala clouds, Tuturro." He patted the boy's head and dragged the little boat across the sand, still wet from the night, and into the sea. As they rowed themselves away from shore the boy looked over the side at the dark water, then looked to his father. His father smiled at him and mouthed the word "Negala."

Before long, the sky opened and spilled rain on them. The boy's father frowned. "If this does not pass, we will turn back to shore." The boy crouched in the little boat with his head down. Big drops slapped the back of his neck. The sea grew angry with the rain, tossing the little boat back and forth and up and down. The boy wrapped his arms around the wooden seat beside him and buried his face in them. His father was now rowing hard toward the beach.

"Hold on Tuturro," he said, "It seems our Negala has grown some teeth." His smile made the boy feel strong and brave, but a moment later a wind joined with the sea and the rain to lift a heavy wave into the boat. It tugged at the boy's arms until they released their hold on the wooden seat and carried him overboard. The wave filled his eyes and nose and mouth, moving down his throat as he cried out for his father. He punched and kicked the water as it pulled him under, rolling him in somersaults and tossing him like a ball.

As the sea drew him deeper, it spoke something to him, and he stopped his fight to listen.

"Do not be afraid, Tuturro," it whispered as it carried his small body away from his father. "You are with me now."

The boy sank down and down into the sea until he found the touch of its sandy bottom. The water felt calm, and he opened his eyes to find that he could see quite well. The salt did not sting; it washed over him with warmth and soothing.

He saw fish of many colors, green and blue and gold and lavender. There was pink coral and bright yellow kelp, and the sand beneath him was white like sugar. The boy had seen these things before, looking over the side of the boat, but now that he was among them, everything was real. A school of angelfish drifted past, parting to the left and right of him, surrounding him in a stain of violet and yellow. He watched them thread into a wall of fire coral and emerge one by one out the other side, each taking a moment alone before becoming a part of the whole again. On the sandy bottom were honey-colored starfish and wide-mouthed clams with thick, pink tongues. Crab and octopus peeked out from algae pockets, and spiny black urchins waited in the sand for something to eat. The boy closed his eyes and let the gentle bottom current mix with him, stretching his limbs away from his body, then floating them back again. His thoughts of the world above the waves, of his father in the little boat, of his mother and sisters in the garden, began to dim.

When the boy opened his eyes again a great sea king was standing before him, wearing a crown of golden shells and a robe made from a thousand purple starfish. His face was like a man's, but he had the flat, liquid eyes of a fish. Still, they held a look of kindness, and the boy did not fear them. The sea king stretched his hand out to him, and the boy took it. The memory of his home and family had almost left him now; he could no longer call to mind the image of his father's face.

"You have come a long way," the sea king said. "I will leave you to rest." The boy did not want rest. He did not want the sea king to leave him. "You are weary," the sea king said. "You must rest." He led the boy to a great castle made of shells and lay him on a bed of kelp. The boy fought sleep as long as he could, but at last he let the warm current close his eyes.

When the boy awoke, he was alone. He called for the sea king, but he did not come. The warm current had disappeared, and his body was shivering. The sand that had been so soft against his skin now scratched. The colorful fish were gone, and he was no longer resting on a bed of kelp, but on something that shook beneath his weight. The smell of it seemed familiar, but his memory could not tell him why. He could not lift his head. He felt a dizziness, and a great pain in his chest. Again, he tried to call out, but the breath stopped in his throat.

He could sense a kind of cloth covering him, and voices that he seemed to know. He felt two strong arms around his body, and a firm chest behind his head, the heart pounding deep in his ears. And somewhere, very close to him, a man was weeping.

"Tuturro," the man cried. "The sea has taken my Tuturro."

The boy coughed out the water, then, that had been sitting in his chest. He choked and coughed for a long time. Everyone grew very still, looking down at the boy without breathing, as if they were saving all the breath they had for him.

When good air finally came to him, the boy reached up to touch his father's face. His father stopped weeping long enough to meet his eyes, and the boy smiled.

"Negala, Papa," he whispered. Then the boy's father raised his head to the sky and cried even harder than before. He wrapped the boy in his arms, bundled him tight against his chest and carried him home to their family, all the while thanking the sea for spitting him out. And the boy knew he would remember this day always.

Felicia Cameron is pursuing an MFA in creative writing at Bowling Green State University. She is an assistant editor with the Mid-American Review and is currently writing a historical fiction novel set during World War ll.

The Blown Harp Lesson

Pam Spence

I have played that piece
        a hundred times,
Not wonderfully
        like a red-tailed hawk circling
                and catching the updraft
But relentlessly
        like water dripping from a tap.

And yet, this morning,
        as I played for you,
my fingers were struck dumb
        and brushed against the strings
like strangers
on the subway
        who took an immediate
        dislike to one another.

My mind was distracted…
releasing carrier pigeons,
  watching as they flew off…
        destined for unknown lands.

My harp thinks perhaps
        we should see other people…
        rethink our relationship…
Get together for lunch…
        …after awhile

Pam Spence has been a writer of many stripes throughout her life: poet, playwright, newspaper editor, reviewer, feature writer, nonfiction book author. While having dabbled in other forms of artistic expression over the years, as expressed in this poem, she is always and forever distracted by the delicious possibility of yet another story.

The Rift

Adam Doyle

I'd been abandoned to face the day alone at my shop. Die-hard Deb had been forced to desert me with late-season flu, and Denver had called off, too, talking in an unsteady voice that went up and down like a broken volume control. He had a hangover or was already stoned. I imagined him sitting naked at the edge of his bed as we talked.

Angry rushes of rain blurred the windows as I bent over the front counter and flipped through glossy pages of an art supply catalog. I was looking for item numbers, trying to call in an order before noon and, as always, wishing that life could be simpler. The online catalog was glitchy and unhelpful, and I kept looking up at the round metal clock on the wall.

The little bell on the door rang, frightened and alone, and a middle-aged man walked in. His blue sweater was riding up on the left side, and he stood in the middle of the shop shaking water from his umbrella everywhere.

"I'm looking for a sketchbook for my daughter," he said in response to my greeting. Far below his receding hairline and just above his glasses, he had a misshapen mole that probably needed a doctor's scrutiny.

"Let me show you what we have," I said and stepped around the poured-concrete counter. I'd had it installed along with recessed lighting in what had been an aging office supply store at the far end of a shopping center. I'd been trying to rid the place of its old trigonometry-calculator feel.

The man bullishly darted in different directions before I guided him with my hand to the right. He was a more extreme example of a type of customer who came in routinely. I'd set up shop in Elmsworth, an affluent, tree-lined area near where I'd grown up. I was lucky that there was enough of an attempt at gentility in the town to support my shop, with a number of dilettantes often coming in to linger over the watercolors or finger canvases that they eventually bought but would probably never use. A few of my regulars had some artistic talent and visited galleries in the city, but most local homeowners saw art as something to be bought by the yard and coordinated with the colors of floors and furniture. That was fine with me; I was just happy that there was no place nearby for a big-box hobby store to move in and ruin me.

As I walked, I glanced through the glass at the top of the front door and saw an unusually large shadow, as if an ogre needed felt or colored pencils. I thought a customer must be struggling through the outer door as the storm attacked, and I watched the shadow grow.

When the inner door opened, I saw the face of Griffith Frost, wet from the rain. Quickly I stepped behind a short row of jars filled with discounted paintbrushes and peered around the edge of them at him.

Griffith immediately saw what he thought he needed and headed to the left. All the angles of his narrow face were as sharp as I remembered them, and his dark brown hair was long and hung over the collar of his shirt. I was relieved that he'd gone to the other side of the shop, away from me. I tried not to watch him but wanted to know what he was looking for. He had stopped near the markers.

I was suddenly aware that I hadn't said anything else to the man in the blue sweater, who had stepped too far down the aisle and was fondling the edges of the tablets of tracing paper as if he were eager for a paper cut.

"The sketchbooks are down here," I said. "Do you know if she needs something specific?" I was slightly whispering.

The man shook his head quickly; it was too much for him to consider.

"Just a general sketchbook, if there is such a thing," he said. "She's just started an art class. And she forgot that she needed one."

He pulled out one close to him and flipped through it.

"Does size matter?" he asked, and I looked over at Griffith. It was the kind of question Griffith would have laughed at when I had known him, his eyes gleeful and condescending.

But at the moment, he was lost in looking for whatever he needed.

"Perhaps just a medium-sized one," I said.

The man nodded.

"I'll take two of them," he said and followed me back to the counter with them. He paid with his debit card, and when I asked him to sign the receipt, trying to keep my voice low, Griffith turned to look at me over the easels. I stared at the man's hand as he signed, handed him his slip and his sketchbooks, thanked him, and wished him a nice day. Griffith was still looking at me as the man headed for the door, and I finally allowed myself to look back at him.

I hadn't seen him since high school—almost eleven years. His hair was heavy and matted with rainwater. He took a few steps toward me, and when his body was no longer obscured by shelving, I saw that his left arm was in a cast and cradled in a black sling, and he was limping. But he was still disturbingly familiar.

As teenagers, we had spent many nights sleeping over in each other's bedrooms, sitting on the floor in our underwear eating whatever we had been able to find in the kitchen, any kind of chips or ice cream or chocolate chips out of the bag, while I stole guilty glances at his body. The size and shape of it had been the focus of my constant attention. Being near him had always been difficult. I had always wanted more. That pull of being close. I looked down at my open catalog as he began to navigate his way through the displays toward me. Griffith and I had parted under bad terms. As he came closer, I stared resolutely at the catalog, my only defense, as I wondered which approach he would use. Would he pretend that we were still friends? Or would he ponder how long it had been? Or maybe he would just ask how I came to be working in the shop.

He didn't do any of those things, and like the Griffith I remembered, his tactic caught me off guard. He stopped just short of the counter and said simply, "You look exactly the same."

That could have been a compliment, meaning that I still looked good. Or it could have been an insult, implying that I should have changed or improved somehow.

"You've—changed," I said and looked down at his cast.

He lifted his arm.

"Car accident," he said, and as he put his arm back down, the Copic markers he was holding fell and slid all over the floor.

His entire body slackened, giving him an air of resigned helplessness. It was too hard for me to watch him struggle for the markers, like a penguin trying to pick up something from the ice with its inadequate flippers, and I stepped quickly around the counter and bent over to pick them up from all the places they had slid. When I thought I had them all, I put them on the counter and then stepped back behind it. The sense of helplessness in Griffith was no longer there. I thought it must have been the broken arm.

"Sorry," he said, and I had to make an effort not to let that word from Griffith mess with my mind.

It was the last word he had ever said to me. We both had been devoted to art in high school. An annual scholarship endowed by one of our hometown's former residents, J. Roscoe Whittleton, who had made a fortune in novelty belt buckles in the fifties (the vagaries and variables of success!), allowed one exceptional student from our high school full tuition at The Langdon College of Art and Design, an expensive school nearby. Griffith and I had been good friends despite hanging out with different crowds and were surprised toward the end of our senior year to find ourselves the most qualified candidates for the scholarship. The final decision was to be based on our last project. I had painted a somber acrylic portrait of my Uncle Eric, who had died of alcoholism. Griffith had made a fearful expressionistic piece that he called 'The Crowd.' The general mood was that mine was better. Until the day before the judging, when it was discovered that someone had cut it to shreds with a knife and then doused the remains with paint thinner for good measure. Some of Griffith's friends had been of the rougher type, especially Jon Scavel, whose family members had a habit of going to prison and who might have done such a thing. A part of Griffith had been attracted to danger, and by the way he had talked to most people, with a distant smile and slightly capricious manner, he had always shown that he felt that he was above everyone and could do what he liked without retribution.

Mr. Dempsey, the art teacher and ultimate judge, had dithered over it, the way he did about almost everything, rubbing his thumb against the bottom edge of his mustache.

"I guess there's no choice in my decision," he said with hesitation.

I had put all of my energy into my final project and had no other piece that was even half as good as the one that had been destroyed. Since I had nothing to present on the day of the judging, Griffith won. He went on to the expensive art school, which had seemed unfair to me since his family had money and mine didn't, and I went to Shepard Business School, which was practical. I saw him for the last time just after graduation when he followed me through the parking lot to get my attention. We stood there in our bright red gowns at a distance from each other, and he just said, 'Sorry,' and I turned and walked away. I never spoke to him again.

"You're working here, Carter?" he asked.

"I own the shop."

Another uncle had died two years earlier and left me enough money to open the place. I had so many uncles.

"I should have guessed," he said. "'Denby's Art Supplies.'"

I wanted to ask what he was going to do with the markers. I wanted to ask what he was going to do at his age and with an art school degree with markers that a teenager might use, but I didn't. Despite what had happened between us, I could still feel the pull of him, and his injuries and rain-soaked clothes were creating a feeling of sympathy in me that I was trying to fight. For so long, I had liked Griffith too much. I tried not to glance at his body, which was ordinary enough, but that I still, to my dismay, felt a draw to be close to. If some people saw the primary expression of love as affection and tenderness, for me, it was the pull of closeness, the simple need to press my body against another as I closed my eyes and exhaled in relief. "I went by your old house the other day," he said. "It didn't look like your father lived there anymore."

"He died," I said as if I was throwing my own father's death in his face.

"Oh. I didn't hear."

The door opened and the bell rang again, and an older woman came in. I nodded at her and smiled, and Griffith flashed her a look of irritation. The old arrogance. I had been attracted to him despite it. His energy and fearlessness had kept me tightly in his orbit. He had never turned his arrogance on me, even though I'd worried about it. He had always been good to me. At least until the end.

"What are the markers for?" I asked him, remembering how he had always claimed that working with markers produced a rather lowly kind of art. I was struggling to overcome my feelings and trying to prove to myself that I was a different person now by getting back at him a little after so many years.

"A special project," Griffith said. "I'm home for a while recuperating, and I just needed something small to keep me occupied."

The word 'small' almost made me wince. As if it was an appraisal of me and my life.

There could have been nothing in it, but I didn't trust him anymore.

"I hope it goes well," I said. "Is this all you need?"

"There's one more. I didn't see it over there. Burnt Sienna."

"I think I have more in the back. Let me check."

As I left him to go back to the storeroom, I could feel the temperature in me rise, and my footsteps felt increasingly plodding. Making a special effort for Griffith Frost, the man who had destroyed my life.

I threw things around a little in the cramped storeroom, tossing cardboard boxes against the stark metal shelves, though not loudly enough for Griffith to hear. Behind one box in the corner, I found Denver's stash, a large plastic baggy filled with bits of shifting green, and that made me even angrier. It seemed to me that Griffith had pointed out the absence of a color of marker to show me that my shop was lacking.

I let out a deep breath when I found the Burnt Sienna, then slowly put the boxes back in place to let my temperature return to normal. When I brought the marker out to the counter, I had calmed down.

"Got it," I said.

"Thanks."

I started to ring up his markers.

"Do you miss the old house?" he asked.

Over the beep beep of the scanner as I waved the markers' bar codes under it, I said, "Not really. Too much upkeep. My partner Matt and I have a condominium."

"Oh," he said. "One of those over on Grantwood?"

His lack of surprise at my relationship with Matt caught me off guard again.

"Yes."

"That's a nice area," he said.

His tone was hard to decipher.

"Is Matt keeping you busy?" he asked, which was a strange question. "I'd like to meet him."

I slipped his markers into a bag and squeezed the paper so roughly that it made a loud crunching sound as I folded the end over.

"He's away on business. Three weeks. Left this morning." I said it as if it was another stab at him, but he just took the receipt.

"That's too bad," he said.

As he signed the receipt, with difficulty because of his sling, his handwriting loose and scraggly, his eyes seemed slightly unfocused, giving him that same air of helplessness. Not like the Griffith I remembered at all. When he was finished, for a moment he didn't appear to know what to do with the slip and seemed disoriented. I wondered what was going on with him. I didn't want to feel any warmth for him. As I took the slip out of his hand, I gave him a tight-lipped smile as I battled the old feeling of being near him. It was much more intense than the feeling of being near Matt, and my smile got even tighter as I thought about that. Griffith had always been the one who was special to me. More special than anyone. But yes, something had changed in him. And it wasn't just that I didn't trust him anymore, making me see him differently. I really wanted to know what the change was.

When we were finished, he took the bag of markers, and we stood there uncomfortably. Suddenly, from somewhere at the back of my head, a storm of emotion came over me, something that I'd been keeping in check. I had a terrible, malicious urge to say something that would wound him. I knew what I wanted to say. It was all I had, my only chance, but I knew it was a longshot, because when we were younger, he had always been so cold to people who expressed a fondness for him. But the burning at the back of my neck urged me on. I decided to risk his derision to see if I could hit a target. He was already injured. Without warning, like a knife attack, I said the words.

"I was in love with you."

I was glad I had taken the chance. His mouth opened slightly, and his eyes flickered. The air of helplessness returned to him, and he was in distress. I had hit a target, like shooting a glass jar on the edge of a fence and shattering it to pieces. He almost dropped his markers. I had no idea what had changed in him, but what I had just said had shaken him. I watched him make an effort to stand up straighter and breathe normally, a visible effort to compose himself.

I enjoyed the feeling of triumph.

But then he said, looking down at his markers, "I was always in love with you." The last words I had ever expected to come out of his mouth. Although I knew that I had just caused Griffith pain, he had done a far better job with me. A deep sense of loss lurched inside me chaotically until I felt as if I was drowning, being pulled by some tidal force that wanted to drag me out into deep water where I knew I would struggle to keep from gulping the waves. I almost couldn't breathe. I looked down at the catalog to try to fix my attention on something, anything, and accidentally made a beeping noise as I knocked the scanner over the breath mints.

As I struggled, Griffith had time to regroup.

"Would you like to come over to my family's house for dinner?" he asked. "Just something to do until Matt gets back. I know my parents would like to see you. It's been so long."

I couldn't believe that he had asked. But his face wasn't showing the old arrogance. As he waited for my response, the helplessness returned to him once more and gave me the upsetting image of Griffith lying on his back like a tortoise, baking in the sun and unable to right himself.

I knew that Matt would never want me to go, obviously, and of course, he would have been right. I wasn't sure why Griffith was asking me. I couldn't believe he would have asked if he hadn't known that Matt was out of town. Otherwise, he would have been obligated to ask Matt, too. He'd already said that he wanted to meet him. I knew the answer I should give him. But this was Griffith Frost. I could feel the pull of his body trying to drag me back into its orbit.

In a fit of reckless emotion, I threw caution not to the wind but into a maelstrom. "Sure," I said. "Why not?"

He exhaled a little in relief but smiled and said, "Good. I'll check with my parents to find a night. Can I call you?"

I gave him the phone number of my art shop, just for a little slap in his face. He didn't seem to notice.

He called me later that day to make plans. The next day after work, I drove over to his parents' house. It was the same imposing house I remembered, solid brick with meticulously maintained bushes in front of it. But the place was older now, and the brick was a little dirty, and the new coat of gray paint on the front door didn't make it look any fresher. I rang the bell, and his mother answered.

"Carter," she said and smiled as she opened the door. "It's been such a long time." She was friendly in a practiced way but tipped her head back a little, with a haughty look in her eyes, as if to look down at me. She was the same as I remembered her; she had the same arrogance that Griffith had always had. Other than the tilting back of her head, she was not letting the arrogance show, but it was there, behind the expensively dyed blonde hair and the clothes carefully selected to look casual but still give the impression of wealth.

Griffith shambled down the stairs as I entered, his broken arm flapping. He stopped a moment afterward and grimaced in pain, but there was no attempt to help him. His mother seemed a little embarrassed by his current state.

Mrs. Frost led us to the oak-paneled drawing-room where Griffith's father was already waiting. When we were younger, I would have followed Griffith to the family room at the back of the house. Griffith's father offered me a drink, and I accepted a vodka—but only one, since I would be driving later—to make sure they realized that I'd grown up. Griffith's father added more vodka to his own drink, which was in a water glass, and which he was drinking like water.

"It's so odd that you've been living back here these last few years, and we had no idea," his father said. I couldn't tell if it was an accusation or proof that I meant so little to them.

"I guess familiarity can be a comfort," I said.

"Mmmmmm," his father murmured and took another drink and looked at Griffith, who had made a point not to drink anything.

We sat down on the hard leather sofas, and Griffith's parents offered no conversation other than little comments about changes that had occurred in the town. Griffith stared at the woolen rug on the floor. To fill the cold silence that followed, I spent nearly twenty minutes talking about the various deaths that had occurred in my family.

"Griffith was near death himself," his father said, looking at Griffith's broken arm, but Griffith didn't respond.

I finally felt out of the spotlight when we sat down in the dining room until Griffith's father asked me what I did for a living.

"He has his own store," Griffith broke in as if he was defending me, which felt odd.

"Art supplies."

The words "art supplies" seemed to have an effect on Griffith's parents, and they both pointedly avoided looking at me.

64

"At least it's practical," his father said. "Our Griffith here decided on one of the most difficult enterprises to be successful in. He was finally making some headway. And then the accident happened."

They were acting as if the accident had been Griffith's fault.

I was sure that both of them wished that Griffith had gone into something that would have been easy for them to brag about. I could see the arrogance in Griffith's mother more clearly now, the self-importance that was angered because Griffith's current condition was doing nothing to support it. The look in her eyes was slyly alert but judgmental. She was lucky to have a husband who could afford for her to be that way. Less successful people had to be more friendly.

When I left, certain that Griffith had invited me over only to bring himself some relief from his parents, he walked out onto the small, unwelcoming gray front porch with me. "Would you like to have dinner with me out sometime?" he asked. "Just something to keep you company until Matt gets back."

The innocent way he had phrased the question made me wonder what he was thinking. Of course, I would have immediately said no, but his face looked pained; he was humbled and uneasy as he asked. It was jarring to see Griffith that way. As much as I tried not to feel sorry for him, it was difficult for me.

"All right," I said.

"I'm afraid you'll have to drive."

I spent the next couple of days thinking about both Griffith and Matt. I told Deb that I had gone to Griffith's parents' house for dinner, and she kept looking at me scornfully, glaring at me through the top part of her glasses. I didn't tell her about Griffith's second invitation. I knew that I shouldn't go. Matt called me every day to talk to me cheerfully about the wonders they were coming up with in new tech. But I didn't cancel the dinner.

When the evening arrived and I showed up in front of Griffith's parents' house, he was already waiting outside as if ready to escape. I had to help him into the car.

"Where do you want to go?" I asked him.

"How about Trimble's?"

Trimble's was a restaurant the two of us had gone to as teenagers. Hamburgers and sandwiches. I had never gone there with anyone but Griffith, even after I had moved back to the area. Even after Matt had suggested it.

"It's not like you to be nostalgic," I said.

"Their hamburgers were good," he said. "I'd like to have one again."

Trimble's was precisely the way I remembered it. Fake wooden tabletops and bright aqua-colored booths. There was no wait for a table, and the server was polite, if not very efficient. I ordered the pot roast sandwich. Griffith ordered the same.

"I thought you wanted a hamburger," I said.

"Oh, well…yeah. But what you ordered sounded good."

I couldn't deny that it felt good to be with Griffith. I kept trying to reject the sense that something missing from my life had finally returned, something that should have been there all along.

I didn't want to talk about his recently sidetracked career, and he didn't mention it. He was interested in my shop and asked me all kinds of questions about it. How long I'd had it, the types of customers who came in. He asked me about different ranges of art supplies, and I droned on for a while as if I was quoting from one of my catalogs. Finally, he ran out of questions.

"I shouldn't be here," I finally said.

"Thanks for keeping me company."

He wanted some ketchup for his fries, and when he picked up the bottle, he had a hard time maneuvering it over his plate. He paused in the middle of the operation before he continued, and I studied his face carefully. It was more than resigned helplessness that was there. I remembered the blank stare he'd had on his face at the dinner table while he had listened to his parents talk about him as if he wasn't there, and suddenly I understood what was different about him. He was lost—but it was more than that. He was like a sailor at sea who had spent a great deal of time alone on a ship and lost part of himself in solitude. He didn't know if there was still any point in setting his sails. Or which direction to set them in, or even how to set them. And it wasn't just because of his injuries. It was something much more. Something that I would never have believed of Griffith Frost: he was not strong. He had been arrogant and superior and certain that he should have everything he thought he deserved, but didn't have the strength to pursue what he wanted alone. He couldn't continue on his own anymore. If he had met anyone since I last knew him, he had not been able to give Griffith what he needed to survive.

Griffith seemed like a small child, and I reached over, took the bottle out of his hands, and put some ketchup on his plate.

"Thanks," he said.

As I watched him eat his fries, I guessed what his life had been like before the accident. He had gone out into the world to fight to make his mark, and he hadn't had the power to do it on his own, as his parents had expected, as everyone had expected. I wondered about the accident.

"What happened to your car?" I asked.

"Oh," he said and looked down at his plate. He didn't want to tell me.

"I ran into a traffic pole," he said. "No one else was injured, though." As if that made the accident all right.

"You hit a pole?"

He pushed a French fry on his plate, trying to get his fingers around it.

"I'd had a little bit to drink," he said. "My license has been suspended."

I watched him put the fry in his mouth.

"It must be hard being back with your parents."

"It's the worst," he said with such emotion that it felt like a hot poker in my face. After dinner, as we got into the car and he struggled with the seat belt, I was reluctant to take him immediately back to his parents' house.

"I can show you the condo if you'd like," I said.

"That would be great."

The condominium was at the end of a row. Two stories with a balcony and a strange alcove over the fireplace in the main room. It was rather plain because I'd never bothered to decorate it, and as I stared at it with Griffith, I realized that was because it had never felt like home. I resisted the feeling that I had never been able to fully experience my life without having Griffith there. I fluffed up the squashed throw pillows on the sofa to make the place look more attractive. Griffith pointed out things that he liked, the moldings and the hardwood floors, as I guided him around. It was interesting to me that just about the only things he didn't compliment were the things that Matt had bought, like the side chairs and the dining table, although I never mentioned that Matt was the one who had bought them.

I offered him something to drink, but he turned it down.

"I don't want it to make me feel more tired," he said, rearranging his broken arm in its sling.

"Do you want me to take you home?"

"No," he said quickly. "Maybe if we could just sit down for a little."

We went back to the living room sofa. Griffith was so familiar that there didn't seem to be a need to say anything, and we didn't know enough about each other's current lives to have a real conversation, anyway. We'd said what little there was to say in the restaurant.

"You should have some artwork on the walls," he said.

"I can't put other peoples' art up on my walls," I said. "It would have to be my own. And I gave that up a long time ago."

He looked uncomfortable and shifted his cast around, and an image of someone that I had tried to repress for years came into my mind: Anthony Worrell.

Anthony had been another student at our high school and had also studied art. He had been very determined but had learned his skills slowly, if he managed to learn them at all. Although he had loved art as much as the rest of us, its creation seemed to be a language that he never understood. As much as he tried to stretch himself, his talent had never matched his desire. He had always been interested in whatever piece I was working on and asked many questions, trying to learn things from me. I remembered that after my final piece was destroyed, I hadn't been able to help noticing the deep satisfaction in his eyes. I knew at the time that he would have been capable of doing such a thing. But Griffith had been the more obvious suspect.

Griffith was trying to scratch under his right arm, but his cast wouldn't let him.

"I hate having dry skin," he said, almost to himself. "At least the winter is over."

"Is it bad?"

He nodded. It occurred to me that I could ask him if he wanted me to rub lotion on him, and I laughed out loud at that thought.

He put his head down dispiritedly as if I was making fun of him.

"Do you want me to scratch it for you?" I asked, to make up for my laughter.

"No, I could never bother you with that," he said as he clawed against the outside of his shirt.

I slid over toward him on the sofa, and he lowered his arm. He looked at me with wide-open eyes, not knowing what was going to happen. I scratched on the outside of his shirt, and he wriggled slightly, but I could tell it didn't bring him any relief. Then I started to unbutton his shirt, and we both stared at my hands.

When his shirt was open, I reached in and scratched his smooth, warm skin at the spot he had been trying to reach, and he closed his eyes with pleasure. Then I put my hands on his chest, and he opened his eyes and looked into mine.

After that I did what I had wanted to do since we were teenagers; I pressed myself close up against him, as close as I could get. It felt just the way I had expected, as if we were two halves that had always belonged together as one and were finally joining. It wasn't just the fulfillment of a silly teenaged fantasy. Being close to him felt like a dream that people rarely allowed themselves, of something deep and warm and satisfying. Something essential that was finally not being denied.

As I held on to him, he tried to undress, to go through the preparations of making love, but I still pressed myself against him, tightly. He stopped moving and let me hold him and pressed his face into my hair. Only when the ancient ache that I had always felt for him started to lessen a little did I finally pull back. We both undressed, and I helped him get his shirt off. Awkwardly we started the movements of making love, and I let him lead the way despite his injuries.

Afterward, he said to me, "I can clear out of here if you want. But unfortunately, you'll have to drive me home."

I didn't say anything but pressed myself up close to him again.

The next morning, I took him home before I went to work. He smiled at me warmly as he got out of the car, and I was glad that he would be able to show his parents that he had done something on his own, even if it was only something as cheap as spending the night somewhere else.

At the store, Deb arrived a little after I did. She undid her long dark blonde hair, then pulled it back even more severely before she fastened it as she looked at me reproachfully. "I saw you on Dover Street," she said. "With him in the car."

"Oh."

"I wonder what Matt is doing right now?" she asked.

"I don't know," I said. "He's away on business."

I knew my behavior had been inexcusable. It wasn't like me at all. I tried to make myself feel guilty. But instead, I sat at the wooden desk in my office, with piles of work around me, and calculated the number of days left before Matt came home, the days I could spend with Griffith before I had to face the consequences. I even hoped that Griffith's cast wouldn't be coming off soon enough to allow him to return to the city before Matt came back. Griffith called on the shop phone, and Deb scowled at me when she realized who I was speaking to. Denver could sense the tension and rubbed his beard for a moment as he decided what to do, then went back to the storeroom, probably to find his stash.

"Are you all right?" Griffith asked.

"I'm fine."

"I'm sorry about last night."

"I'm not."

"Oh," he said. "Okay. So, then, can we see each other again?"

"Um, yeah," I said. "I'll call you in a little while."

Deb looked away from me as I hung up. She picked up a box of watercolor kits for children, an idea of hers that had been selling well, and slammed it on the counter.

"What about Matt?" she asked as she started taking the kits out of the box.

I really had no idea what to say to her. It wasn't her business, but I was glad someone was sticking up for Matt, even though I knew it should be me.

"He's a big boy," I said awkwardly.

"And I suppose Griffith is bigger," she said icily.

"Well, he does have an extra inch or so," I said, in response to her tone.

She threw the box of watercolor kits onto the floor and stomped back to the storeroom. Griffith didn't question me when I made it clear that I wanted to see him every night from then on. Sometimes we went out to eat, and sometimes we just went back to the condo. I was careful that we never used the bed that Matt and I slept in. Griffith and I always slept in the guest bed, which almost made things worse, because it started to feel like our room. But I didn't let it bother me. When Griffith and I invaded each other's bodies each night, it felt so natural, so unlike the way it always felt with Matt.

Matt could tell something was wrong when I talked to him on the phone.

"So, what's going on?" he asked.

"Oh, just all kinds of busyness."

"You seem different," he said. And I was.

Before Matt returned, Griffith didn't pressure me in any way. But he made his feelings clear.

"I wish that we could stay together," he said.

I didn't answer right away.

"I know."

I didn't say anything to Griffith about a future for us. But as soon as Matt came home, carrying on with all his new tech information and trying to sound upbeat, I knew that he and I were over. I couldn't believe how quickly my feelings for him had deteriorated, as if they had never been there. I wished that I felt guilty about it.

At least I didn't wait. I told him about Griffith the first night he was home, although I didn't give him a name.

"You haven't been sleeping with him, have you?" he asked. He was standing there with his feet pointing outward like a duck, which I used to find endearing. Now it just looked ugly.

When I didn't say anything to that, he put his hand to his forehead and said, "Oh, fuck." I couldn't think of anything to tell him other than that Griffith affected me in a way that I couldn't control, and that underneath I had always wanted to be with him (though a part of me still wasn't fully sure that I could trust him—but I wasn't letting that stop me.) But of course, I couldn't tell him any of those things.

"So, who is it?" Matt asked.

Reluctantly I told him it was Griffith Frost.

"You mean that creep from high school? The one who ruined your life?" He had a look on his face that made me feel as if I was leaving him for a known serial killer. But as he fumed, I could only wonder that if Griffith—or someone—had ruined my life, then wasn't my life with Matt just a part of the ruin?

"You told me you wanted a simple life," he said.

I held back from telling him I did want a life that was simple, but not too simple. I refused to hurt him further by letting him know that with Griffith I had finally drunk from the wellspring of life, and tasted its golden nectar, and couldn't go back to evenings with Matt eating pretzels and drinking diet coke while we binge-watched old episodes of Unsolved Mysteries, most of which had been solved by now anyway.

Matt made a big scene. His bags were already packed from travelling, but he packed another one to give himself a chance to throw things around, and to give himself time to yell at me about my betrayal. When he left, he told me I would regret my decision and seemed to think that we would get back together eventually, if not soon. That I would call him and ask him to take me back. But I was just glad when he was gone.

I called Griffith.

"Matt left," I said.

"For good?"

"Yeah." I didn't say right away that that meant I wanted to be with Griffith.

"Are we going to keep seeing each other?"

"Yeah."

A turbulent time followed. I got an apartment, and Griffith moved in with me. Matt and I sold the condominium. All the way through it, he acted as if he couldn't believe it was happening, and even called Deb at the store to complain about my behavior.

"You said you wanted a simple life," she said to me. I remembered saying that at some point to someone, but I couldn't believe that I'd said it to as many people as I apparently had, as if I'd paraded down the streets of our small town, skipping and playing the lute and singing about the joys of a simple life.

After we signed the last papers for the sale of the condominium, I had a last chance to talk to Matt.

"You really know that I'm not the love of your life," I said.

Matt looked defeated.

"Yeah," he finally said. "But we had a pleasant time together, didn't we?"

"Yes. We did."

Despite my love for Griffith, I was still slightly wary of him. But Anthony Worrell was also in my mind. I realized that Griffith could have simply been the easiest scapegoat. After all, he had never done anything before to hurt me. I knew how much he needed me now, and I wondered if that was love. I got my answer when we talked about my art supply shop.

"Don't ever sell that," he said. "It's so good and real. It's such a part of you, a part of everything I love about you."

After his injuries had healed, Griffith went back to the city. He had to find a new apartment, which I helped him with, looking through small and somewhat dirty hovels for something he could afford, because his parents were still supporting him financially, but only barely. When we found a place without roaches or bullet holes in the walls, I helped him clean it, and he moved a bed in along with his art supplies. We saw each other as often as we could.

I spent time with him in the city, and he came back to Elmsworth occasionally. The inroads he had made in the art world, I knew, could take a while to reforge, if he could do that at all, because it was easy to be forgotten in that unsympathetic world.

Although I didn't say so to Griffith, I never expected him to make any progress. He was not a bad artist, but his success was always an incredible longshot, and despite my love and support, I knew that Griffith was damaged, which would hurt his chances. Sharks circle when they smell blood.

We lived between the two different apartments for nearly three years. He had a lot of false starts and was often dejected. So many times, I went into the city and bought a pizza or some other takeout and sat with him on the floor of his apartment as we ate it by candlelight.

Afterward I would hold him in my arms until we both fell asleep.

I increasingly expected that one day he would return to Elmsworth for good and make a life with me there. I was looking forward to it, although I didn't want to crush Griffith's dreams. I pictured myself in my art shop, and Griffith teaching painting. Perhaps to children. It amused me to think of him getting irritated with them when they held their brushes incorrectly.

But to my surprise, Griffith finally came up with two series of pieces that looked promising. One was a group of pencil sketches that had to do with time, and the other was an emotionally charged series about love, a strange mesh of colors, mostly blues but with some red, with vague outlines of bodies pressed together and joining in different places. I could tell by looking at them that they were about the two of us.

A gallery owner came and spent some time scrutinizing them. His name was Ogden Nelson, and he was bald and had manicured fingernails and an aging but well-preserved face. "These are clever," he said of the time-related pieces. Then he looked at the others again. "These are something more. I have a place for them. We'll see what they do." The pieces sold. Griffith was pleased and smiled and nodded as the gallery owner related the news. But I knew him well enough to see that he was more concerned about my reaction to his success. He hovered near me afterward and asked me questions about it, most of which were unnecessary.

"I'm happy for you, Griffith. For us. It looks like we made the right decision. And now you have some concrete progress to show your parents," I said.

About a year later, he had a show of his own in a tiny gallery. One night in the middle of it, when he should have stayed at the gallery, he came back to Elmsworth and took me out to dinner. We ate at this small, outdoor Mexican place that specialized in taquitos, my favorite food. He made me sit down and then kept running back and forth between the table and the window with everything he'd ordered.

"Let's take a walk," he said after we had finished.

It was a warm night, and we went around the corner to Langdon Park, named after the city's founder, where people recently had been found having sex in the bushes. He led me to a bench and asked me to sit down. I realized what he was doing and tried to stop him from kneeling in front of me.

"Griffith, please," I said. "Let's just discuss this the way most people do."

"No, I want to make sure that you understand that my love is genuine."

"Griffith—"

"I know I'm not much," he said, cutting me off and looking downward with the humility that he so frequently showed when he was with me. It was reassuring but heartbreaking, and I tried to pull him up off the ground, but he stayed there stubbornly. "I love you," he said. "You know how much. And if we could get married, I don't think there's anything else that would ever make me feel more complete or happy with the world."

"Of course I'll marry you, Griffith. Now get up."

He had bought a ring, and as he struggled to get it out of his pocket, I slid down onto the ground and put my arms and legs around him.

"Let's get out of here before they think we're having sex," I said.

We had a small ceremony. Griffith let me make all the arrangements but asked if we could hold it in my shop. I picked a Saturday and closed for the ceremony. I didn't want his parents there, so he didn't invite them. A handful of our friends came over. Deb was there, and Denver brought his girlfriend, who kept nodding and smiling at the gay guys getting married. I wanted a really gay wedding cake, so I had a lavender one made with lots of flowers and had two grooms put on top.

Deb had softened toward Griffith.

"I have never seen you happy like this before," she said to me. Then she turned to Griffith. "Don't fuck it up."

The more successful Griffith became, the more he relied on me. He always asked my opinion of his work before anyone else. He encouraged me to take up painting again, but I realized it was not for me. Being with him had shown me that I never would have wanted to do what he was doing. I needed more warmth than the art world could provide. I had Griffith, which was all I really wanted. So many nights when we were at home together, I would wrap my arms and legs around him and think, "He is mine. Griffith Frost is all mine."

We moved to a nicer apartment in the city, with so many windows and a bit of a view, and I spent most of my time there, running the business of our life together.

Deb looked after the shop. Whenever we went to one of his showings, or any exhibition, I watched Griffith go out into the throng of people while I stood at the side of the room. I would study him and wait until he looked up, like an ostrich surveying the landscape, searching for me. He never failed. He always needed to know where I was. He would come over as soon as he could and put his arm around me and pull me close.

"My better half here," he always told everyone.

I remembered one particularly important exhibition his agent wanted him to attend, and I had to struggle through it because the harshness of the art world was wearing me down. It exhausted me. But Griffith's work was at an important stage, and I wanted to be there for him. I was very tired, and almost holding on to the wall. He kept asking me what was wrong.

"Do you want me to take you home?" he asked.

"I'm all right."

"No. I'll take you home."

When we got home, I told him that I was just worn out from the worldliness of his life, and he pressed his full body against me and held me until I fell asleep. He was an intelligent man and had figured out early what I wanted from him most. He pressed himself against me constantly. He did it one weekend when I was in the kitchen cooking, and wouldn't stop, until I had to tell him, "Griffith, I'm almost in the guacamole."

Our life was like a shimmering, golden thing that nothing could touch, and I was so glad I had made the choices I had made. Griffith always made sure I knew I was the most important thing in his life. It was a precious time.

So, I was bewildered one night as we were dining at the house of some friends when Griffith brought up high school and the contest. The two of us had never spoken about it to each other, let alone with other people.

We were with Samara and her husband Wen, who had made a roast chicken that we were eating on their patio. I was always happy with simple food, things that I didn't have to peel through layers of to figure out what I was eating.

"The new exhibition is going well?" Samara asked.

"It wasn't at first," Griffith said. "But it came together when Carter made his visit."

He reached over and grabbed my hand.

"I wouldn't be here without him. He makes everything work."

He said that kind of thing frequently, and I smiled at the table.

"And it all began with something horrible," he said. I turned to look at him.

"Something horrible?" Wen asked.

"We were friends in high school," Griffith said, and I dropped his hand. "We were both in the running for a scholarship to The Langdon College of Art and Design. Carter would have won. But someone slashed his final piece just before the last exhibit. That's the only reason I got the scholarship."

"That's terrible," Samara said. "Did you ever find out who did it, Carter?"

"No," Griffith said.

I was confused and a little angry as we went home, but I didn't say anything. I just stared at the street lights as we passed them. As we locked up the apartment and went to bed, our routine was normal, and we were both quiet.

I wanted to ask him why he had brought the contest up, but I didn't. I got into bed. He turned off the light and slid into bed with me. But he didn't get up close to me; he was a little distance away. He didn't start his movements to make love, the way he usually did after we had been out to dinner. We lay there silently, and the room around us felt large, and the walls felt very far away. Then I heard him speak.

"I slashed your painting," he said quietly. "It was me."

A dark fire burned quickly through my body, through every inch of me, and after it had flared out, I felt hard and heavy. I held myself very still.

"You waited all this time, until after we were married, to tell me that," I finally said.

"Yes."

Immediately I got out of bed and left the room. I didn't want to do anything as clichéd as sleeping in the spare room, so I went out to the dining room and sat in a chair. It was hard and cold, and the floor was cold under my bare feet. After a while I went over to the sofa and lay there awake until morning came.

I listened to him get up and go through his morning routine. He came out and stood at the sofa behind me, and I imagined all the things he wanted to say, but I didn't look at him. He stayed there for a while before he left, and I could hear the front door close gently. I stayed on the sofa until I finally fell asleep.

I made him dinner that night like always, but when he came home, I still didn't speak to him, mostly because I had no idea what to say or do. We went through the next few days without speaking. I wasn't giving him the silent treatment. I knew he was waiting for the verdict, but I couldn't give him one. I didn't know it myself.

I thought I knew the reason why he did it. He did it because his parents never would have paid for art school, and art was his passion. Enough of a passion that he would betray our friendship, and his love for me. I went over and over it in my mind.

I knew what other people would have said if I had told them about it. Deb would have said, "Pack your bags," then shown up at my door carrying a bazooka and wearing a gas mask. She would have pointed out that I had abandoned Matt for Griffith, even when I had my doubts. Others would have said, "But he was so young. People make mistakes." I couldn't be sure which direction to go in. I thought of practical things. It would have been such a mess for us to split up, financially and otherwise. And I would have been alone. I kept thinking about the watercolor art kits at the shop and going back to ordering those and living that life again. I wondered, if I stayed with him, if we'd wind up having one of those dead marriages as so many people did. It used to be easier for gay people to leave each other. But we were married. More than anything I wondered why he had told me. It would have been so easy to keep it to himself. It would have been easier for me, too.

As I tried to decide on our fate, I did the things I usually did. I made our meals. I ran errands. I told him things he needed to know. We slept in the same bed at night. But we didn't say anything important. And I knew he was terrified. When he was home, he often came near me, trying to get me to look at him, but I wouldn't.

After a week had passed, he finally said something at dinner one night.

"Will you come down to the studio with me? There's something I need to show you."

I thought about it, then nodded.

We drove down to his studio in the darkness. When we arrived, he only turned on a few of the lights. On an easel in the center of the room was a covered painting. He led me up to it, and he looked at me as he lifted the cover.

It was a painting of a fracture in the earth. A rift. It filled the painting, from the upper left corner to the lower right. It was so naturalistic in its fine detail that it almost looked like a photograph, and I walked up to examine it. The smaller fissures along its sides went deep into the ground, like the ragged edges of an open wound, and there was an awful, searing pain in its lines as if Griffith had painted it with his own blood. The chasm at its center was black and pitiless, and I could imagine falling into it. As real as it seemed, it was also unreal, like a phantasm, slightly hallucinatory, as if some malevolent spirit was bound into it. And in the somber hues of its colorings, which seemed overlaid on top of it as if they had come with time, there was an immense sadness in it, unbearably wise and knowing and infinitely aware of its own existence. Its combination of qualities made it extremely difficult to look at, as if it was a picture of someone dying. The overall effect of it was horrifying. It was an ugly thing. As we stood there looking at the painting together, again I wondered why he had told me. Was it guilt? That would have been to make himself feel better, not me. And he had created this painting only for me. I knew that. To show me something about himself. And I knew he had told me because he had wanted me to know; because he had thought I deserved the truth. He had needed to tell me what he had done, what he had been capable of, and let me decide if I wanted him or not.

"If I hear any attempt at an apology from you," I said, "if I hear the word 'Sorry,' especially, you and I are finished."

I could hear his breath trembling, and he took a step away from me.

"No one is ever going to buy this painting," I said.

"I know."

I reached out to it and lifted it off the easel.

"It's mine," I said.

I put it in my office at the shop, around a corner near the copy machine, where Griffith will rarely see it, but where I can look at it whenever I wish. Deb doesn't know what it is, but she avoids it. It shows me the rip in the soul of the man I love. I can hear something in it talking to me, a voice from somewhere inside Griffith coming to me in a whisper, speaking about the burden of monstrosity, and regret. I am getting used to it. I don't know what that says about me. Like the Picture of Dorian Gray, I have a picture of Griffith, but my picture is of something unchanging, of something deep inside him that no one else will ever see.

And it causes me pain sometimes. I wonder if simplicity is for the faint of heart.

Adam Doyle was born in Los Angeles and spent part of his childhood there before his family moved to Ohio. He is a graduate of The Ohio State University, where he studied creative writing. He enjoys writing about human relationships, especially family dynamics that have to do with trust and estrangement. Drawing from his life experiences, he also likes to write about the ordinary lives of gay characters.

The Guts that Come with Love

Schyler Butler

Zip-tied to the fence
across the street
from a dilapidated building
next to this high rise
in another revitalized downtown:
the faces of but fifty or so
Black people murdered
in the last five years
in this city alone.
The residents call it art,
the activists, a public announcement,
absolutely no one: a reminder
of what resources Black people have
to fix anything
              (can't even fix themselves)

and what resources white people have
to fix anything
              (can't even fix themselves).

Schyler Butler's work appears in *Hobart*, *African American Review*, *Narrative Northeast*, *Juked*, and elsewhere. Currently, she lives in Columbus, Ohio.

The Sheriff

George Pallas

Another scorching day in southwestern Arizona began to give way to evening as the sun started its slow but inexorable slide toward the peaks of the Santa Rita Mountains. It had been a hot day for late September, but soon, after the sun went down, the desert would become cold indeed. A sidewinder, *Crotalus cerastes*, slithered off the large, flat rock where it had been sunning itself and, using that species' peculiar method of locomotion, lurched its way off into the desert. Ahead of the snake, a roadrunner crossed the trail and scurried to safety. The roadrunner, in turn, flushed out a jackrabbit resting in the copious shade of an ancient saguaro cactus' upstretched arms. The jackrabbit hopped away in search of a resting place where roadrunners wouldn't disturb him. With the approach of evening, the desert was settling down for the night.

And yet, all was not quiet in this part of the Sonoran Desert, for off to the east a small dust cloud was visible. The cloud grew steadily larger and soon the sound of distant hoofbeats foretold the arrival of a horse and rider. Presently, they came into view. The horse was on the brink of exhaustion, with foam flying from his mouth. The rider, intent on maximum speed, stayed bent low over the horse's neck, except when he looked over his shoulder, which he did frequently. He was a man on the run, no doubt about it. But shortly after reaching the aged saguaro that formerly sheltered the jackrabbit, he reined in the horse to a slow walk, apparently satisfied he'd shaken his pursuers if, indeed, he hadn't imagined them in the first place.

Now, the rider dismounted near a clump of green and, to his relief, discovered the vegetation shielded a small spring. He let the spent horse drink first before filling his hat with water and taking a drink himself. The sun had now completely slipped below the peaks of the Santa Ritas. "I reckon this is as good a place as any to bed down for the night," he said to no one in particular. Then, after a few more anxious glances toward the direction he'd come from, he hobbled the horse and staked the reins to the ground. Next, he unlimbered his bedroll and stretched it out on the sandy desert floor, He had no food for either himself or his mount, although the horse could snack on some of the grassy plants around the spring. The rider, however, would go hungry. A small price to pay, he thought, for his escape.

Daylight waned quickly, replaced by a spectacular canopy of stars. There was no moon tonight so, not wishing to risk a fire, there was little to do but try to sleep. A bedroll on the desert floor with a saddle for a pillow was not the most comfortable arrangement, but he'd slept that way enough he didn't give it a second thought. Yet sleep wouldn't come. It wasn't discomfort that kept him awake. Instead, it was the day's events replaying over and over in his head. After trying unsuccessfully to push the memories aside, he gave up, opened his eyes, and looked up at the winking stars, giving in to the reflections that troubled him.

The rider went by the name of Big Kid Josie. It wasn't his real name, but folks had called him that for so long, it seemed more natural than the name his parents had given him. In fact, it suited him well. He was tall, nearly six feet, with a mop of thick blonde hair that fell down past his collar and was visible even when he wore his ten-gallon hat. Despite being well into his thirties, his beard was so light and sparse he went clean-shaven. He looked like a big, overgrown kid.

For the past several weeks, Josie traveled with his sometimes-friend, Mexican Pete. Just as Josie wasn't a kid, Pete wasn't Mexican. His dark complexion and black, drooping mustache suggested the moniker and it had stuck. The pair didn't have any fixed destination, rather they ambled from town to town looking for games of chance that might offer the opportunity to make a little money. They had ridden into Nada del Norte earlier in the day, shortly after noon. Nada del Norte wasn't much more than a wide spot in the trail, but it did have a few businesses that served to anchor the handful of ranches that dotted the area. Reaching a clapboard building with a sign ambitiously touting itself as a saloon, the pair dismounted and tied their horses at the rail outside.

"Saloon" turned out to be an embellishment. Inside, Josie and Pete found a dirt floor with a few tables for card games. The bar consisted of a stout plank stretched between two pickle barrels. Bar patrons had to stand; there were no stools at the "bar." Over in a corner, two men sat opposite each other at a square table. The deck of cards between them was an obvious invitation to a game, so Josie and Pete introduced themselves and took the two vacant seats. Josie made sure to sit facing the door. He'd read how the famous gunslinger and sometimes lawman Wild Bill Hickok met his end in a Deadwood, Dakota Territory saloon. Hickok, sitting with his back to the door, didn't see "Broken Nose" Jack McCall come in, and McCall shot Wild Bill in the back of the head. Josie wasn't about to have the same thing happen to himself. Mexican Pete, however, didn't seem to mind that seat.

The man to Josie's right had a head of thick, wavy black hair and, not surprisingly, introduced himself as Curly. He had a big nose that matched oversized ears and a small scar on his left cheek. The other man admitted to going by Three-finger Jake, an obvious reference to the missing thumb and forefinger on his right hand. His laconic explanation was that he'd lost the digits during the war, whether fighting for the Union or the Confederacy he didn't say. Maybe that was because he didn't want to offend anyone, or maybe he no longer cared. It didn't matter to Josie.

The four men settled in to play poker, five-card stud. They also chipped in for a bottle of whiskey, which the four card players shared. They were silent except for the occasional "raise," "call," or "deal" needed to move the game along. That, the purr of shuffling cards and the clink of hard money tossed into the pot were the only sounds at the table. Josie noticed that Three-finger Jake proved quite adept at dealing with his left hand even though he said he was naturally right-handed.

As the game progressed, the saloon gradually began to fill up. Now all the other tables had card games going, and would-be players crowded around them waiting for a chance to get a seat. Drinks flowed freely, too, and the noise level rose accordingly. At Josie's table, the cards had fallen fairly evenly most of the afternoon. But by the time their second whisky bottle was nearly empty, Mexican Pete had a noticeably larger pile than anyone else.

Pete was dealing when, without warning, Three-finger Jake shoved back from the table, drew his gun, and shouted, "You dirty son of a——." The cocking his revolver hammer obscured the last word, but his meaning was clear. The gun was pointing straight at Mexican Pete's nose.

Somewhere someone hollered, "Whassa goin' on?"

"I caught this chiseler dealing from the bottom of the deck!" Jake yelled back.

Mexican Pete looked worried and kept his hands on the table. "I ain't done no such of a thing!"

"I seen ya!" Jake roared.

Curly nodded. "I seen it too."

Spectators and kibitzers lost interest in the other games and crowded around the corner table where Josie, Pete, Jake, and Curly sat. Even some of the other card players temporarily abandoned their games to join the jammed circle. "We don't tolerate no chiselers in this town," Jake said evenly. A chorus of agreement spilled out from the saloon patrons surrounding the table. Two men from the crowd grabbed Mexican Pete, one on each arm and yanked him out of the chair.

"Now wait a minute, fellas," Pete said, clearly frightened now. "Y'all can keep the money, me an' Josie here'll just ride on out."

"Taint' good enough," said an anonymous voice from the crowd.

"No, taint," agreed someone else. "No, we catch somebody cheatin' in a friendly game of chance, we string 'em up!"

The saloon murmured agreement. "Yeah, a necktie party!"

"Come on, we'll show 'em!"

"Somebody get a rope!"

Josie's heart pounded in his chest. He hadn't *seen* Pete deal crooked. He was, in fact, paying more attention to Three-finger Jake's left hand. But Pete *had* been known to cut a corner or two in the past, something Josie warned him about more than once on this very trip.

Josie started to protest but two burly men grabbed him, too. Someone produced two small lengths of rope and tied Josie's and Mexican Pete's hands behind their backs. Then they dragged the two outside and hoisted them up onto their horses. One man from the crowd grabbed the bridle of Josie's horse while another did the same for Mexican Pete's before leading them away from the saloon. Soon it was clear that their destination was a small clump of mesquite trees just outside town. Josie watched as someone slipped a noose around a still-mounted Mexican Pete's neck. Where it came from, he hadn't any idea, but there it was. Pete's goose was certainly cooked and, just as certainly, Josie would be next.

The crowd was now an unruly mob, eager to serve "justice" to a supposed card cheat. They reveled in the moment, their mood ugly. Angry men shot baleful looks at Josie and Pete as their murmured threats became louder and more specific. But Big Kid Josie discovered something. Whoever tied his hands behind him didn't make such a good job of it. With a little effort and a lot of patience, he managed to get his hands free. He still had his gun belt, but there was no way he could shoot his way out of this scrape; the mob was too big. His only hope was to run.

Every member of the crowd had dismounted except for one man on horseback. He was saying something Josie couldn't hear, but from his attitude and pose it appeared he was either reciting an indictment or passing judgement. Big Kid Josie and Mexican Pete traveled together and sometimes gambled together, but they weren't really *friends*. Still, he hated to see Pete meet his end at the hands of a lynch mob. But there was nothing Josie could do now except try to save his own neck.

The man on horseback reached down and smacked Mexican Pete's horse on its hindquarters, causing it to run off. Pete dropped and his life ended. Josie picked this exact moment of maximum distraction to spur his own horse and begin a mad gallop to get away. With their attention focused on Mexican Pete, the angry vigilantes didn't notice that their other prisoner had freed himself until they heard the galloping hoofbeats of his escaping horse. Desultory shouts to go after the fleeing rider briefly filled the air. But mobs are funny things. Usually, one or two or maybe a small handful of men are instigators, yet mobs lack true leadership and organization.

Seldom is it possible for such a disorganized group to make plans and quick decisions, and so it was in this case. While the crowd dithered and tried to decide what to do next, Big Kid Josie fast retreated toward the setting sun on the western horizon. Which is how he found himself sleeping under the stars in the Sonoran Desert.

***

Sheriff Lucas Grant was somewhere in his forties. He had small obsidian eyes set deep in his weather-beaten face. Most people when they first met him noticed his prominent chin and his bristly walrus mustache. He was almost bald but concealed that fact by wearing his pearl-gray Stetson almost constantly. The joke around town was that he even wore the hat to bed. Grant stood more than six feet tall in his sock feet and, despite a slight paunch, was strong and tough. Quick thinking was not his forte; instead, he was slow and methodical. But he would be a formidable opponent in almost any kind of showdown.

Sheriff Grant was more of a businessman than a lawman. It was his saloon, for instance, where Big Kid Josie and Mexican Pete had their fateful card game. He also owned the mercantile store and had an interest in the bank. Yet Grant was all that passed for law in Nada del Norte. Even if he paid less attention to keeping the peace than he should, it was better than having no sheriff at all. And Grant wasn't one to get in a lather over a little extra-judicial hanging as long as the money kept rolling in. What Grant *couldn't* abide, though was the idea of a chiseler playing cards in his saloon. Not that it mattered to him if the games were honest; he only rented the tables. But if word got out that the games in his saloon were crooked, it would be bad for business. So, when he heard about the supposed crooked card game, Sheriff Grant decided to chase down Big Kid Josie and bring him in. Even though nobody *saw* Josie cheating, guilt by association was guilt enough for the sheriff.

Before midday the next day, Grant saddled up and methodically followed Josie's trail out of town. He was, everyone acknowledged, an excellent tracker, with decades of experience hunting both game and men. The trick was not to hurry, but in this case, it didn't matter. Big Kid Josie, fleeing for his life, followed the trail due west and made no attempt to cover his tracks. As for a posse, Grant figured he didn't need help rounding up one tinhorn card cheat.

It took him most of the afternoon, but before sundown, Sheriff Grant found the spring where Josie had bedded down the night before. Since the sun would be down before long, he decided to camp there for the night himself. Not worried about pursuers as Josie had been, he gathered some dried mesquite wood and soon had a small fire going over which he cooked a simple supper and boiled a pot of coffee. After dining in this fashion, he kicked sand over the fire and spread his bedroll out on the sand. These gamblers might be tough enough in the city or town, but out here in the desert, most of them were as helpless as babies. Grant doubted he'd have much trouble tracking Josie in the morning.

***

Big Kid Josie was cold. With the sun again dipping behind the Santa Ritas while he rode, he shivered so much it was an effort to stay in the saddle. Last night on the desert floor had been miserable. He spent the whole night huddled under his thin blanket trying to keep warm and fervently wishing he could risk a campfire. A cup of hot coffee would have been truly welcome, but it was impossible to have a fire without giving away his position. He wasn't sure anyone had followed him. After all, he hadn't seen any pursuers. But after what that mob did to Mexican Pete, he wasn't taking any chances. Nevertheless, bedding down under the open sky again tonight didn't have much appeal. He hoped he could find some sort of shelter that would both conceal him from anyone following and protect him from the elements.

Dusk was fading into darkness when he spotted the abandoned barn that seemed to be the answer to his prayers. It was part of a cluster of buildings that appeared to be a deserted ranch situated near the trail. What had once been the ranch house was nothing but a blackened foundation, a single stone chimney reaching forlornly skyward. It had obviously burned down long ago. The other buildings were either too small or too decrepit to be useful as shelter. Except, that is, for the barn. It stood intact with a good roof. A pile of hay that would make for a more comfortable bed survived in the hayloft. This, he decided, would be his bunk for tonight.

Josie wrinkled his nose when he walked into the old barn. The smell of old manure was still pungent and, although not pleasant, it was an odor that wasn't unfamiliar. He tied his horse in one of the stalls and selected what appeared to be the cleanest one to sleep in, Then, he climbed into the loft and before long had pitched down a sizeable pile of the hay. Not only did the hay provide padding for his bedroll, spreading some over him after he bedded down gave some extra insulation from the cold desert night. With little sleep the night before, no food, and a long ride through the day, he was asleep in no time.

As Josie had run from the lynch mob during his waking hours, so he did again in his dreams. Awake, he never saw his pursuers, but the men who chased him through his dreamscape were angry and menacing. There seemed to be hundreds and each of them carried a bona fide hangman's noose with which to string him up to from the immense gallows visible in the distance. Every pursuer was heavily armed, too. And no matter how hard he tried, he seemed to be able to move only in slow motion, allowing the mob to close the distance between them and him.

Josie shook himself awake to escape the phantoms. Hiding out in the desert wasn't what he had in mind when he chose to be an itinerant gambler. He thought gambling would be an easy way to make a pile, but it hadn't worked out that way. He did win more often than he lost, and he made enough to get by. But he wasn't raking in big money. Good as he was on the small-time circuit, his attempts to play with the big boys in cities like Denver and San Francisco had ended badly. Choosing gambling as a career had been a mistake, he thought, as he finally drifted off to sleep.

Sleep began to give way to wakefulness and as it did, a vague unease took hold of Josie. The first thing he saw when he opened his eyes was a six-shot Colt revolver pointed at his face. At close range, it looked as big as a cannon. The man behind it wore a gray Stetson, a bushy mustache, and a huge grin. "Well," the man said, "lookie what I got myself here!"

Startled as he was, Josie had enough of his wits gathered about him to avoid making any sudden moves. "Who the hell are *you?*" he asked.

The man with the gun laughed, then pointed to a tin star pinned to his vest. "Me? I'm Sheriff Grant. I'm gonna take you back to Nada del Norte, where I 'spect some of the boys will want to arrange a necktie social for you."

"If you're the law, ain't you supposed to prevent lynchings?"

"Well, son. I might be the law, but out here we make our own law. An' I don't take kindly to chiselers cheating in my saloon."

"*Your* saloon?"

"Yeah. *My* saloon. Now let's get you up real slow-like. I want your gun belt. I already got your saddle rifle. So, you and me'll ride into town real quiet and peaceful. Like we was pals or somethin'." Grant threw back his head and laughed heartily. Then his face became serious again and he said, "Let's you get yourself up. Now!"

Josie decided that protesting his innocence would be futile and did as he was told. He slowly got out of the bedroll, then gingerly unbuckled his gun belt and handed it to the sheriff. He brushed hay off himself before shaking out his bedroll, packing it up, and preparing to ride. The pair set off to the east toward Nada del Norte without, Josie glumly noted, having breakfast.

"I hear they call you Big Kid Josie," Grant said. "Well, you don't look so big now, does ya?" Josie remained silent. If that was the sheriff's attempt at conversation, he'd failed miserably. Josie said nothing as they rode on, while Sheriff Grant bragged now and then about his prowess as a lawman. Without anyone to guard his prisoner, sleep for Sheriff Grant would be impossible, so he pushed the two on through the night. It was all Josie could do, exhausted and famished, to stay upright in the saddle, but somehow, he managed.

Nada del Norte glittered in the morning sun—if, indeed, such a drab place could be said to glitter—when Sheriff Grant and Big Kid Josie rode slowly into town the next day. The desert heat was already oppressive and only a few people scattered along the wooden sidewalks bothered to watch as the sometimes-lawman brought his prisoner in. But Grant intended to make a show anyway. He paraded Josie past the town's few buildings, then turned back toward the jail, which also housed the sheriff's office. Upon reaching the jail, he turned his horse to face Josie and said, "All right, get down."

As noted, Sheriff Grant was more of a businessman than a lawman. Maybe if he'd been a little more diligent as sheriff and searched his prisoner carefully, what happened next wouldn't have happened. But it did. In a flash, Big Kid Josie reached into the top of his boot, pulled out a Sharps pepper box pistol, and fired twice. A puzzled look crossed Grant's face, followed by one of consternation before his eyes glazed and he fell from the saddle with a heavy thud, stone dead. The fall knocked his pearl gray hat off, exposing his bald pate to public view.

Josie swung down from his saddle and went over to inspect the body. Sheriff Grant was clearly dead, but he took the former lawman's six-gun from its holster and placed it in his own belt anyway. Then he unpinned the tin star from Grant's vest and hefted it in his hand. It was heavier than he expected. Maybe it was made of something besides tin.

A man standing outside the jail door stood gawking. Josie motioned for him to come over, which he did. "You the sheriff's deputy?" he asked.

"No, Sheriff Grant said he didn't need deputies." He stared at the dead man for a long time, then he looked up at Josie and continued. "Nobody much liked Sheriff Grant. Makin' money meant more to him than keeping th' peace." He carefully sized Josie up as he spoke.

"So, how come he was sheriff if he was so unpopular?"

"Weren't nobody else what wanted the job."

"What's your name?"

"Mike Oliver," was the taciturn reply.

Josie's thoughts whirled. Since gambling hadn't been what he expected, maybe it was time for a change. The office of Sheriff was now vacant and, well, it was an opportunity Josie decided he didn't want to miss. If the townspeople didn't like the idea of him taking over, they'd have to come up with somebody else. And, apparently, nobody else wanted the job.

With a flourish, Big Kid Josie deliberately pinned the star Grant had been wearing onto his own vest. Then he looked at Oliver. "There's a new sheriff in town, Mike Oliver, and I'm appointing *you* as my deputy." He paused briefly, then asked, "This town got an undertaker?"

Oliver nodded.

"Good. Tie up Grant's horse, then get that—" he pointed to Grant's body in the street— "over to that undertaker. Pronto."

"Yes, sir, *Sheriff!*" Oliver said, promptly springing into action.

Big Kid Josie stood in the doorway of the jail and surveyed the town. It wasn't much but, he decided, this was going to be *his* town now. Maybe lawing wouldn't be such a bad job. It would at least be a welcome change from a rootless life of a man constantly on the move.

A wide grin spread over Josie's face as he went inside the jail and plopped himself down at the sheriff's desk. The simple act of sitting behind that desk imbued him with a sense of permanence missing from his nomadic life as a card player. He patted the star on his vest. "Yes," he said to himself in the empty office, "I think I'm going to like being the law here *just fine.*"

George Pallas is a native of Tennessee, growing up in the Nashville area. He moved to Ohio after graduating from Vanderbilt University and started a career in information technology. He has a published mystery novel, *Stalking Horse*, a story in the Ohio Writers' Association's *Outcasts: An Anthology*, and maintains a true crime blog at georgepallas.com Now retired, George writes from his home in downtown Columbus where he lives with his wife, Sharon, and t heir dog, Sheldon Cooper.

Unbecoming

Devon Ortega

We hurt ourselves—what do
we care of these strangers,
these strange bodies and
unfamiliar minds? We hurt
ourselves—asking, "Can
you feel that?" As if our
pain will translate through
the air. See what I'm doing
for you? How I carve myself
into your image? What do
we care of these strange
unfamiliar expanses of flesh
that contain our vulnerable
hearts that we are only
trying desperately to
expose?

Devon Ortega obtained a bachelor's degree from The Ohio State University and a master's degree in creative writing at Ohio University. She was the recipient of the 2011 Gertrude Lucille Robinson Award for poetry. Her poetry and short fiction have appeared in *Barren Magazine*, *Azure Magazine*, *Door is a Jar*, among others. She is currently the fantasy editor for *The Worlds Within* magazine and lives in Pickerington, Ohio with her husband and four children.

Red: A Fairy Tale

Jim Hodnett

It's the same as always, at least at first. He is running toward a rainbow, but this time it doesn't disappear as he approaches, nor does it even recede. It grows larger. Excited, he runs faster, traversing the vast, open field with a lightness and ease he has never felt before. The soft earth and damp grass disappear behind him. Once he reaches the rainbow, once he is underneath and can look straight up to see only the lowest band, the violet one, he turns to his right and starts heading toward the end. He is not sure why he turns right. As he presses on, he wonders if it might not have been better to go left. The path he chooses isn't easy. He must surpass barriers: stone walls, barbed fences, steep hills. And he has to get around formidable objects: tall, barren trees; large, jagged rocks; empty, ghostly houses. He keeps looking up, keeps checking so he stays on course. The violet band is his navigator. He is encouraged when he sees it curving lower and lower toward the firmament. At last, he arrives at the rainbow's end, a trunk as wide and daunting as two sequoias. He rests for a moment, panting as he braces his palms on his thighs, and looks around. Of course, there is no pot of gold, no prize, no answer. He should have known that. There are only gnarly, ugly roots. The roots are the colors of the rainbow bands that they connect to and feed. They spread over and into nearly an acre of ground, their multicolored branches intertwining in a confusing pattern, an ill-conceived, chaotic fabric. He feels exhausted, dismayed. Something grabs his shoulder, shoves hard.

"Jason, wake up!"

"Huh?"

"Wake up! You're snoring!"

Jason's heavy lids open. He can see Darren's face not six inches from his own. Even in dim light, he can make out the black stubble and the frowning eyes. "Sorry," he mumbles, turning on his side, away from Darren.

"You know you snore on your back! Can't you just stay on your side? Jesus! Now I'm awake! And it's only four-thirty!"

Jason nuzzles his cheek into a pillow and tucks a second one between his knees. "Sorry," he repeats.

Darren blows a breath of disdain through his lips. "You sounded like a damn freight train coming through the house! And fuck! Now I've gotta pee," he says, as though that were Jason's fault, too. He gets up and stomps to the bathroom. He doesn't close the door all the way, so Jason can hear the loud gurgles and splashes as his piss hits the toilet water. When he returns to bed, Jason pretends to have already fallen back asleep.

"Shit!" whispers Darren as he settles into the mattress. "Shit!"

***

Though he doesn't will it, not consciously anyway, the dream resumes where it left off. At the end of the rainbow again, Jason becomes fascinated by one set of the roots, the red ones.

He follows them with his eyes and feet, trying to see where they go, or rather where they come from. Soon he is on his knees tracing their paths. More and more closely he holds his face to the ground. He begins to dig, pawing at the dirt with his fingers to expose the tinier and tinier filaments. The smaller they get, the redder they get, a fiery, glowing red—hot to the touch. He is able to trace some of the blazing roots down to a size barely larger than capillaries. He wishes he had a magnifying glass. Where can he get one?

Again, a shove on his shoulder.

"Hey, you awake?"

Jason keeps his eyes closed as he answers. "I am now. What time is it?"

"Six-thirty." Darren scoots over and hugs him from behind. He runs his palm over Jason's chest and stomach. "You wanna?"

Jason moans. "I don't know. I'm really tired."

"That's okay. I'll do all the work. I'm already ready." Darren presses himself against Jason's thigh.

"Okay," says Jason. He knows how this works. Darren feels he lost something during their exchange in the night. Now he is reclaiming it.

A half-hour later, Jason lies in bed listening to the rush of shower water. Darren warbles off-key melody fragments from time to time, none of them from the same song. First Aretha, demanding R-E-S-P-E-C-T. Then Dolly, pledging undying devotion. And finally, Gaga, unable to extricate herself from a crazy-bad romance. Jason cups his pillow over his ears and stares at the ceiling. He wishes he could finish the dream, find the answer he was looking for. But sleep is no longer an option.

He remembers, years ago in college, a session when his counseling center psychologist, Dr. Mandarin ("But please call me Monica") had prompted him, "Tell me about your dreams, Jason." At the time, he had shrugged, "Don't remember any." He wouldn't have told her even he had. He was only in her office because his parents had refused to pay for another semester unless he "worked on himself." But now he knows what he would say to Monica: "They're about rainbows, almost every night."

"Chasing them?" Monica might have asked.

"Lately I've been catching them," he would've answered, "but it doesn't seem to help."

Once the shower water shuts off, Jason gets up, puts on a robe, and goes to the kitchen to start coffee. Just as the coffee maker beeps to announce it has completed its task, Darren bounds into the room, dressed for work and looking not at all sleep deprived. "So, what have you got planned today?" he asks as Jason hands him his coffee. Darren's attractiveness is undeniable. He has a full head of thick, brunet hair despite being in his late thirties, plenty more on his body to match, and a solidly toned physique that presses against his clothing in a way that makes an unmistakable masculine impression. Often when Darren is near, Jason feels painfully conscious of his own white, hairless, skinny-limbed body and angular face.

"Not much," Jason answers. "I work the dinner shift tonight, so I'll be home late."

"Okay. How late?"

"Ten-thirty, probably. I don't close."

Darren peels a banana and devours it in four bites. "You know, it'd be fine with me if you quit that job, or at least got a nine-to-five. You're hardly ever here in the evenings."

"I like tending bar," replies Jason. He has poured himself a cup of coffee and is sipping on it, one arm in front of his chest. His robe is closed all the way to his throat.

Darren rolls his eyes and smirks just slightly. The meaning is clear: bartending is a loser job. He takes another sip of his coffee, then pours the rest into a travel mug. "Yeah, okay. We'll talk about it this weekend." The way he says it makes it sound like more of an edict than a suggestion. "But now I gotta run. Nine o'clock meeting." He shoulders his work satchel and screws on the lid of his mug. Then he grabs Jason by the small of his back, forcefully pulling his body up against his own, and plants an aggressive kiss on his mouth. The suddenness of the moves causes Jason to teeter. Darren slaps his rear. "See you tonight, Babycakes."

Jason says nothing as Darren exits the condo. He returns his arm to its position across his chest and looks around the large open room that comprises the kitchen, dining space, and living room. It is full of furnishings Darren had purchased before Jason moved in: dark, heavy, wooden tables, a plumply upholstered sofa and side chairs, and huge, framed photographs of ominous, clouded skies and rocky, desert landscapes. That first night that Darren had brought him here, after their Grindr-arranged date at Headfirst Bar, he had felt exhilarated by the sight of it all, could not wait to be pulled into the spacious bedroom with its generously pillowed bed and ravaged on its luxurious sheets. He has spent almost every night here since, moving in only two months after that first date—quite an incautious act in retrospect. But what had he to lose? Not much, to be sure. He had vacated a studio apartment above a garage in a sketchy neighborhood. The only view from its solitary window was a gas station. And then, of course, there was his easily riled landlord, who, it had turned out, owned an arsenal of assault rifles.

***

The woman who perched herself unsteadily on a padded stool at the long, polished-wood bar at Moon River Bistro was seventy-five if she was a day. Of course, what she was doing right now had probably aged her, given her skin that leathery, wrinkled look and made her eyes the sunken fog lights they were. So maybe she was only sixtyish. Jason addressed her, "I'm sorry, ma'am. Smoking is not allowed here."

"Yeah, I know," she said in a gravelly voice. "Say, you wouldn't happen to have an ash tray, would you?" She tapped the tip of her cigarette on the rim of an empty highball glass. She was wearing a lacy, calf-length, eggshell dress with an open, silver brocade jacket over it. The top of the dress under the jacket was daringly low cut, exposing wide cleavage nearly as wrinkled as her face. Shockingly, her purse and shoes were bright red.

"Ma'am, it's a city ordinance..."

"Yeah, yeah, okay. I'll put it out." She took in a long, final drag, blew the smoke up but not necessarily away from Jason's face, then pushed the half-burnt stick into the ice of the glass she had just used as an ash tray. She gave Jason a reproving look and pursed her lips. "You happy now?"

Without making eye contact Jason took the ash-stained glass from the bar, plucked the doused cigarette from it, and poured its ice into the sink behind him. He dropped the cigarette into the trash. Then he grabbed a rag and began wiping down the bar in front of the old woman.

"Sorry, ma'am, I'm just doing my job."

She had been watching Jason with furrowed brows. "I just bet you're sorry," she said. "Bet you're sincere about it, too. Bet you're a good rule-follower, aren't you?"

"I try to be..."

"Well, you owe me all the same. What time you get off?"

"Ten, but I..."

"So, meet me at the Raging Unicorn. You know where that is, don't you?"

"Yes, ma'am, it's right across the street, but I..."

"But you don't like old women?" Jason looked at her with wide eyes. "Or maybe don't like women, period?" Jason opened his mouth as though to say something but couldn't think quite what. "What's his name?" she demanded.

"I'm sorry?"

"Your boyfriend, or husband, lover, partner—whatever you queers are calling each other these days."

"Darren... if you must know."

The old lady scrutinized Jason through narrow eyelids. "You didn't smile when you said that. What's yours?"

"What's my what?"

"Name!"

"Oh. Uh, Jason."

"Okay, Jason. I'm Linda. See you about—what, ten-fifteen?"

"Well, I'm..."

"Don't be late." She slung her purse strap over her shoulder and walked with a heavy-footed stride to the door, despite her three-inch, red heels. Once she reached the sidewalk, Jason watched her through the restaurant's tall, plate glass window. As she stood at the crosswalk, she riffled through her purse for a moment, then pulled out a cigarette and lighter. After her first drag, she threw her head back and blew a cloud of smoke from her mouth. Then she looked directly at Jason, as though she knew he would be watching, pursed her lips into a kiss, turned and crossed the street.

Harvey, Jason's co-worker at the other end of the bar, who had been watching from the corner of his eye since the moment Linda had blown smoke in Jason's face, looked at him and smiled. "Jason's got a girlfriend! Jason's got a girlfriend!" he taunted in schoolyard fashion. Jason adored Harvey, pudgy and haphazardly groomed though he was. Still in his early thirties, he had already started to let himself go. Yet his smile was ready, and his kindness was unfailing.

Why did he have to be straight?

"You're just jealous," taunted Jason back. They both laughed, and Jason didn't give Linda another thought through the rest of his shift.

***

At ten p.m., Jason leaned over his end of the bar and gave it a final swipe, grabbed his tip jar, and walked into the kitchen. He took off his apron, threw it into the laundry bin, and counted his tips. Not much, even when he added the ones from credit cards. Slow Tuesday night. Harvey would finish up with the last few customers. It was his turn to close. As Jason finished his preparations to leave, he thought about the drive home and the routine once he reached there. Darren would be in bed or close to it. He might have a drink or two in him, which meant he would either ignore Jason or criticize him. He seemed to be capable of affection only in the mornings. Jason left the restaurant, saying goodbye to the kitchen staff, Harvey, and the hostess. He stepped onto the sidewalk, glanced across the street at Raging Unicorn and saw Linda, sitting at a table at the window. She raised a stemmed glass, looked him in the eye, winked, and gave a come-on-over nod of her chin. Jason shook his head slowly in disbelief. *For real?* He turned to go but then thought again about what awaited him at home. He pulled his phone from his pocket and texted. *Have 2 close after all. Will b late. CU in the morn.* Then he stepped into the street, black and shiny after a light drizzle, and headed toward the Raging Unicorn. Linda gave him a big smile as he approached, but just as Jason reached the bar's door, he heard a ping. *Whatever*, Darren had texted.

When Jason passed through the doors of the Raging Unicorn, he had to blink a few times before his pupils adjusted to the dim light. In the three years he had been tending bar at Moon River Bistro across the street, he had never been inside the Unicorn. It had always seemed to be populated by persons younger and hipper than he, and the name seemed quite precious. The first thing he noticed upon entering was a huge white wooden cut-out of a prancing unicorn on the wall behind and above the bar. It was outlined in rainbow-colored neon lights, especially the mane, tail, and horn. The second thing he noticed was Linda, who had moved from her window seat to a stool near the end of the bar, the unicorn in the background above her head. She waved him forward. "What'll you have?" she asked. "On me."

"Just a club soda. I gotta drive home."

"Are you nuts?" Linda scoffed. She turned to the bartender. "Make this man a Manhattan, Pete, and one for me, too."

"But…" started Jason.

"You like Manhattans, don't you?"

"Well, sure," Jason said. "And I make a good one, too. At least that's what people tell me." For some reason, he felt a need to establish some credentials with this aggressively maternal woman.

"Of course, you do, if that whiskey sour you made me across the street was any indication. How long you been bartending?"

"Oh, eleven years or so. I started when I was in college."

"What's your degree in?"

"Nothing, never finished."

"Well, that sucks. Why not?"

Jason smiled at Linda's salty language. It seemed so at odds with her clothing finery, although not so much with her face and personality. "It's a long story. I guess I just wasn't quite ready for it. Goofed off, watched too much TV, zoned out on music. Then my parents cut me off, and I ran out of money."

"The hell they did! 'Cause you're gay?" Jason shrugged noncommittally, but Linda sneered, "The bastards!" Jason startled. He had never heard anyone call his parents bastards and had never even allowed himself to think it.

At this moment, the bartender set their drinks in front of them. "I put them on your tab," he said to Linda.

"Thanks, Pete. Hey, this is my friend, Jason. You two should hang out some time. You got a lot in common. I mean, you're both 'bartenders.'" Linda made air quotes with her fingers when she said *bartenders*, then cackled as though she had cracked a witticism worthy of Truman Capote.

Pete, a tall and slender man with a shaved head reached across the bar and shook Jason's hand. "Nice to meet you, Jason. Pay no mind to Dolly Levi here. She's harmless." Jason smiled and felt his face flush. Pete's hand was large, and his grip was strong.

"Now don't tell him that," said Linda, before Jason could find words to respond to Pete.

"I want him to think I'm a *femme fatale*."

Pete chuckled. "Oh, you're that, all right. No doubt about it." Then he turned to Jason.

"You tend bar across the street, don't you? I've seen you come and go."

Jason flushed again. He'd been noticed. "Yeah, well, that's pretty much my life," he said, "coming and going."

"Well, maybe you need a little excitement," said Pete, raising his eyebrows and smiling suggestively.

Linda interrupted. "Now just hold your horses," she said to Pete. "This man is my date, at least for tonight. Don't you have other customers?"

Pete glanced around the nearly empty bar. "Not really, but as you wish, madame." He bowed and made flourishes with his hand in front of his torso. Then he smiled and winked at Jason before turning and walking to the other end of the bar. Jason watched Pete as he busied himself wiping some wine glasses and hanging them on an overhead rack. His shaved head reflected the colors of the neon-lit, rainbow unicorn.

Linda extended her arm and snapped her fingers in front of Jason's face. "Hey, over here!" she said, directing his attention to her.

"Sorry," said Jason, looking shamefaced.

"It's okay. Can't blame you. He's a looker." She offered the rim of her glass, and they toasted. "You know, I knew you'd come," she said.

"Really?"

"Yeah, you're a pleaser. I can tell."

"I am?"

"Yeah, I can spot one just like that. Used to be one myself."

"Well, that's hard to believe."

"Yeah, well, I wised up. But enough about me. What's the deal with this Darren person?" she asked.

The abrupt shift in the conversation was disorienting. Jason frowned. "What do you mean?"

"Well, clearly, you're not happy. You never look happy when his name comes up." Linda took a sip of her Manhattan and peered at Jason from above its rim.

"You're making a lot of assumptions, aren't you?"

"Sure am, and they're right, aren't they?"

"No!" Jason was feeling annoyed. "I mean, Darren's okay. He can be nice. He bought me a car…"

"What are you—a prostitute?"

Jason bristled. "No. Are you?"

Linda threw her head back and laughed. "Good for you, kid!" she said. "Well, if I am, I'm barking up the wrong tree tonight. That's for sure!"

Jason didn't laugh with her. "Well, I just think you have no right. You make it sound like I'm Holly Golightly or something."

Linda stopped laughing and set her nearly empty Manhattan glass on the counter. "Well, aren't you?"

That was the final straw. "Look!" said Jason. "You don't even know me! You can't tell me who I am and what my life is like! What do you know about it?"

"So, you're angry at me, huh?" Linda's expression was sober.

"Well, yeah. As a matter of fact, I am!"

"Good. Wasn't sure you had it in you. You didn't say a word when I blew smoke in your face and dumped a cigarette butt in that highball glass."

"Well, I was at work, just doing my job," said Jason defensively. Then he went on attack. "Besides, those things are cancer sticks. They'll kill ya, ya know."

Linda cocked her head for a moment, then nodded in agreement. "Oh, yeah. No doubt about that." Then she added, "Bet you never smoked, did you? Not even once."

Jason shook his head.

Linda rolled her eyes, "Like I said, you're a good rule follower. Super nice guy, too." She tilted her head back and downed the last of her Manhattan. "Hey, Pete! Time to settle up."

Pete was at the other end of the bar talking to a customer and gazing up at a soccer match on the TV screen hanging on the wall, just beyond the unicorn's horn. His head was still reflecting its neon lights. He turned around, nodded at Linda, and went to the cash register. A minute later he approached with a credit card slip and a ballpoint pen in hand, both of which he placed in front of Linda. She hastily wrote in a generous tip and signed her name in an oversized scrawl. "Gotta go, Babycakes." She leaned across the bar and kissed Pete on the cheek.

"Where ya going?"

"Time to work another corner. You two studs are scaring away all my customers!"

Pete looked confused but smiled, nonetheless. He gave Jason a whattaya-going-to-do look. While Jason returned his eye contact, Linda stepped forward and cradled him in a gentle hug. "You take good care of yourself, Sweetie." Then, as she left the bar, red purse slung over her shoulder and red heels clacking on the wood floor, she called out without looking back.

"He's all yours, Pete. New and improved."

After the door closed behind her, Pete looked at Jason with a bemused smile. "What's she talking about? New and improved?"

"I'm not sure."

"Well, that's not an unusual feeling after a conversation with Linda. She likes to leave you guessing."

"You've known her long?" asked Jason.

"Not really. Well, sort of. She's been coming in here a couple of nights a week for the last few months. Bends my ear about one thing or another, usually stirs up a little trouble with another customer, then leaves." He looked at Jason's half-empty Manhattan glass. "So, you ready for another?"

"No. Thanks, though. I shouldn't even finish this one. I've got to drive home."

"Are you sure? It's on me," offered Pete with a hopeful look on his face.

Jason smiled, "Still, I better not."

"Well, if you won't take a drink, will you take this?" Pete handed Jason his business card.

"My cell number's on the back."

Jason held the card with both hands and stared at it. Then he gave Pete a drooping gaze.

"Actually, I'm in a relationship."

"Oh, I'm sorry. My bad," said Pete, looking confused. "Linda told me you were single."

"She did?"

"Yeah, she did. Look, I apologize. She saw me watching you leave last night and said she would go 'scout you out' for me tonight. I told her not to, but you probably have an idea by now how well that works."

Jason nodded and twisted his mouth into a knowing smile.

"So anyway, she came back earlier tonight, said she had talked to you, and that you were single. So again, my apologies." Pete reached to take his card back, but Jason pulled it up to his chest.

"No," he said a little too firmly. "I mean, if it's okay, maybe I'll keep it all the same?"

Pete's reply sounded cautious. "Yeah, sure, but I'm no homewrecker. You need to know that."

Jason gave a solemn nod and placed Pete's card in his shirt pocket. "I wish I could finish this," he said, looking at the Manhattan Linda had bought him, "but I need to go…home." The word *home* had never felt more foreign on his tongue.

But home he went. When he arrived, he found Darren in bed. An empty cocktail glass sat on his nightstand, and he was snoring loudly. But that was not the reason Jason went to the living room, lay on the couch, and pulled a kaftan over himself. Before long he fell asleep and entered his dream. He stood at the edge of that open field and looked at the rainbow in the distance, taking in its graceful arch. It seemed to spew like a fountain from a break in dark clouds through which sunlight glowed. But he felt no need to chase it. He knew—in that way that people can know things in their dreams that they can't know when awake—that as long as his eyes could grasp the rainbow's beauty, it was already his.

***

One evening four weeks later at Moon River Bistro, Jason untied his apron and threw it in the laundry bin. He had already stuffed his tips in his wallet. He said goodbye to the kitchen staff, then walked around the front of the bar. As he passed by Harvey, they exchanged a high five. "Good luck, Roomie!" said Harvey.

"I'll give it my best," he replied. He walked out the front door, stood on the sidewalk and took a deep breath. The air was warm and redolent with the scent from a blooming magnolia tree outside Moon River's door. He crossed the street and walked into The Raging Unicorn. It was a moderately busy night, and it took a few minutes for Pete to notice him standing at the bar. When he did, he smiled and walked straight up to him. "Well, hello, Stranger," he said. "What are you doing here?"

"I came to collect that free Manhattan you promised me."

The smile that appeared on Pete's face deepened his dimples and accentuated a slight bend in his nose, an imperfection that Jason had not noticed before. For no reason he could explain, it made his heart melt. "Comin' right up," said Pete.

When he returned with the drink, Pete set it in front of Jason on a cocktail napkin. Then he held up a shot glass half-full of brown liquid. "There was a little bit left in the shaker," he said and winked. Jason raised his stemmed glass, and Pete gently tapped the shot glass to its rim. Jason took a sip of the Manhattan, but Pete downed his liquor in one swallow. "And how have you been, Jason?"

"Good, good," he replied. He looked at Pete for a moment, then gulped. "Okay. I'm just going to say it. I was wondering if you would like to hang out with me some time. Like, I have Thursday off."

"I thought you were in a relationship."

"Not anymore." Jason could feel something float up and spin around inside his chest when he said that—like a flake in a snow globe someone had just shaken. It was something he had been feeling frequently the last two weeks. And he hadn't been dreaming about rainbows, either.

"Wow! Are you okay?" asked Pete.

"Yeah. I moved in with my friend, Harvey. He just broke up with his girlfriend. It was kind of messy for both of us for a while, but it's better now, a lot better."

"I bet it was messy. How'd your ex take it?"

"Well, he didn't like it. He got very angry."

"Oh yeah? What did you do?"

Jason raised himself to his full height. "I got angry back."

"Well, fuck yeah!" exclaimed Pete with a smile. He held up his palm, and Jason slapped it. But then Pete's smile faded. He looked down at his hands and twisted a ring on one of his fingers. "Linda would have been proud of you," he said.

Jason pulled in his chin. "Who? Who would have been proud?"

Pete raised his head and looked at Jason with sad eyes. "Linda. You know, the old lady who introduced us?"

Jason's lips formed a crooked smile. "Oh, yeah. Her. How's she doing?"

Pete took a deep breath. "Jason, how would you feel about our first date being a funeral?"

Jason did not respond. *Cancer sticks. They'll kill ya, ya know.* He felt his throat close and a tear well in his eye. Pete leaned over the bar and rubbed Jason's shoulder with his palm, a palm large and warm enough to cradle a heart and keep it beating. "It's okay, my man," he said. "She was fearless. Died with no regrets."

Jason looked into Pete's kind eyes and open face. He nodded, then wiped a tear from his own eye—a perfect, clear, pearly drop, shed for a gravel-voiced old woman who wore bright red shoes and told him he was selling himself short. Again, he looked at Pete's face—a princely face.

Before his brain had time to filter, the words tumbling out. "Could I kiss you?" he asked.

"Yes," came the reply.

Jim Hodnett is a retired educator and psychologist. He has been writing short stories and memoirs for more than a decade. His works tend to focus on the experiences of gay men in America. He shares life with his spouse of nearly three decades, Joe Heimlich.

The Last Susan

Christina C. Moore

Morning Susan begrudgingly reminds herself to bring pajamas up for Evening Susan. While she hates having to do it every day, Evening Susan refuses to go down into the musty basement. She does, however, expect a freshly laundered set of cotton pajamas to be laid out on the bed by the time she gets home and complains loudly if she has to so much as open a dresser or, God forbid, venture down to the laundry area.

"Why do I have to do everything for her?" Morning Susan asks aloud to no one in particular, "she never does me any favors. I end up scrambling to get us ready for work every day because she can't even drag herself down a flight of stairs to pull the knob on the washing machine. Would it hurt her to refill the automatic coffee maker before she goes to bed? Or put a fresh roll of toilet paper out?"

"Well, she does work all day," a nasal voice suggests from the far corner of the basement.

"Stay out of this mother!" Morning Susan shouts, her own voice reverberating off concrete walls, "and no, she doesn't work all day. All she does is lay on the couch and scroll through social media."

"But she's exhausted. She needs downtime," the voice persists.

"Well, don't blame me!" Morning Susan snaps, "Blame Ms. Steward. She's the one who wears those horrible shoes with the tiny heels. She could afford to hire a maid if she weren't so cheap."

"The cleaning lady comes every Saturday," the nasal voice intones, "I raised five children practically on my own, and do you think I ever got some lady just to clean my house?"

Susan turns up the sound on her ear buds hoping to drown out this intrusive presence from the depths of her past. The last thing she needs is to argue with her dead mother before work. It's past seven already, and she still must finish preparing the work clothes so that Ms. Steward can get dressed.

She pulls shirts out of the dryer and onto the concrete floor. When she finds the shirt for Tuesday, she wads the rest into a ball and stuffs them in a plastic basket. She will regret this tomorrow when yet another shirt needs to be ironed, but she doesn't have time to fuss with it now. As she pushes the basket aside, she notices the black pin stripe peeking out from the side of the pile. This shirt was missing when Susan loaded the washer this morning. She had emptied the hamper looking for it. Yet here it is coming out of the dryer covered with what, in the dim light, looks like a huge coffee stain. One of the other Susans must have hidden it in the washer last night, probably so Morning Susan would not see the stain.

When Susan holds the shirt directly in front of the light, the brownish discoloration reveals itself, and it's definitely not coffee. She doesn't want to know how this shirt got blood all over it, but it's a damn shame. Had she gotten to it right away, she could have soaked it in dish detergent preventing the stain from setting. Now that it's been through the dryer, the damage is most likely permanent, another piece of clothing to be thrown away. Evening Susan, with her lazy habits, strikes again.

She grabs today's shirt and runs the iron directly across the thin fabric, not bothering to smooth out the seams. This shirt is always worn under the herring bone sports coat anyway, and so it doesn't need to be perfect. She's tired of the constant starching and ironing. Besides, she hates this blouse with its tiny buttons and fussy frill. Some days, Ms. Steward goes to work looking like she ought to be selling Edwardian hats rather than holding down the city's most powerful law firm.

While she's been asked to do more around the house, Evening Susan will never help with preparing the work clothes. She doesn't even bother to put dishes in the dishwasher after she uses them. *Fat, pampered, and lazy is what she is.*

She spends most of her share of the day sitting on the couch in front of the huge television, eating chips directly from the bag. Half the time she walks in with fast-food, dropping empty containers on the counter rather than in the trash. The lingering grease stink makes Morning Susan's stomach lurch. Ironically, Ms. Steward thinks Morning Susan ought to be the one who does something about the extra weight they're all carrying, wake an hour early to run a few miles on the treadmill. When she gets back upstairs, Morning Susan will eat a piece of cold pizza directly from the fridge just to spite her.

Ms. Steward emerges as Morning Susan squeezes her way into the elastic shaping garment. The blouse takes forever to button, and she wishes Morning Susan would remove it from the weekly rotation. The dainty lace on the collar gives off an antique vibe, and Ms. Steward is trying to look younger these days. Fresh from the dry cleaners, the sepia suit she wears on Tuesdays is still wrapped in paper. She discards the paper on the closet floor, a habit which infuriates Morning Susan. Since this is the day she often meets with new clients, she needs to look formal.

Rumors circulate amongst the rank-and-file of a Friday massacre. Her name has been mentioned with reference to the chopping block more than once these past few days. These rumors are partly true. The fat will be trimmed this Friday. The partners are meeting Thursday afternoon to vote out one of their own, and most of the juniors are hoping it will be her. Of course, she already knows who they're voting out, and it's not her. The very idea is laughable. She brings in twice as much money as her male counterparts—good solid corporate cash, the kind that gets paid promptly and never dries up.

No. The "cranky old bitch" is safe this time around. They are meeting to vote out the pedophile. Lewiston's estranged wife found the wrong sort of porn on his laptop and turned it over to the police. Unbeknownst to Lewiston, he's days away from being served an arrest warrant, and the partners need to get rid of him before that happens.

Besides, Lewiston plateaued years ago, stopped bringing in new clients as soon as he made partner, taking his promotion to mean he could spend more time with family-- as if that did him any good. Most of what he makes now is through poaching clients. The other partners have been looking for an excuse to remove him for months, and there is no more thorough way to get rid of someone than with a dose of child pornography.

Somewhere, deep inside, another Susan chuckles at the image of tubby old Lewiston in handcuffs and an orange jumpsuit. This other Susan appears briefly just below the surface of the mirror causing wrinkles and cracks to appear through heavy makeup. But this is a mirage. As soon as Ms. Steward realizes something else is there, it fades into the background. "I must need Botox," she tells her forty-five-year-old reflection.

"Yes, you do," the reflection responds as it affixes a blond wig over its gray-streaked bob.

She decides to wear the tan pumps today, the same ones she wore yesterday. However, when she pulls them from the walk-in closet, they are mangled. One heel has completely broken off and the soles are scratched and discolored with asphalt. It looks like she walked home down some country road. "What the hell happened to these things?" Ms. Steward asks aloud. In the empty house, no one answers.

Nearly five hundred dollars down the shitter, she throws the damaged shoes against the far wall leaving a nick in the blue paint, frustrated that her best pumps were ruined during the night, and she can't remember how or why.

She grabs a lesser pair of shoes, lighting a cigarette to calm her nerves.

Normally, she would wait until she's in the car to smoke, but Morning (aka Sabotage) Susan is going to have to deal with the lingering cigarette odor. It is after all Ms. Steward who pays the bills in this place. She treats herself to a second cup of coffee and ten minutes of silence before she grabs her purse and heads out to the car.

For a second, her heart clutches in her chest. The spot where the Bentley should be parked is empty. It takes her a moment to realize that someone pulled it into the garage last night rather than under the carport. Since Morning Susan rarely drives, it could only have been Evening Susan, but unless the weather is bad, she is usually too lazy to bother with the garage. Why then did she use the garage last night? Regardless, she should have left a note to spare her the jolt of pure terror, particularly on this morning when her nerves are already frayed. Next time she might end up with a heart attack.

Ms. Steward sometimes makes it all the way home on her own, but usually it is Evening Susan who pulls into the driveway, emerging as the Bentley shoots through the mountain tunnel, the emotional halfway point between work and home. Occasionally, she is annoyed by this. She would love to drive her own damn car for a change...or be the one to feel the sensation of taking off these horrible shoes at the end of a long day and sinking her feet into slippers. Evening Susan enjoys most of the simple pleasures, while Ms. Steward is expected to pay the bills.

At least Evening Susan is finally taking initiative in securing the car. Thieves are everywhere, even in this zip code, and they can smell a Bentley like a shark can smell chummed water. Ms. Steward has been leaving notes begging Evening Susan to please secure the car in the garage, and after a month of nagging, she must have gotten through.

She doesn't notice the damage until after she pulls into the parking space marked "Reserved for Susan Steward, Esq." Even then, she only spots it because she drops her keys and must lean down to pick them up. There is an indentation on the right side of the front bumper, as if she's hit someone's dog. She mentally throws up her hands. Even minor fender damage on this car can run up a bill equivalent to ruining ten pairs of expensive shoes.

She gets to her feet quickly. She doesn't want to be spotted looking too long or hard because she still does not know what happened last night, and she might not want someone else noticing the strands of hair embedded in the frame just below the grill.

Quickly she gets back in the Bentley and drives towards the car wash a mile further down Broad. This problem needs to be solved before the morning round-up which begins in half an hour. It would be uncharacteristic for her to be late for a meeting with her juniors. While acting uncharacteristic never proves anything, it is always suspicious.

On her way to the car wash, she calls her go-to coffee shop, ordering a container of coffee and box of random pastries to be charged to her personal account. The juniors might arguably find this sort of spontaneous reward to be uncharacteristic, but they can hardly complain when she is being nice to them for a change. It will also give her an excuse to be up to five minutes late if need be. She is going to let two of them go at the end of the week, and so this can be her special treat.

The car wash takes less than ten minutes. She is the first and only car in line. Normally, she would pay to have the car hand washed, but she can't risk having someone notice anything disturbing stuck to that bumper. While she cringes her way through the abrasive tunnel of scrubbers and spray, the jet of cleanser blasting the undercarriage should take care of any residual materials. She will of course have to double check. If the hair is stuck on the metal, it might still be there. While hair is incriminating, DNA will convict.

On her way into the coffee shop, she drops her keys again, further under the car this time. The car wash has done its job. There are a few strands of hair left behind, but she quickly yanks them off, leaving them to the morning breeze.

It was a blonde, whoever it was.

And suddenly she feels a pulse of dizziness pass through her, as a fragment of memory flashes through her skull. It's like a photograph taken from the past, using her brain as a camera. A single image, a blond head lolling back against her breast as she heaves the bulk of an unconscious person across pitted asphalt. Scarlet flows across pinstripe. I could not have done such a monstrous thing, she thinks. *Could Evening Susan have done something so terrible?*

When she finally looks up, she is startled to see an edgy young woman with long blue hair staring down at her, balancing a white box on one hand, while carrying a cardboard coffee take out container in the other. Dammit. Of course, they would bring the coffee out to her. She's a regular customer who drives a distinctive automobile.

"Dropped my keys," Ms. Steward smiles up at the woman, "Never get old, it's impossible to get back up again."

"I see you dented your car," the barista responds.

"Yes, I hit a dog last week. A collie, I think... something like Lassie."

"You hit a dog? That's terrible!" She exclaims a bit too passionately.

"Yes... it was. These cars are so expensive to repair. I'll need to take care of it sometime next week."

The young woman falls silent, watching as Ms. Steward struggles to her feet fighting to regain her balance on kitten heels. The young barista tersely loads the coffee and pastries into the back seat of the Bentley as Ms. Steward hands her a fifty for her efforts.

When she is alone in her car, two dark eyes stare at her through the rearview mirror. They are Susan's eyes. "If you had an accident, why didn't you call the police?" she asks, "I could have gotten us off."

She does not expect an answer, but the truth gradually reveals itself as she waits for the red light to turn. The police could not be called because of the time spent in Halstead's office yesterday afternoon with the other three partners. The Golden Hour, when male higher-ups gather at the end of the day to talk shop and smoke cigars, happens every day around six. She had never been invited to join them before, but yesterday for the first time, she was beckoned inside. The other partners had been amused when she lit herself a cigar and poured two measures from the best bottle of scotch in the office. Lewiston was there too, and they exchanged jokes pretending as if they had not been secretly planning to fire him for the past week.

She does not know what her blood alcohol level was when she left for the evening, but she is willing to bet that she would've blown more than .08.

Regardless of other mitigating factors, this incident will be viewed in one way. Susan hit a person because she was driving drunk. Even if she can minimize criminal charges, the other partners will throw her out on that curb with old Lewiston and her future in the judiciary will be over. Her only option now is to not get caught.

When Ms. Steward arrives back at the office, she encounters Lewiston puffing on a cigarette near the front entrance, (a huge no-no, even for the partners). "I thought I saw you pull in earlier," he remarks. He has obviously been watching and waiting for her this morning.

"You did," Ms. Steward replies, no use lying at this point. "When I was half-way to the door, I got a sudden urge to turn around and buy coffee for my juniors. They've all been working so hard. Please be a dear and help me carry these boxes over to the conference room."

He gallantly carries both boxes while she holds the door. "We need to talk," he says.

"Sure, we can talk. Have Jane schedule an appointment for early next week."

"Not soon enough."

"See if she can pencil you in somewhere later in the week then," she responds, and instantly he is dismissed.

She cannot help but notice that when he places the takeout on the conference room table, he does nothing to dispel the general assumption that it is he who is providing the goodies. The juniors thank him heartily on his way out the room, their bright eyes following him with sheer adoration. He was the one they all hoped to be working for when they entered the firm. Won't they be shocked when the shit tornado blows through here later this week? *Enjoy it while it lasts*, she thinks.

After lunch, Ms. Steward goes out to smoke her second cigarette. There is a bench for smokers at the side of the building, but she lights up near the front entry because a man in a shabby blue suit is scrutinizing her Bentley. He has an officious looking series of badges hanging just below his drooping gut. Had she practiced criminal instead of corporate law, Ms. Steward might have recognized him.

"Are you Susan Steward?" He asks, one meaty palm extended in her direction.

"Yes, I am." she responds cheerfully, switching her demeanor over to Official Susan, the version of her who attends church and speaks at Rotary Club meetings. Official Susan cannot function separately from Ms. Steward because she is more of an adaptation than a truly autonomous identity. This is the version of Susan that she plans on using when she makes a run for that seat on the municipal court bench next year. "How can I help you?"

"It's a shame about this Bentley," he comments, "Beautiful car."

"Yes, but it'll be good as new once I take it in for repair."

"Did you hit something?"

"A dog. Poor thing."

"What a shame," he comments dismissively. Luckily, unlike the barista from earlier this morning, the detective does not hold undue sentimentality for dogs.

"But you are not here to talk about my poor old Bentley," she purrs.

"No. I'm here to talk about your associate, Lewiston," he walks with her as she heads through the garden and towards the smoking bench. "You already know what they found on his computer…"

"Yes. I'm greatly disappointed in him. The sexual exploitation of children is one of the great evils of this world," she replies.

"Agreed. That's why I do what I do. The problem now is that Lewiston is claiming that while he enjoys a bit of the legit stuff from time to time, he was not the one who put the kiddie stuff on his laptop. He seems to think someone in your building borrowed his laptop and transferred those photographs over."

Ms. Steward coughs, a nicotine cloud bursting forth from her mouth, "I bet they all try to point the finger elsewhere," she chokes.

"They do," the detective laughs, "But this one might be telling the truth. Innocent until proven guilty right?"

"Or so I learned in law school," Official Susan quips, stifling another cough.

"Do you know what metadata is?"

"Sure. Automatic data attached to digital files."

"It's a bit more complicated than that, but you got the gist," he replies as if she is just another promising young police recruit.

"We always check the metadata because that's what leads us to the really bad guys, the perps who create this stuff to begin with. And our computer guy thought there was something interesting about the metadata on Lewiston's machine."

"Do tell," Official Susan responds, masking her alarm under the allure of shared conspiracy.

"The folder was not created on his computer. It was transferred over from an external device, probably a flash drive."

"He could've bought it online or from some shady street vendor."

"Sure, but why would he transfer the files to the computer where the wife might find them whenever she orders groceries? Why not just access the files directly from the flash drive and then lock it away in a drawer?"

Good question, Susan thinks.

"You have the mind of a lawyer," Official Susan responds, "Pity you don't work for us."

"I'll let you know when I'm back on the job market. But joking aside, we have to follow all leads. The DA is worried he won't get a conviction if Lewiston goes around claiming one of you set him up…as absurd as that sounds. Any chance we could take a look at some machines in your building?"

Official Susan laughs for real now, "Detective Gerhardt, we are a legal firm! Getting access to any device in that building is going to take one hell of a warrant. It's not that I don't want to help you out, but I can't just show you a computer. I would be violating attorney client privilege."

"I understand, but I thought it was worth a shot. Lewiston seems to think you're still on his side despite everything that's happened."

"What did he say happened?" She is authentically curious as to why Lewiston would think that she is on his side.

"Apparently, he was given some of your accounts, one quite recently. Does Nolan Hills ring a bell?"

"Yes, Nolan Hills was initially my account, but clients are always free to change representation."

The Nolan Hills case was only the most recent account of hers that Lewiston poached. It involved industrial pork producers accused of introducing pig waste into a shared irrigation system, contaminating a nearby lettuce harvest, which in turn caused a nationwide E. coli outbreak via a popular fast food chain. Susan wanted to take the case to court. All she needed to win was to prove the bacterial strain present in the pork waste was different from the one contaminating the lettuce. Instead, Lewiston had cozied up to old Nolan, giving him the "old boys'" treatment, while warning him of the inevitability of a negative judgement costing ten times what it would cost to settle out of court. In the end Lewison convinced Nolan Hills Farms to cut their losses by cutting more checks.

"So…you're not mad?"

"I'll always be mad at Lewiston for taking my case. I lost a million-dollar paycheck," Official Susan replies, "But I've moved on."

Her brain is suddenly filled with a stench so overwhelming that it causes her to gag…Another memory. A flash-drive sinking into a pool of pig slurry.

She snaps back to find Detective Gerhardt examining her quizzically,

"What is it? What's wrong?"

"I keep thinking how bad that damn farm smelled," she replies with a forced giggle, "If Lewiston wants to deal with all the pig shit, let 'im."

They share a chuckle before parting ways. Ms. Steward suspects this will not be the last time she sees Detective Gerhardt.

*****

The body is found sometime during the day by a woman out walking her dog. Ms. Steward watches the story on the local news. A reporter conducts a roadside interview with the woman whom Susan vaguely recognizes as a neighbor. Her dog looks just like Lassie.

That her crime is discovered so quickly comes as a shock, but there can be no doubt that this is the man from her vision: unknown white male in his late twenties, transient, found in the tall grass at the side of the road leading directly to Susan's house.

Thank God the guy was just some drifter and not someone's son or husband. If there's no one around to champion his cause, this whole thing could fizzle out in a matter of weeks.

She wonders if he was alive when he was dragged off the road, and then she remembers the flash of crimson blossoming across the front of her shirt. If he was still bleeding, he was alive.

She spends the rest of the day sitting at her desk staring at the rows of black binders covering the far wall. All she accomplished is recorded in those folders, her legacy to the world, a monolith of black vinyl against an office wall. Everything in those binders will mean nothing if she does not cover this up. If anyone found out what she did last night, even the best criminal lawyer money could buy would not be able to keep her out of prison. But there is another voice too, a voice long suppressed, who is saying the opposite. A young woman just out of law school is pleading with her to come clean, telling her that the law really does mean something and there is such a thing as right and wrong.

At around six, she is startled by an explosion of laughter from down the hall--Lewiston laughing at one of Halstead's pointless jokes. The Golden Hour has begun, but she was not invited this time around.

She decides to leave an hour early, making her way down the back stairwell rather than using the elevator. The sun has already set behind the mountains. It must have just rained. The dark pavement of the parking lot has become a mirror in the moonlight. Two Bentleys, one in this world, the other in the world of reflection, hum to life when she presses the fob.

As she cruises down the coastal road, fog rolls in off the ocean. *It was no one's fault. Anyone could've hit that man,* she thinks. *He should've known better than to walk down that winding road in the dark.* Another voice shouts from the back of her mind, *Susan should have stopped. Susan should have reported the accident to the police and gotten an ambulance.*

Before her, the tunnel beckons, its rows of halogen lights pulling her forward as if into an alternate universe, a universe where only one Susan exists, a Susan who is whole and complete.

As she speeds through the tunnel, she realizes that Evening Susan is late. Ms. Steward checks for her in the rear-view mirror. Instead, she sees the Other Susan, eyes black as tar, skin cracked with time. A disheveled young man with flowing blond hair and a tattered rucksack sits blankly in the seat beside her.

"Where's Evening Susan?" Ms. Steward asks.

"Gone," the Other Susan responds in a nasal voice which sounds so much like her long dead mother. "She disappeared as soon as she heard that hideous thump below the car. I had no choice but to take over."

"Will she be back?"

"I don't think so, and don't care either. She was the weakest amongst us and was holding us back."

"Did you kill her?"

"No, my companion here killed her," she replies, gesturing towards the young man, who sits with empty eyes and clenched fists. Blood trickles down from a gash across his forehead, soaking the clean white upholstery of the Bentley, but that hardly matters at this point.

"How do I get out of this?" Ms. Steward asks.

"You make a choice," the other Susan answers, "You can choose to continue forward with me, or you can turn around and choose this young man here. If you choose me, I'll protect you and push you further than you ever thought possible. You'll keep your house and this precious Bentley. You'll win your seat on the municipal court…and why stop there? Once you get started even the Supreme Court is not out of reach. When the partners approach your bench, they will do so with deference…but if you choose him, people may not be able to see him, but they will know he is there. You will wear him like a chain around your neck. They will eventually find out who it was who hit him and dragged him off the road leaving him to die. You will go to jail, and he will move on. The other Susans will abandon you until only the real Susan remains, and you will atone…but you will get to keep your soul."

Ms. Steward remains silent, as the Bentley clears the tunnel exit. She does not know the right answer. She does not even know what Susan she is at this moment. Legions of Susans scream from within.

"Which is it, Susan? Your life or your soul."

In the end, it is the Bentley that makes the choice for her, speeding on into the night past lines of yellow police tape towards home.

Christina C. Moore works at Ohio State University Libraries in the Bibliographic Initiatives Department. She has a BA in Art History and Anthropology from Oakland University. *The Last Susan* is her first published work, reflecting a childhood love for the Twilight Zone and Alfred Hitchcock movies.

Aubade

Karen Schubert

I

My grandson's voice breaks
the dark, *is it morning?*
-—if yes, he flips the switch,
Zips the blinds, cannonballs
his mattress on the floor. He rises
like the sun, like someone
coming up the stairs,
open for business, inevitable.
Before we slept, he asked me
when we wake up, call me Shark Boy, ok? That
makes me Lava Girl
and I chase him with molten hands
but it's 20 minutes to remote
kindergarten, my yoga mat
leans in the corner for gym class.
If you look in my window
you will see a woman cooking oats
and having a second chance.

II

Monday and alone, all night
My mind churns like my daughter's
rock tumbler, polishing regrets.
The morning alarm tosses me
from a dream. My neighbor's
muffler chugs off, garbage truck
rumbles past without stopping
at my empty stoop-—I'm trying
to catch a whole sleep in
7-minute nets. Slow woman
at work, I cup coffee, its
milky fog, squint at the heron
colored sky, check the calendar
for clues I am already sure of.

III

Dawn, give me another fanfare.
Tomorrow I'll be the goldrusher
in James Michener's *Alaska,* skating down
the frozen Yukon clutching a jar
of sourdough starter to my chest
like an organ. I'll be my young self,

making promises to God that were more
hymns to you, Dawn, hungry for light
under the oaks that cathedral my city block.
When I get another spin, dance me
into the morning, crack open like a jar of
good sauce, coat my day like fresh paint.

Karen Schubert is author of *The Compost Reader* (Accents Publishing) and five chapbooks including *Dear Youngstown* (Nightballet Press) and *I Left My Wings on a Chair* (Kent State University Press), winner of a Wick Poetry Center Chapbook Prize. She is director and co-founder of Lit Youngstown. On her grandson's recent visit, they ate pistachios, caught fireflies, made jewelry with salt dough, and went to the ice age (living room) via a time machine (door) with their pet fox (cat).

Grandma Teague and Me

S. Mia Ling

<blockquote>

Grandma Teague, I am thinking of you, wherever you are, even it is floating way above us in the ethereal white clouds in the company of God, Jesus, and the rest of your beloved Holy Trinity. Grandma Teague I am thinking of you and loving you and asking for your forgiveness for never seeing you again on this earth. I am thinking of you and crying, and hoping you are happy in Heaven the way you always wanted. I am missing you so bad. I wish I could feel your bony hand on my head. Do you remember me, Grandma, the little girl you used to take care of?

</blockquote>

Our first meeting was not auspicious.

My mom and I were on one end of the front porch, where I was clinging to her and crying so hard the floorboards shook. I had entwined myself in her legs as she was trying to get to work, tearing her new white stockings in my grubby embrace.

My mom always lied to me and said she would be home soon, when in reality, I had learned she would often be away at work for days. I expected that she was lying to me again.

At the other end of the porch, was a long-boned, skinny stranger.

"You see that nice lady over there?" Mom pointed. "She's going to be your grandma from now on and take care of you. You better stop crying or she won't like you."

I squinted. She did not look like a nice lady. She did not look like anyone's image of a grandma. She looked tall and ghostly in her faded housedress and loosely hanging apron. Her skin was pale and grayish, and her hair was the color of a rusted coat hanger.

"No!" I cried, tightening my grip. "No! I don't like her!" I was going to be swallowed up by this scary ghost.

"Hush now. You have to call her grandma so she will take good care of you," my mother reasoned in her soft melodious voice. "She's going to teach you all sorts of things while I am at work all day, so you won't have to be alone. I won't always be worrying about you because I will know that she's feeding you and telling you stories. You'll end up loving her, you'll see."

For answer I just screamed louder than ever. Mom was becoming angry and looked at her watch impatiently. She disentangled me from her legs and carried me over. When we were almost there, I dared open my eyes. The scary ghost lady enfolded me in her skeletal frame and said to my mother." Go, go quickly. She'll be just fine. You'll see."

"Call her grandma," admonished my mother one final time before she left.

I was blubbering and snot was dripping out my nose. "Grandma?" I said choking, "I need a Kleenex."

She laughed at me shaking her head and carried me into her home where she found me a starched white handkerchief and wiped my face dry.

In retrospect, of course my mom was right.

But this thing, of calling complete strangers auntie or uncle, or if they were older, grandma or grandpa, made me feel weird. My mom had told me that it was a mark of respect. Like you were loving them as you would love someone in your own family. She assumed that they would like it.

104

But I was not sure people really felt good about suddenly becoming part of our family. Whenever my mom would call them uncle or auntie, I would see the surprise on the strangers' faces. I was also wondering if maybe they might consider it an insult. I had heard kids on the street yelling at some old folks, "Hey Grandpa canja hurry it up, y'old slow poke?"

But Grandma Teague didn't seem to mind. She was happy to take care of me and earn the extra money.

We lived in one half of the duplex and she, the other, all by herself. Her husband had died many years ago and her only daughter was grown up and married with a family of her own.

Living in that duplex was convenient. We just had to walk across the front or back porch and there she was. Mom and Dad had to be careful not to yell at each other or throw things because she could hear everything. So if they swore it had to be in Chinese. That was how I learned all those words that didn't really sound bad at all but apparently were things children should never say like: "*Ni wan ba dan* (you are a mixed turtle's egg)" or "*Ni sheng jing bing* (your nerves are inflamed)."

The first day in Grandma's house she poked her finger into me and said, "You are a skinny little thing, look at them bones." She put her hands around my waist and her fingers overlapped. "We going to put some meat on them bones, missy."

That is what she had decided to call me, Missy. My Chinese name Ming Hsing sounded almost the same to her and Missy was easier for her to say.

She started to whip up a meal explaining, "I don't ordinarily cook, for just one person it's too much trouble. Ever since my husband died, I haven't wanted to cook, got no reason to. I used to be a normal weight person. Now I just live on my snuff and chewin terbackie and that's enough for me." So saying she pulled out a can from underneath her bed and spit into it." But now I see I'm going to need to cook for you and so I guess I'll be putting some weight on my bones too and my doctor will be glad of that, so thank you Missy!"

She looked at me again and shook her head. "I never saw a chile so skinny. You shore do look downright sickly if I say so myself."

No one had ever said that to me before. It was true that I sometimes played all day running around by myself and didn't eat until my mom and dad got home at night. Even then I didn't want to stop playing and sometimes they would have to chase me all around, begging me to eat something. I thought it was fun to have them chase me and beg me to eat. I was proud of being able to run faster than them. Sometimes my mother would cry because I wouldn't eat.

Before Grandma took care of me, I was often sick. The glands on both sides of my jaw would swell red hot and painful. I would barely be able to drink, even plain water. Mother would put warm compresses on my swollen glands and after a few days they would get better.

After she bustled around in the kitchen, we had a lot of food on her enameled kitchen table. Green beans cooked in bacon fat and white mashed potatoes with gravy pools. Big pieces of fried chicken with a peppery crust, sour slices of red beets. Before we ate, she made fold my hands and bow my head while she said, "Thank you Lord for bringing this poor Chinese chile to my house to help out me out with my poor aching bones and for what we are about to eat. Amen."

"Amen," I repeated after her.

But the biggest surprise was at the end of the meal when I thought we were all done. "Pshaw, we still got dessert," she said.

She brought a transparent red jewel shaped like a star to the table. The jewel wobbled and reflected the lights of the kitchen.

Grandma said to me "Quit staring chile. It's just Jell-O. You hadn't never had any Jell-O before?"

"You can eat it?" I asked.

"Yessiree Bob, it's mighty good. "

She dipped a spoon into the beautiful sculpture and tore a bit away. Then she plumped a giant spoonful onto my plate.

I tried a bit. It was hard to keep it from wiggling off the spoon. It was cool and wet and melted like sugar in your mouth. As soon as it hit your tongue it lost its shape. I liked it very much.

Her half of the house was arranged front to back with all the rooms in a row. First a tiny living room filled with trinkets and hand-crocheted antimacassars. Then a small guest bedroom which had a bare single bed, a beat-up cardboard suitcase, and some of her daughter Flora Belle's old toys, and from which she extracted a small rubber doll baby for me. Then came her bedroom, and finally the kitchen with a space for an eat-in table and followed by the porch and backyard.

Her bedroom was bigger than any of the other rooms. It smelled of rose water and tobacco, pine sol, clean laundry, and her missing husband. Above her bed was a cross-stitched pane "Home Sweet Home" and a brass cross with Jesus nailed to it. On the shelf were all her husband's old shaving things, a short brush, soap, cup, and razor. At night when we prayed, she never forgot to bless him and recommend him to the Lord.

But of all the marvelous things in her house, none was more awesome than Grandma herself. She did not stop toiling for a second. As soon as she finished one task, she was on to the next. One of the things she did to earn extra money, was laundry for other people.

She had the kind of washing machine that had rollers on top to wring out the clothes after they were washed. The machine was fat and round and made a jolly sound until it came to the end when it would whump and wobble around as if its insides were about to rupture. Louder and louder were the explosions in a rhythmic dance until Grandma would shriek "What in tarnation? Lord forgive my swearing."

The wringer was stubborn and hard to work. It seemed like a devil had invented that machine expressly to pinch your fingers or whack your elbow when you were least expecting it. I stood next to Grandma and helped feed the laundry in between the two wringers, while she turned the handle.

When we had wrung out as much water as we could, we carried the laundry out to the back yard to hang in the sun.

When she hung the item up on the drying line, she kept clothespins in her mouth as she was going up and down. It saved her going to the cloth bag hanging at the end of the line each time. But now that she had me, I would carry the bag behind her and carefully hand her a clothespin whenever she needed it. She would snap each item with a quick wrist action before she hung it up. The clothes swung there in the wind as if they were having a jiggly conversation with each other.

After the sun had dried the laundry all afternoon, she brought it inside in a big basket. The laundry smelled good. She sat me down on the bed while she showed me how she did the ironing.

I had never seen anyone do ironing before. My parents for sure never ironed anything. We didn't even have an iron. They said, "Ironing is for laundrymen. We are not laundrymen, we are intellectuals."

Grandma sprayed starch from a can on each item and then with a steaming iron carefully pressed the various linens, the tablecloths, the shirts, the handkerchiefs. The sweet smell of the starch and steam entered my nostrils and circled around my body; I longed for the day I could iron. It seemed to me the best thing in the world for I liked how flat and evenly she pressed the cotton. I loved to see the wrinkles magically disappear. How the white shirts with their stiff collars seemed to gloat self-importantly afterwards, assuming a noble shape.

Grandma Teague knew how to do so many things that I had never seen anyone do before. She showed me beans growing from a vine in her backyard that went all the way up some wires to a pole. She plucked the beans by hand and took them inside where she rinsed them. I liked helping her snap off the ends and hear them pop and then peel the stringy lining. She seemed pleased to have me help her. And that I hadn't peed in my britches a single time.

We went to deliver the fresh clothes to the family that had requested it. It was the pastor's family. His wife and children stared at me, and I hid behind Grandma.

"Who's she?" asked the wife narrowing her eyes and pointing at me.

"She's my new grandbaby," said Grandma proudly.

"Ain't you got enough grandbabies of your own? Have to go around getting some from the other side of the earth now?" snorted the pastor's wife.

"Can't ever have too many," said Grandma proudly.

"Kin she speak English, you know, Amerkan?"

"Sure, she can, and please and thank you too. She's got better manners than any kid I done took care of so far," she remarked tartly and glared at two boys who were pinching each other behind their mother's back.

"Well, she don't steal, do she?" the pastor's wife was counting out the money.

"Her, no she wouldn't hurt a fly."

"Well, you'd best be careful, you can't really trust no Chinaman. But they're better'n the colored I suspect."

"Well, I imagine so. Her folks got culture. They're studying to be doctors."

"Doctors? Both of 'em? "

"Yessiree. And her mom works awful hard, sometimes two or three days in a row before she can come home."

"Well, I'll be darned. God bless her heart. You bring her by to play with the boys sometime, wontcha? After church. She does go to church, don't she?" She wrinkled her nose suspiciously as if she had just smelled something really bad.

"Of course, of course, I'm gonna bring her, soon as I kin git her the right clothes," exclaimed Grandma.

The woman gave Grandma the money and another big load of laundry to carry back.

When we were out of sight, Grandma turned to me and said "Some people! The nerve of her thinking you can't speak English. When you can speak whole lotta heaps better'n her!"

***

It was the anniversary of my mom and dad. Their five-year anniversary. They liked telling the story of how my dad had "courted" my mother by taking her out for lemon meringue pie. This was while they were in China and lemon meringue pie could only be had at a fancy "Western" restaurant.

My mother thought that was the most romantic thing that had ever happened to her. When she wasn't mad at my father, she said that lemon meringue pie was her favorite food in the whole world.

Grandma had somehow heard the story and she decided to make them a lemon meringue pie. We were all hoping that they would be happy on their anniversary and not fight.

We had the whole afternoon to make the pie. Grandma put on her worn out apron that she had sewed out of a flour sack. She pinned back her hair in a net, rolled up the tattered sleeves of her house dress so I could see all the freckles and wrinkles on her arms and lined up all the ingredients we would need on her linoleum counter.

A lemon meringue pie! I had never seen any pie being made before. I felt that something momentous was about to change my life.

First, we had to make the crust. She took out a huge bag of flour and measured it with a glass cup. Then she poured the flour into a red and white metal cup-like thing with a handle that she made me turn so that the flour would grind against a wire net at the bottom and magically out would flow finely aerated flour sprinkling the bowl underneath. She said it was called a sifter which would puff up the flour with air so that we could get the exact right amount.

That little sifter thing really got me.

It was hypnotizing to hear the grating noise and then see the flour magically appear as if I had actually created it by turning the handle.

Then she mixed the other ingredients for the dough. She took out a wooden rolling pin and rolled the dough nice and even. "This is what I crack Billie with when he don't act right" she joked, waving the pin around. Billie was her grown up nephew who had a pompadour like Elvis Presley and sometimes came to visit.

She rolled the dough expertly, flat with no cracks at the edges. My job was to add a pinch of flour if she thought the mixture seemed too sticky. She greased a pie pan with Crisco and flour and rotated the pan, so the flour flowed from side to side. The flour flew into the air like white dust motes, and you could see the sun cascade off the individual flecks.

After the dough was rolled very thin, she said, "Here comes the tricky part. We gotta move this dough from here to there without it breaking. If it breaks, we gotta start all over again."

She gingerly raised the delicate cape of dough and placed it gently on the greased pie tin. My heart was pounding with apprehension about that translucent piece of dough failing to hold together. But it did and we breathed a sigh of relief. She trimmed off the edges and gave me the leftover bits to shape into an animal.

By now we were both coated with flour. It was in all the wrinkles and crinkles of her face and even in her hair and hair net. Her hair was even whiter than usual. I sneezed and clouds of flour went flying off me. We laughed and that made me sneeze more. I must have sneezed about five times before the flour settled.

She had yet another amazing gadget, a thing that could roll and make little pin pricks on the crust. She let me roll the pin-pricker thing all around the crust and make tiny little tracks.

Next, we had to make the pie filling. Grandma had lemons from her back yard which she made me squeeze. Three times on each side and then once more for good measure, to make sure that every drop of juice was wrung out.

"I got bad artheeritis." she moaned. "Can't do nearly all the things I ought to. Bless the Lord, we have to be grateful for the things we got and not go complaining about the things we cain't never git no more."

"What's artheeritis Grandma?" I asked her.

"See my hands," she said and cracked her knuckles. Her knuckles were red and swollen. "Don't you go cracking your knuckles," she said. "It ain't good for you." Then she popped the last ones again.

"Why do you have that?" I persisted.

"When you're old and have worked as much as I have, you'll get it too. Just you wait and see. Shoot, you sure have a lot of questions."

Getting old sounded terrible. Her hands were still strong and active, but she had to take pills all the time and she was always rubbing liniment on her sore hands.

But she didn't let anything stop her. "Watch this here," she said, "how I crack them eggs." She tapped the egg on the edge of the counter and the egg broke evenly in half.

We only needed the egg yolks for the lemon filling, and not a bit a shell could fall in. After she cracked the egg, she cradled and rocked the two halves of the shell back and forth, hypnotically, like a magician, so that the clear viscous liquid dripped sinuously into a bowl while the yolk remained safe and unbroken in one half of the shell. She wouldn't let me help with this part.

"It's too 'pacific for you. We're gonna use them egg whites later and not a drop of yolk can come along. Even a smidgen of yolk will ruin our meringue, bless the Lord."

We mixed the lemon and egg yolk and sugar and poured the mixture into the pie shell.

Finally came the meringue. The egg whites whirred swiftly in the electric beater.

"Watch it, watch it, watch it," ordered Grandma. "It's about to turn."

Suddenly the clear liquid suddenly became a whitish mountain stiff with tiny crystalline peaks. She gave me a rubber spatula to shape the meringue over the lemon filling. Then we set the pie to baking.

Grandma was plumb tired from making that complicated pie. She sat down, took out her false teeth, placed them carefully into a glass of fizzing water and rested, something I hardly ever saw her do. I looked at the teeth carefully. They were attached to pink gums and floated about like a mouth that wanted to say something. Grandma's face had become concave, like a deflated balloon and she talked with a muffly sound. From a coffee can underneath her bed, she took out a pinch of brown stuff and stuck it in her cheek while she closed her eyes happily.

"That won't take but three quarters of an hour to bake and then we'll see if it's worthy of eatin'," she sniffed.

It was that time of day when the sun is starting to cool down. The shadows are starting to be long. When if you've worked hard all day, it's okay to have an icy glass of iced tea and maybe a nap. Grandma suddenly seemed as tired as a drunk man and started snoring while half collapsed on the bed.

While she rested, I played with a rubber doll baby she had found that used to belong to her daughter when she was a kid. She had given me some old handkerchiefs for diapers and so I had the baby drink water and then pee and then drink and then pee some more. That doll really couldn't do anything more but pee and drink. I would change the handkerchiefs and let them dry on the bed railing.

After a while I could hear the snoring stop.

"Grandma," I asked her, "why do you eat that brown stuff. Does it taste good?"

"When I'm real tired, it gives me energy," she said, little brown dribbles spilling out of the corner of her mouth. "I know the Lord says it's a vice. But He's forgiven me time and again. It's my one failing. That chewing tabakker."

She brought out a spittoon and suddenly let a long brown swoosh of liquid spurt out from her mouth to an arm's length away.

"Well time's a wasting," she remarked.

She took out the pie. It smelled like the fruit tree in her front yard. The meringue tips had turned golden brown. A little piece had broken off the edge and she gave it to me to try.

Mother was very impressed with our efforts when she came home. My father got back half an hour later. We were all waiting for him so we could eat the pie. Grandma cut us each had a huge slice and we washed it down with sweet iced tea.

The pie was tart and sweet and crunchy and soft all at once, ten different textures melting all together. My cheeks puckered and saliva poured out of my mouth. I could see why my mother had fallen in love after lemon pie.

The four of us ate the entire pie. There was not a crumb left. My mother was smiling. She seemed delighted.

But we weren't sure about my father. Sometimes just when things seemed perfect, he'd have an anger fit and no one would know why. We all turned to stare at him anxiously.

He seemed more inarticulate than usual. He grunted. His face turned red. Blobs of lemon and crust stuck to his lips. A few crumbs had wandered onto his white shirt.

Then he burped and broke out in a big grin.

"Good pie," he chortled enthusiastically. He took out a five-dollar bill and pressed it into Grandma Teague's hand.

"I like lemon pie," he exclaimed.

Jesus

Mother was working over the weekend, so it was me and grandma all week-end long. Arkansas was known for its swelteringly humid summers. Grandma was going to church, and she decided to take me with her.

We walked there, a long walk through the hot dusty town. People were sitting on their front porches and fanning themselves. Before we had even gone five blocks I was wet with sweat and wishing for a popsicle or even a bite of cold Jell-O. Grandma had on a light housedress she had made herself out of salvage flour sacks printed with small flowers. She liked to say that that material was *indestructionable*. Because it had come all the way from wherever flour was made to the store and then to her house. Grandma was thrifty and she never threw anything away. Everything had a use. Even people.

If we met someone panhandling on the street, Grandma would haul out her tiny coin purse from the big black satchel she carried, and hand the person a nickel or dime. Like as not, she actually knew the person or someone in their family and would start to jawing with them. She would encourage them: "I know, yer farm ain't had no rain this month, it's a tough month for y'all, don't worry, Lord will provide. You kin come by my house, you know I'm a widder and I always need a hand." Then she would add, pointing to me: "By the way, this here's my new grandbaby. Ain't she cute?"

And I would be cute, because she had dolled me up, braided my hair and put ribbons in the plaits, washed my face.

When we got to the church, she took me in with her through the big front doors. I couldn't believe it. The church had air-conditioning. We headed straight for the front pew where the cooling was the strongest. It was a beautiful place with tall multi-colored windows and pots of fresh, sweet-smelling flowers. Soon we were singing songs from a book and yelling back at the preacher, words like "I believe!" "I testify!" "Amen!" and waving our arms. I copied everything Grandma did.

Then came an even more exciting part. The doors and fence in front of us suddenly parted and a little pool of water appeared behind them, right next to the preacher. Grandma was excited and she pushed me forward. I stood in the cold water up to my ankles, then the preacher unexpectedly poured a stream of water on my head and said: "I now baptize you in the name of Jesus, Lord and the Holy Ghost." He crossed himself with his hands going up and down and then sideways, the way I had seen Grandma do.

Water was dripping off my head afterwards, even though Grandma tried to blot it off.

So she decided I should go outside and dry up in the sun and join the other kids at Sunday Bible School. She was still emotional. "You done been baptized, you're saved! Thank the Lord. You've been saved! Do you know what that means? It means we can be together in Heaven!"

I asked her, "Isn't Heaven where you're supposed to go when you're dead?"

"That's right," she answered rapturously. "It's a great place, everything is nice there, you would love it, clean and proper. No one even has to do any work. The angels come and do it all. And delicious food, all your favorites, and it's all free."

"Hmm," I said, "but how do they know what I like to eat?"

"Oh, they're watching you all the time. Even when you're asleep."

"But I don't want to be dead," I protested.

"Oh," she laughed, "that won't be for a long time. But it's better to get in good with them now, so they know you, it's like money in the bank, the sooner you do it, the longer time it's got to get interest and pile up."

Grandma sure was practical. I guessed it would be a good idea to go to Heaven, after I died, if it was a long, long time from then.

Sunday Bible School was fun, there were swings and a playground. We got coloring books and did crafts. And then, we learned about Jesus.

"Jesus died on the cross for you," the teacher told us. "They put nails in his hands and made him hang that way until he died." They showed a picture of his hands with the nails and the blood. I felt the nails going into my hands. I imagined the pain of the first nail entering. I imagined the torture of hanging there, all my weight radiating out from that one nail on each side. I imagined the pain until I felt nauseated. I blinked away the tears. Why did they have to do that to Him? "That's why we all have to be good," said the teacher, "to make it worth it. "

I promised that I would never tell a lie. I promised to turn the other cheek even if someone was mean to me.

Walking home, I asked Grandma about it. "God made everything, and Jesus was the Son of God," she said.

"But why did He make mosquitoes? They're a bad thing."

She had an answer for every question, "That's for Him to know and us to find out."

I told my mom that I had gotten baptized, but she didn't seem too keen about it. She said that maybe Jesus was good, but she wasn't sure about all the rest of them. She had never heard of a Holy Ghost. She said that maybe it was like one giant ghost that was bigger than all the others.

She especially hated the missionaries that had come to China. She said that they were a bunch of hypocrites, look at what they had done to China, come and stolen everything, scraped the gold off the emperor's palace, taken all the people's land. They even sided with the British when they tried to get the Chinese people hooked on opium.

She took me with her to the grocery store. Between the green onions and the cashiers, was a bookstand with magazines and soft covered books including one called "Great Love Stories from the Bible."

"It's all the dirty stories from the Bible," Mom whispered to me. "Like how the King saw Bathsheba taking a bath and got married to her, by sending her husband away to battle."

I thought it was weird that her name was also about her taking a bath.

School

At the end of a year with Grandma, I had grown several inches and she was sewing me new clothes for my first day at school. She had made me a matching sun bonnet and I felt pretty. Grandma had arthritis of the hands, still she had managed to braid my hair into matching pig tails and my mother had bought me new red ribbons.

Grandma knew how to do everything. She could sew on the sewing machine, she could do embroidery. She bought me a little embroidery hoop and I sewed the picture of a little dog. She let me try my hand at starching and ironing. I helped her make a cake, coated the pan, and licked the frosting off the beaters. She could cook and clean way better than my mom who never did any of those things.

All that year she babysat for me, fed me, taught me many things. And many nights I slept with her in her bed. I got to know her tobacco-y smell and the way her body ricocheted when she walked. I got to anticipate when she would call me or need me and what I should do to help her. She got indignant when she saw people being mean to me and yelled at them: "Thass my grandbaby y'all talkin about."

At school they said I was smart because I could read already. I don't remember how or where I learned to read, but it seemed natural to me. When the teacher talked about certain letters meaning certain things, I already knew it.

At the end of the school year, my mother announced that we were moving away to South Dakota. She told me to kiss my grandma goodbye. I cried. I loved her now.

She cried too. She gave me a little white Bible inscribed with my name and asked me to write to her every day.

I did write to her in my best script, almost every day for a month. I gave all the letters to my mom. I'm not sure if she mailed them, because I didn't have the address or any stamps. Mom said she would look up the address and mail them for me. But she was always busy. I never got any letters back except one.

It said: *Dear Missy, we sure do miss you down here, it is so darn hot the tar is bubbling, remember Jesus loves you, don't forget your prayers and swear on the Bible never to tell any lies nor any of the bad things that people do up North. Love, from your white Grandma who loves you to the stars.*

I read that letter about a million times until my mother threw it away one day. I cried, but Mom said," She was a nice lady, she took good care of you, but she wasn't your real grandma anyway."

S. Mia Ling moved states almost every year as she was growing up, but Ohio seems to be the one that stuck. She left and came back, left and came back. White folks ain't all bad and many are downright lovable. There's a lot to appreciate in every part of the world and she has passaged in over 70 of them.

At the Crossing

Kathleen Nicklaus

On the cusp of two worlds,
    they wait for the crossing:

the fetus dreaming,
    a sea trout feeding,
        my father in hospice,
           (and I by his side).

They float, unknowing, in sediments fragrant,
    deep blankets of silt, sandy-sweet with decay.

The bay is salty,
    the umbilical winding,
        the I.V. keeps dripping,

        And somewhere the muffle of thunder or rain.

They are drawn to the surface
    by glimmers of movement,
        by something that beckons, pulling them near.

Stippled and urgent,
    a glimpse of the shoreline.
        The membrane is silver, a trembling mirror.

Then the talons—The catch!
    The shock and the gasp.
        Wrenched from the warmth into blinding light
           from the dark they have known into dazzling bright.

Then weightless, aloft, and another world seen.
    The struggle is brief, and the body gives way.

        And somewhere the echo of thunder and rain.

Born and raised in the Columbus, Ohio area, Kathleen Nicklaus attended Worthington High School and Otterbein College before moving to Lakeland, Florida, where she teaches college English and humanities. She wrote the poem, *At the Crossing*, in the first days following the death of her beloved father, Robert T. Nicklaus.

The Insatiable Appetite of Eight Billion Wolves

Jeffrey K. McKee

Time and numbers can be tricky things. Time is relative not just in an Einsteinian way, but also in the way we perceive it. To a 6-year-old child, a year is a long, long time between birthdays. Yet as a dear friend in his 90s once told me, "My typical year lasts about 3 weeks now." Add in geological time, with Earth being 4.54 billion years old, then the timescale of a human life looks minuscule. What impacts could human lives have in such a short amount of time? It turns out to be quite a lot.

As for numbers, they are also subject to varied perceptions. When talking about economics, we toss around numbers like billions and even trillions of dollars. But how much is a billion? I ask my students if they think they've lived a billion seconds. Some shoot up their hands confidently, others were not so sure, having never thought about it. It turns out that a billion seconds is nearly 32 years, shy by about 4 months. Being the scientific nerd I am, I calculated and celebrated with a party on the day of my billionth second. We had a grand time, but sadly I just noticed that I have barely missed celebrating on the day of my second billionth anniversary. Tempus fugit in a short human life.

This essay deals with both time and numbers, and how they apply to people and life on Earth. If you are the kind with math anxiety, do not worry as I do all the math and it's all just for perspectives and thought experiments. If you are comfortable with math, be prepared to come away from this reading with at least a touch of math anxiety, as the numbers are profound.

Time and change will surely show...

Our world is evolving rapidly. We see changes in real time that used to go at a much slower pace. Technological developments provide a vivid example. Stone tool technology took a long time to develop. By about 2.5 million years ago our ancestors created the first stone tools, the Oldowan industry. The tools were simple, just one rock knocked against another to create a sharp flake used in scavenging meat. That industry lasted over a million years as our ancestors' only lithic technology. So, by two million years ago, it was still Oldowan version 1.0, and in parts of Africa Oldowan 1.0 lasted another half million years. The population numbers of these diminutive pre-humans were small and their environmental impact immeasurable. They were just another incidental part of the evolving African ecosystems.

Contrast Oldowan tools to today's technology. In terms of a human lifetime for somebody my age, it took a long time, to go from rotary land-line phones to car phones, then to flip phones on cellular devices. And now our smart phones have advanced so rapidly that they can do more in an instant than the room-sized computers could do with punch cards, back when I first learned computer languages in the 1970s. Recently I had a bright young intern helping me update a dataset regarding my research on human population size and animal species diversity, or "biodiversity" as we call it. When certain software questions came up, he would grab his smart phone and look up the answer. I told him that when I started this line of research there was no such thing as a smart phone, but to him it is something that has been a given norm for his entire life.

Now let's translate these temporal observations to nature, on a global scale. Our planet is metamorphosing at an increasingly rapid rate. In evolutionary biology we often talk about fits and starts of the origins and extinctions of species; sometimes when it rains it drizzles, other times it pours. We refer to the five mass extinctions of life known from the paleontological record, the most recent one being 65 million years ago when most of the remaining dinosaurs were finished off in a relatively short amount of time. Today something else is awry. This planet, with its current though diminishing abundance of plant and animal species, is rapidly losing the diversity of those life forms on which we depend. It started after Oldowan gave way to hunting technology used by a larger bodied human ancestor whose populations grew beyond Africa, leaving behind a small but noticeable trail of mammal extinctions. Now our planet is verifiably in a full-blown 6th mass extinction, and the first one caused by a single species.

How does that happen? Quite simply we humans are squeezing out other species of animals and plants as well. Research by myself and others has demonstrated a close correlation between human population density in each country and the number of animals threatened with extinction. I started this research when the human population was about to reach 7 billion in 2011, being concerned because we got to 3 billion when I was only two years old. The next big milestone of 8 billion will come in 2023. This is despite a devastating global pandemic, and despite deadly wars and famine. To do some interesting and sobering math, that means that we will have 1.76 humans on Earth for every year of its existence, all occurring in a mere moment of geological time. Pause a human moment to think about that.

Meanwhile, it is estimated that we are losing between and 1 and 43 species of plants and animals per *hour*, with the typical estimate being around 11 extinctions in the time it takes you to read this essay. Maybe the estimates are wrong and don't take enough into consideration, like new species evolving to refill the gaps. So, let's imagine that we have a net loss of just one species per *day*, given the best estimate of 12 million species on Earth today. At that low rate, all life forms on Earth would be extinct in less than 33,000 years. That seems like a long time from the perspective of a human life, and maybe you can still sleep soundly tonight, but again through the lens of geological time, that is just a blip out of 4.54 billion years.

The loss of other species due to human expansion is not just a tree-hugger's lament, though such lamentations are worthy of consideration. It also has practical consequences. For example, pollinators of our agricultural base are disappearing. Even the iconic monarch butterfly that adorns the cover of this anthology is a pollinator of many wildflowers and has recently fallen into the category of "endangered species." Digging deeper, the microbial regenerators of our agricultural and forest soils are becoming weakened. Yes, it is tragic to lose poster-sized mammals such as the rhinoceros, but we are losing species big and small, plant and animal, that have less of a visual presence than an ecologically impactful scale, causing a threat to the sustainability of Earth as we know it. Some say that it is arrogant to think that we tiny little humans can alter the abundance of life and the atmosphere as well. To the contrary, it is arrogant to believe that 8 billion people and their technologies would have a negligible effect.

Seasons pass, the years will roll

So why the title about wolves? That idea harkens back to human sensitivity about ourselves. Human overpopulation and associated biodiversity loss should be cause for great consternation, but few other than academics and a handful of others even talk about it. Certainly, politicians would never touch these third-rail issues, lest they get burned at the polls by voters who have never really thought about it, or in some quarters even consider the topics to be impolite. We don't want to talk about population size because we are humans and the subject conjures up complicated issues such as cultural norms, 'population control,' family rights, family planning, birth control, abortion, and more. Many also don't want to blame ourselves for the loss of species that couldn't adapt to a planet over which we have dominion.

We need to think about this on a different level and use a thought experiment in which we take humans out of the equation, along with all of their cultural and emotional baggage. We can substitute some other animal for humans and see where it takes us. My first thought was eight billion lions. That's fun to envision but it just doesn't work, because lions are such different creatures from humans. I also decided against other primates; whereas they are much closer to us biologically, they can also invoke too much sentimentality, and we need to think further outside the box.

So, I settled on wolves—eight billion wolves on planet earth. Why wolves? Well, they are similar to humans in many ways. They are about the same body mass and eat about the same weight of food per day as an average human. Wolves are also social and territorial, like most humans. They are not an exact match for our species, as we will see, but they are useful for getting us beyond our discomfort with discussing human overpopulation. Also, given recent successes with the reintroduction of wolves at Yellowstone National Park, both environmentalists and politicians alike are happy to talk about wolf ecology, at least temporarily when it is convenient

With all that in mind, I embarked upon the thought experiment and took the lowest pack size, and the lowest territory size for a pack, calculating individual wolf needs across the total land surface area of Earth. On that basis, I figured that it would take 530 Earth-like planets to sustain eight billion wolves. That is quite an insatiable appetite and didn't make sense. I warned you that numbers can be tricky. But I still like to play with numbers, so I recalculated with greater wolf efficiency with the maximum number of wolves in the smallest territory, according to the best wolf data I could find. In this latter scenario, eight billion wolves would need only 128 planets with the land surface area of Earth. Keep in mind that in this simple thought experiment we have wolves living in deserts, mountains, Antarctica, and so on. But it is clear that sustaining eight billion wolves would be more than a bit problematic, and even politicians might pay attention.

The wolf problem raises the obvious question of how humans get away with having so many people on just one planet, if we have a similar body size and a similar amount of daily food consumption. There are many potential explanations, but here we'll concentrate on just a few. First of all, we eat lower on the food chain. There are no vegan wolves, so they can't live on nuts and berries, and thereby need more territory to find meat. Secondly, we have agriculture to concentrate nature's energy into a host of consumable foods. Wolves are not likely to domesticate the animals they eat. We also have artificial energy to do a lot of our work for us. A pack of wolves can't use fossil fuels to carpool to the site of a kill, or even harness a horse to get there.

This thought experiment could go much further and become more fanciful, such as wolves inventing Oldowan-equivalent tools or wolf politicians ignoring the problems, but I want to get to the main points. I just asked how we were getting away with such large human numbers, when wolves could not. Well, the fact of the matter is that we are not getting away with anything, not even for ourselves. Around 9% of humans around the globe are chronically undernourished, and that increased to over 10% during the Covid-19 pandemic. More than 11% of our human population lacks access to safe drinking water. Despite the best efforts of many, such statistics grow worse on a daily basis for the simple reason that we cannot keep up with 227,000 more people each day. Keep in mind that the growth figure is net gain, births minus deaths—compound interest on our bloated human population—and that is a lot of mouths to feed and people to provide with clothing, shelter, and dignity.

We are also not doing well for the other species on this planet. Mass extinctions seem to move in slow motion in the framework of a human lifetime, but in geological time, what is happening today is a mere instant of an eon, cropping millions of years of biological evolution. Our own species has evolved to live in the here and now, to react quickly to the threat of a nearby predator, or to seize an opportunity at the moment it presents itself to gather food, slake our thirsts, or have sex. The long-term consequences were of no concern to our evolutionary ancestors, and so they tend to be far from the forefronts of our modern human minds. So political seasons pass, and the years roll on as this train wreck unfolds before our eyes with indifference and inaction.

Yet if wolves were overrunning the planet in the way we humans are, the animal extinctions would probably happen more quickly, and it might better awaken the human instinct for survival. We would cull the wolves or plot ways to disrupt their reproduction. Already we cull elephants in South Africa's Kruger National Park because their unbridled population growth would wreak havoc on the ecosystem. Yes, African elephants, endangered by humans elsewhere on the continent, need smaller populations for the parks ecosystems to be sustainable. Why can't we see our own havoc on the global ecosystem and act responsibly? Because we are humans, not elephants or wolves.

Finding responsibility for sustainability is not all that difficult. No, we don't need to cull humans. I tell my students, after they understand the concept of billions, that there are two ways to curb the growth of the human population and its consequences: increase the death rate or decrease the birth rate. Those students are unanimous with me in preferring the latter. Let's disrupt our rampant reproductive patterns with the responsibility that comes with knowledge. Our human head count matters to the sustainability of our planet, and we can achieve that by simply reproducing less. Reducing the number of babies born is easy because we know what causes them. Reproductive responsibility is not tough science.

How do we achieve reproductive responsibility without invoking the 'population control' that many fear? I had to answer that question on the spot at the Woodrow Wilson Center in Washington, DC. I was presenting my scientific findings on the close relations between human population density and species threatened with extinction to delegates from the WHO and the UN, among others, after which they asked me what to do about our explosive population growth. I balked and said that I'm just the scientist presenting my findings, and that they were the policy makers who should be leading the way. But they insisted. So, my answer came from perspectives I had read before, and have since become what I call the 'three pillars' of slowing and halting human population growth.

The first pillar is simply basic education. This not just education about people and the environment, although that is important, but education in general. Better educated people tend to make better life decisions and reproduce less. The second is obviously a widespread availability of contraception, along with proper education on the uses of the many options for preventing unwanted pregnancies. Finally, the third pillar that many overlook: the empowerment of women. This is not just the employment of women, but the empowerment of women to make decisions in the home, the community, the city, the region, and the country. Country after country who have seen women become more prominent in decision-making have also seen fertility rates drop to more sustainable norms.

If we are to minimize the consequences of the mass extinction we are in, conservation efforts must continue and even expand, but it is now clear that all conservation must factor in the effects of our growing human population. Environmentalists and conservationists tend to dislike me when I suggest that if we don't curb the rate of growth human population growth, that all of their noble efforts will come to naught. But they would be the first to act in the prevention of such a calamity as eight billion wolves. Eight billion humans are profoundly too many as well, especially compounding in such a brief sliver of a time.

Jeffrey K. McKee is a native Ohioan who is currently a Professor of Anthropology and The Ohio State University. He spent a decade living and teaching in South Africa, where he led excavations at two fossil sites of our early ancestors. He applies his knowledge of our evolutionary past to the problems of contemporary biodiversity losses across the globe.

Fair Flip
Charles O'Donnell

The first Vietnamese Encephalitis victim I saw was twenty-nine, but he looked ninety. Cable news channels had him on an endless loop with a warning every ten minutes about how sensitive viewers might "find the images disturbing." Disturbing, hell. He scared me shitless.

His skin was papery and white, head rolled sideways, mouth wide open. You know that painting, the one with the guy on the bridge holding his head with both hands screaming his lungs out? That's what he looked like, only not screaming, or even moaning. He was brain dead, but his body hadn't caught on yet.

That was Nam-NC patient zero. A month later they clocked patient twenty thousand. Ten thousand of them were dead.

I was holed up in my apartment with my roomie, Doug. His full name was Douglas Fir. The name fit because he was big as a tree, and I never saw him afraid of anything. Patient zero, though—no older than him, laying like a corpse on a slab, scared him like a little girl. Scared me, too, but life goes on. Garbage still piled up, and we still got hungry. "No way'm I going out there," he said, any time something needed doing, like taking down the trash or buying food. So, I did it. What the hell. With neither of us working, stuck in that apartment until the plague passed over, even a trip to the dumpster was a vacation.

Nam-NC was so nasty that the government sent us masks along with the checks. "Put on the mask," Doug'd tell me every time I opened the door. "Like this." He showed me step-by-step.

"They put the instructions on the box, Doug," I said, and they did, in pictures with no words. I held it up. "See? A baby could do it."

Me and Doug each got checks, and between us we could buy food and beer, and if we stiffed the landlord for part of the rent we could manage for a few weeks. Yeah, it was rough, but it's not like we lived like kings anyway. Doug cooked chicken at KFC and I stocked shelves at Kroger. I didn't miss *that* grunt work. I *sure* didn't miss the guys at the store, all peons like me. We worked our butts off until the weekend came, got two days off with a case of beer and some weed if we were lucky. Then Monday'd come and it'd start over, week after week, until we die, I guess. It's a life.

Just not the life my mom had in mind for me. She always figured I'd go to college and *be* somebody, like *she* did after she got pregnant with me. She raised me by herself and went to night school until I was eight and she got a job in a place that gave out free legal advice. *Pulled myself up*, she said about a million times. But that wasn't ever going to happen for me. I barely made it through high school. I never would've graduated at all, but schools don't like to deal with problem kids. They used every excuse they could to pass me. And now there I was, a burned-out wreck going no place, and there was Mom, a lawyer with an out-of-work stock-boy son she never talked about.

With all the restaurants closed, KFC put Doug on furlough. I could've kept on at Kroger, because food markets were still open, but Doug wouldn't let me. Really, he said he'd rather eat half-rations than let me chance it out in the world. I know that sounds like he was worried for me, but I think he was really worried about himself. But maybe he cared about me a little bit.

Hell, if I was gone, who'd take out the trash?

The only time the TV wasn't on was when we were both asleep, which was almost never. Reports covered the carnage non-stop, with a count of the sick and the dead on one side of the screen and some reporter wearing a mask on the other. All of the reporters stuck to government guidelines on mask-wearing, to set a good example for the viewing public, I guess, but mostly because they were scared shitless themselves. We could hear it in their voices, even if we couldn't see it behind their masks.

One day, Doug was sprawled all over the couch and I was stretched out on the floor in front of the TV when there was this government doctor explaining the *pathology* as he put it.

"The virus invades the cerebral cortex," he said. "The blood-brain barrier, which normally protects the brain from pathogens, is ineffective against Vietnamese Encephalitis. Once in the brain, it causes widespread disruption of neural pathways. Normal cognitive functions are affected. As mental activity declines, the body atrophies."

By then I was on my third beer and Doug was on his fifth. While the doc was saying *declines* and *atrophies*, they panned through a ward of victims, like refugees in a concentration camp. It made my throat close up. I couldn't even finish my beer.

"The course of the disease is undetermined. Some patients succumb in days, while many others have lingered for weeks. No one is known to have recovered, but, tragically, half of the cases have ended in death."

Half. The toss of a quarter. That thought kept me inside when I was home and sticking to the guidelines when I wasn't. A coin flip's just too easy to lose.

By week six the count was 25,000 dead, 25,000 still hanging on, with no end in sight. The second government check came and spent. Doug volunteered to take down the trash now and again (though he still wouldn't buy groceries). We were so tired of isolation we were getting lax in our observances of the protocols, but we got righteous again when our neighbor Agnes, a lady about 70 years old and on Social Security came down with it and they took her away. We heard that she didn't last three days.

Then one day: BREAKING NEWS—PATIENT ZERO RECOVERS. That stopped the world from spinning.

"From his hospital room in Walnut Creek, California, Perry Brooks, the first recorded Nam-NC pandemic patient, talks about his ordeal."

The guy's face filled the screen, looking drained but a million times better than the horror show he was last month. His hair was combed, his face was clean and shaved. He was in a robe, not a cheap one like they give you in the hospital, but more like the thick ones they have in hotels. In fact, he looked damn good, considering, like he was a celebrity who *belonged* on TV, and not only because he'd cheated death.

The last time we saw him, he was knocking on heaven's door. His eyes were hollow, like two holes dug side by side in the graveyard. Not anymore. Now they glowed like they could be windows on an old house and living in the house was a family with a mom and a dad still married, and they all ate meals together, and talked about what they did with their days, and put logs on the fire in the fireplace and celebrated Christmas with presents.

"I don't remember much," he said. "Darkness, mostly, nothing but endless black interrupted by flashes."

"Flashes?" the news guy asked him.

"Dreams, I suppose. Some were people, but no one I knew." His eyelids drooped like he was slipping back into a coma, and his voice got weirdly intense, like a voiceover on some Discovery Channel show about ancient times. "I saw throngs of laborers straining to haul monumental stones on sledges over sandy ground. Mounted warriors riding into battle, spears held high, naked but for the paint on their bodies and faces. Children at play, mothers in childbirth, artists at their craft, lovers in their beds.

"Some were animals: flocks of flamingos rising like flame from the Camargue, lions lolling on the savannah, bison herds blackening the plains. I saw teeming seas: schools of tuna, pods of whales, coral reefs to dwarf anything made by humans.

"I saw visions of the universe: galaxies condensing from primordial gases, planets spinning in their orbits, stars exploding."

He was talking like God sat beside him while he slept and touched his face, and put all God's knowledge inside him, like downloading from the Internet.

"It seems you remembered a lot," the news guy said.

The virus guy, Brooks, opened his eyes and smiled. "Just a trifle."

"A trifle?"

"Compared with all there is to know, it's nothing."

We saw a lot of Perry Brooks after that. All the TV shows booked the first Nam-NC survivor, who turned out to be wicked entertaining. And smart. Jesus, he was fucking brilliant. Jimmy Fallon had him on with that astrophysicist guy, deGrasse Tyson, all via webcam, of course. They got so deep into black holes and shit that Jimmy had to go to break before he lost his viewers. Colbert booked him with Jane Goodall and Perry taught *her* a thing or two about chimp behavior. And the thing was, before he got the plague, he was just a working guy like me or Doug. He pre-treated the wheels and sprayed down the bumpers at a *car wash* for chrissakes. Now he was entertaining audiences multiplying fifteen-digit numbers in his head like a party trick. That went on for about a week.

Then the novelty wore off. Because more sick folks came out of it, and they were all geniuses, too.

A cashier from Portland wrote an opera in French and staged it from her basement, singing all the parts herself.

A landscaper in Guadalajara solved some math problem that had baffled mathematicians since the 1800s.

An Uber driver from Des Moines beat Google's chess-playing supercomputer eight games out of ten.

There were thousands of them, so many that the news shows stopped talking to them one at a time. Instead, they were a group—the *Survivors*. It was scary, in a way: There was a whole bunch of new Einsteins in the world, and they were taking over.

I don't mean like they staged a coup or anything. Instead, they *did* things. They did art, science, inventions, music, writing—if anyone other than a Survivor was doing anything, nobody knew about it. They were the only ones who mattered—Doug, me, and everyone else, not at all.

Then the Survivors got busy on the virus. A group of fifty or so announced they were just weeks away from a vaccine.

Weeks. That's how long I had.

***

"I'm going back to Kroger," I told Doug.

"No, you're not."

I pulled on my hoodie. "Yeah. Someone's gotta pay the bills."

"We're doing okay."

But we weren't. We had maybe fifty in cash, and we were two months behind in the rent. We were eating canned peas from two years ago. I wanted to go to the food bank, but Doug said the place was a Nam-NC breeding ground. He made me promise I wouldn't go anywhere near it.

I went for the door.

"Are you really doing this just for the money?" he asked.

"Yeah. Why else?"

He turned up the sound on the TV. A hairdresser from Liverpool was giving an update on the vaccine. It was days away, she said.

"You want it."

"You're nuts."

"You do. You want in before they cure it."

I didn't answer. I just stood there with my hand on the doorknob.

"It's a fucking coin flip. Fifty-fifty chance you'll end up dead."

"Only if I catch it."

He flexed his jaw muscles the way he does when he's majorly pissed at me. He shoved his hand in his pocket and pulled out a quarter. "Call it," he said.

"No."

"*Call it!*"

I could see I wasn't going anywhere until I played his stupid game.

"Tails."

He flipped. It came up heads.

"That doesn't mean anything," I said.

"Wanna do-over? Two out of three? C'mon."

Damn him. How long did he think he could keep this up?

"Gotta go," I said, and I was out the door.

"Put on the mask!" he yelled, but I was already down the stair.

***

I stared at the sidewalk while I walked until a guy passed me from the other way. His eyes got huge when he saw I wasn't wearing a mask. He went wide around me, and I watched him as he trotted off.

I took a deep breath. It was the first outside air in weeks that I hadn't sucked through two layers of cloth. It felt good. It tasted *fresh*.

The trees made a sound in the wind I'd never heard, like crinkling paper. They were a color I'd never seen, green only more intense, like they'd been sprayed with party paint and set on fire. A police siren shot through my brain. Rubble from a broken car window covered the street like a rhinestone jacket.

The Kroger was five blocks away, not far from the food bank. I thought I might pick up some free food on the way home.

I wondered how Mom was doing. We hadn't spoken since before the pandemic.

I wanted to hate Doug, but I couldn't. It was a fair flip. Fifty-fifty. Coulda gone either way.

Like Nam-NC.

It's just, you know, no two-out-of-three.

Charles O'Donnell writes thrillers with high-tech themes in international and futuristic settings. His works include *Shredded* and *Shade*, two cautionary tales about the potential for technology to either augment reality or to replace it entirely, and the erosion of privacy in a world in which everything is shared online, and nobody reads the terms and conditions. Charles's short stories have also appeared in a number of literary journals, including the *Dark Ink Press Fall 2018 Anthology*, *Dreamer's Creative Writing Year 1 Anthology*, *Carcosa Magazine*, and the *Esthetic Apostle*, among others. Charles lives with Helen, his wife and life partner in Westerville, Ohio.

On the Way to Proximata

Joe Graves

Maisie's pencil glided along the surface of her new sketchbook, nearing completion of her first sketch. She was inches from finishing the line that would connect the moon's horizon with the setting earth when the graphite snapped. The broken bits scattered over the page like an undiscovered cluster of supergiants. She blew the fragments off the page and bit the pencil to secure more, but it was too far down. She spit the bits out of her mouth and turned toward her tent, not far from the dome's wall, where she bumped into her husband, Huxley.

"We need to talk about Proximata."

She closed her sketchbook. "We have plenty of time to decide. Can we discuss it after the ceremony?"

"We can't keep putting it off."

"We won't. We will sit down and discuss it right after the ceremony."

"Promise?"

She nodded and slid the sketchbook into her back pocket. "For now, let's enjoy the view." She gestured to the moon dust beyond the dome.

Huxley laughed at first and paused. "It's not an excellent view. It's beautiful in its own way, I guess."

Maisie agreed. It was beautiful in its own way. It was beautiful like the last moments of one's life are beautiful if the life was well-lived. It was beautiful like a sketchbook with pages filled with drawings and sketches, its binding broken and cover torn. It was beautiful in a way that is also painful and sad.

"Did you hear about the attack?" asked Huxley, grabbing her arm.

"Senescents?" asked Maisie.

"I should say 'the supposed attack'—the ship jumped only minutes after it arrived. No casualties. No attempts to hack anything. It's unfortunate it happened today; now everyone will be talking about it and—"

"No one will talk about it. This event is all about Rupert, he made sure of that." Or at least that's what she hoped. She didn't need her husband getting into any political debates at a retirement ceremony.

She looked at her pencil and considered whether she'd be able to get away again to finish when a notification popped up on her wrist.

"Our shuttle is closed for repairs; we're going to have to walk."

***

Her mentor, Rupert, was retiring after four dozen cycles of regeneration. He wanted to be laid to rest in the greenhouses he built cycles ago. His greenhouses were some of the best in that solar system if only because they were the oldest. Maisie had joined his lab three cycles after he finished them and had been working for him as a biologist ever since. Huxley tagged along, even though the moon was not much of a destination back then.

Rupert's retirement took place in a large hall through the yellow tunnel that ran under the dome. By the time they got there, Maisie was sweaty and annoyed, and the room was so full of visitors that the large space felt small and forced Maisie and Huxley against the back wall.

"We should try and find some seats," she said, gesturing to the path that had opened up in the crowd. They started towards it when she noticed the room getting quiet and the path getting larger. She grabbed Huxley when she saw what everyone was staring at: a senescent. She was old and her back was bent over, she walked with a thin cane, and old clothes draped over her like the dust of the moon outside the window. She had white hair, smashed against her head, thin enough to expose her scalp. It was the first time Maisie had ever seen a senescent this close up. Far closer than she wanted. She had to have gone at least a dozen cycles or more without regeneration. The woman took another step into the room and the room gasped in sync and pushed each other against the wall, and Maisie grabbed Huxley and tried to pull him back with them, but he wouldn't budge. So, she covered her face, even though she knew senescence wasn't contagious. Everyone covered their mouths— everyone except Huxley. His hands were in front of him, open, as if to invite her to grab them—with no gloves, mask, or anything. He took a step towards the woman, becoming the bravest man Maisie had ever seen.

"Everyone, remain calm," said Maisie, uncovering her mouth long enough to speak.

"Huxley will take care of this—he's an expert with these people. He'll know what to do." Huxley studied sensecents and oversaw one of the labs back on Earth where they attempted to reincorporate them into society.

She looked at him, smiling, but he ignored the announcement. He walked over and extended his hand to her. She looked up at him, her eyes sunken into her face. She smiled, and he guided her to him, her legs thin as poles, and when she got close, he placed his arm under hers to help her stand. They talked by the door for a while— a lot longer than anyone was comfortable with, and then instead of escorting her out of the room towards security, he walked her down the aisle to where Rupert lay. Maisie ran up to him.

"What are you doing?" she whispered through gritted teeth. "Security will be here soon, and if they see you escorting her towards the front instead of out of the room—"

Huxley brushed her aside, and Maisie was so confused by the whole interaction, all she could do was watch. They made it to the front, and he helped the woman climb the step to look into the retirement bed. Huxley let her reach down to touch him. The old woman's fingers were knotted and thin and unclean.

Maisie caught up to them and pulled her arm back.

"Don't let her touch him!"

"Please, babe, relax. It's fine."

"We have to get her out of here! She shouldn't be touching him." But it was too late. Before she could finish warning him, the security had arrived. They ran to the front, contained the woman, knocked her onto her back and dragged her out. Then, two other guards escorted Maisie and Huxley out with their wrists bound behind them.

***

Maisie and Huxley were put in a holding cell a few miles outside the colony.

She sat with her back to Huxley, staring out the small window towards the shipyard. He reached and touched her shoulder. "I'm sorry, Maisel."

She had nothing to say to him. They had given up a half cycle for this trip, and it was all for nothing; the ceremony went on without them. Not to mention it was possible they'd be flagged and stopped on every trip from here to as far as Plotu—questioned without reason, for the rest of their lives! They might as well head to Proximata, or even further, if they could. What was Huxley thinking?

Huxley reached over and put his hand on her shoulder again. She shrugged it off.

"Are you going to be mad at me forever?"

"You should have escorted her to security, like protocol requires. You of all people should know that. What were you thinking?"

"Maisel, I'm sorry. I forgot where I was. I'm sorry—I mean it." She turned towards him. "Why let her contaminate him like that?"

He looked at her for a good minute before answering.

"She was his sister."

"Don't be a fool. Rupert didn't have a sister."

"That you know of. She said she was his sister. And anyway, what reason would she have to lie?"

"I don't know why they do what they do! You're telling me that Rupert, with three dozen cycles of regeneration, was outlived by a senescent? How is that even possible?"

"They live a lot longer than rumors would have you believe—some reach four dozen cycles on their own without regeneration. I've met a few. Not many, but there are cases that suggest they can. Plus, she told me she was much younger than him—so it's possible."

"Don't come at me with your research. He'd never have a senescent for a sister. It's unnatural."

"I'll have you remember, growing old is natural. It's reversing those effects that isn't."

"Please don't talk like that—not here."

He looked away. "I believed her. I could tell she was telling the truth. She wanted to see him. Sister or not, she loved him." He turned to make eye contact with her. "You could see it in her eyes. She wanted to pay her respects, that's all. She wanted to say goodbye. It seemed like the right thing to do."

The cell door opened and they both got quiet.

The guard didn't say anything other than to gesture for them to follow him. Huxley went first, head down.

The guard led them down a hallway to a room with a table under a dim light and he attached their wrist to the magnetic strip on the table, binding them. They sat with their backs to the wall, staring at the door.

"Will you let me do the talking?" asked Maisie.

Huxley didn't respond.

"Just let me do the talking, ok?" she asked again.

He didn't answer, and before she could ask again, the door opened and a security official walked in. He placed his briefcase onto the table, opened it, and pulled out a chip reader.

"You know what this is?" he asked.

They nodded.

He turned it in the air, examining it. "One tap of your wrist and you'll be flagged as friends of terrorist."

"That's really not necessary. We're so sorry about the whole—"

He slammed it on the table, and she got quiet. "I had planned to come in here, to scan your wrist, flagging you for good, and then let you be on your way. That is until your boss called and pulled a few strings. I guess your work back on Earth gives you certain privileges." He picked the reader back up, twisting it in the air.

Maisie made an audible sigh of relief and sat back. "Oh, thank you. Thank you!"

"But you're not on Earth, so I want you to hear this," pointing the reader at them, "and hear it plain and simple: senescents are terrorists. Period."

Huxley sat up and opened his mouth to speak but paused. The guard noticed and pointed the reader at him, as if to challenge him to talk. Huxley looked at Maisie, who shook her head, forbidding him to speak, but then he looked back at the official.

"Do you have something to add?" the official asked.

Maisie held her breath, using every bit of her will power to silence him with her thoughts.

"Not all senescents are terrorists," said Huxley. Maisie turned and wide-eyed him. "Based on our research, less than 10% engage in terrorist activity, and the ones who do, often do so out of desperate circumstances. It really is difficult for them, you know."

"Difficult?" asked the guard. "Let me tell you about difficult. My partner was in the base when they attacked last year. His body was ripped from head to toe; it took two cycles for the pods to put him back together, and he's never fully recovered. He's spent every half-cycle in the pod since. He'll never walk straight again. Not to mention his memory loss—he don't even know who I am anymore. So don't talk to me about difficult."

"I'm sorry for your friend, but—" said Huxley, but before he could finish, the guard grabbed his reader and shoved it into Huxley's bound wrists. It beeped. Then he turned the reader towards Maisie. "Do you have anything else you'd like to add?"

Maisie shook her head.

"Then you're free to go."

He took the reader and placed it into his briefcase, slammed it shut, and walked to the door. As soon as he opened the door, their wrists released from the table. Before the door could close behind the guard, a notification popped up on her wrist informing her that their flights back to earth were placed on hold due to a change in her husband's security clearance.

***

That night Huxley slept in the sand out by the glow lamps and Maisie slept in the tent.

The next morning, she found Huxley standing along the wall, staring out the window, Earth nothing more than a small marble in the distance slowly falling. She walked up and bumped into him, knocking his mug over and spilling his tea.

"Careful now," he said, as the spill drifted to the dust below them. He turned to her and she smiled. He grabbed her arm and put it under his, pulling her close. "I should have kept my mouth shut." He looked down at his wrist, hers nestled next to it, and rubbed his device. "I'm sorry about everything, especially missing the ceremony."

She could tell he was sorry—as sorry as anyone could be. She'd be mad at him for a while—she was confident of that—but there was no need for him to know how long. "It's ok."

"I know you wanted a chance to say something at the ceremony."

"That's the least of our problems now, don't you think?"

He nodded as they stood, watching Earth set. She grabbed his cup and took a drink and then gave it back to him.

"Proximata doesn't sound like such a bad idea now, does it?"

"Even with my status?"

"Absolutely. With a senescent incident on your record, you look like a regular space explorer. Plus, I know for fact, no one else is signing up to go as far as Proximata, not in the state it is. Except for those running from something."

"You make it sound like I've become an outlaw—it's not as bad as that."

"We could use a fresh start, that's all."

"Every cycle is a fresh start," he said, smiling.

"Very cute. But you keep shooting off proverbs like that and I'll go with someone else."

"No, you can't do that. By the time you got there, you wouldn't have many cycles left.

Not enough to get back anyway."

"So, if we go, we go together, and retire on Proximata?"

"It's the only way."

One cycle later, they boarded a ship, with a small crew, and left for Proximata. Their pods were assigned and ready before passing the station on Mars, and soon after they were put to sleep.

***

Maisie wiped her breath from the curved lid of her hibernation pod. Under normal circumstances, she would have been cleaned and dried before gaining consciousness, so the fact that her arms were still dripping with gel revealed the level of the emergency. She sat up and looked out over the edge through the glass, but her eyes were still blocked by gelatin. Through the haze, she could see a fleet of ships silhouetted against a distant star. Across the room someone ran back and forth handling the controls. She hit the eject button, and the glass lid of the pod opened up; the figure noticed and ran over.

"Maisel, what are you doing up?"

It was Huxley's voice. "What the hell is going on? How far are we from Proximata?"

"We're three jumps away. I was just doing routine pod maintenance in between jumps when this colony of senescents showed up and started hacking our system."

"Let me out." She tried to wipe the gunk from her eyes.

"No. I was about to jump again when you woke up. I have to get our pods closed and then we will be ready. It will only take a minute."

He pushed her back into the pod and closed the lid. She thought about protesting, but she knew he'd get the pods turned back on a lot quicker if she didn't. She placed the respirator over her mouth. With the emergency protocol already in place, she felt the gelatin wrap around her body before the gas had finished putting her to sleep.

***

They designed the pods for long-term space travel, allowing a person to sleep in suspended animation indefinitely. The technology not only suspended them in sleep but rejuvenated the body. When they first discovered this side effect, the pods were used as often for rejuvenation as they were for space travel. With the right rotation

129

of time in the pods, a person could stay young-looking for a lifetime. It was too good to be true, and it's why it eventually became illegal to do anything else. Those who didn't were known as senescents. Rooted in their backward ways and religious beliefs, the senescents refused this treatment and had no choice but to live on the run, pulling ships and colonies together from what they could steal from the young and civilized.

Maisie expected to run into senescents, but she had no reason to fear them. As her husband explained, the vast majority were peaceful and the ones who weren't had outdated technology.

When she woke up, the gel had been drained and she was clean and dry, she assumed everything was as it should be. She took a few breaths and waited for the container to open, and then blinked to wipe the leftover gel from her eyes.

She could tell that they weren't floating in space; they must have landed. She got nervous wondering what Proximata would end up being like and whether it was a good decision to leave Earth's orbit for a Class 2 colony. She looked at her wrist device to confirm her location but couldn't make it out. She lifted her head and looked up. The lights were bright silhouetting two figures standing over her. She couldn't see them at first, until one shifted their stance and blocked one of the lights. They slowly came into focus. Then she wished she hadn't seen them at all. Or wondered if it was all a hibernation dream. Either way, a young girl, at least five cycles before her prime age, stood over her. She was too young to be a member of any respectable ship or station. The only time the young roamed the galaxy were as children of senescents. It was possible that people could lock into a prime age early, if they bribed the right doctor, and sometimes the prime age looked younger than one would assume, but the second figure confirmed her fears. It was an old man, bent over, with thin arms, wrinkled skin, and skeleton fingers.

She jumped from her pod.

"Slow down. It's going to be ok. Do you know where you are?" the old man asked.

She refused to answer. She pushed her naked body against the far wall and grabbed a uniform from the hook and used it as a shield. She looked around but couldn't see more than a few meters in front of her. The lack of clear sight forced her nose to work overtime, and the ship didn't smell right. It smelled dirty. It smelled old. It smelled like a senescent—like a life without cleaning agents or mist showers or regeneration. She reached for her wrist and hit the panic button. She hit it repeatedly and she couldn't understand why the alarm failed to go off. She wiped her eyes again and when she opened them, the old man was standing dangerously close.

"Here, you have to be freezing."

He handed her a post-hibernation robe.

"Where is Huxley? Where is my crew?" she yelled, grabbing the robe.

"If you sit down, we will explain everything."

The old man gestured to a seat.

She wrapped herself in the robe, and as soon as it was tied at her waist, she bolted for the exit. But before she could turn the corner, she ran into someone. She blinked and with him standing right in front of her, she recognized him. "Huxley! What is going on?"

He grabbed her.

"It's going to be ok." Then he looked behind her, nodded, and when she turned, the old man was standing there with a respirator. She tried to fight it, but Huxley held her tight, and with the mask to her face, she fell back asleep.

She spent her dreams thinking about how Huxley held her like that. His grip was firm, and he wouldn't budge. She remembered the time they got into a fight and he had gotten angry; he grabbed her like that. He hated himself for a half a cycle as a result. She forgave him, and he promised never to do it again, and he hadn't—not until just then. She had never been more disappointed in him than in that dream.

She woke up, leaving most of these details behind, but keeping the feelings they created with her. It was with this feeling that she found herself curled in a ball, laying in soft dirt. A glow lamp behind her cast shadows against the surrounding trees. She tried to remember her dream so she could roll over and tell Huxley all about it. He'd apologize, even if he hadn't done anything wrong. He always apologized for her dreams. She pulled the blanket close and took a deep breath.

That's when she noticed it.

Small, green, fern-like plants grew within her reach; plants she had never seen before. She reached her hand out from under the blanket, brushing the black dirt, and plucked a small one, roots and all. She brought the roots, packed with soft silt, to her nose.

"You shouldn't touch that—not without gloves," said a man behind her. His voice was deep, like his throat was filled with gravel. She turned over to see him standing in a dark cloak and a wide-brimmed straw hat that hung low on his face.

She sat up and scooted back, dropping the fern and turned to check her wristband for her location and time, but her wrist was empty.

"Who are you?"

He shuffled next to her, dragging his feet, and grabbed the plant lying next to her with his glove-covered hands. He tossed it and then grabbed her hands, wiping them with a wet cloth. "We're allergic to most everything here. I'm going to put gloves on you, ok?" He didn't wait for her permission.

"Where are we?" she asked again.

He pointed to the sky and walked back to his seat. Maisie looked up to find she was sitting under two small moons that shined like spotlights on a stage; the stars danced in patterns she didn't recognize. The view of the sky was obstructed only by the leaves above her. She was in the wild, free of a dome or station or tent. Between her and the old man, sat a real fire, not a glow lamp, the smoke drifting up towards the ceiling-less sky.

The old man sat down on a short stump. It tilted as his frame shifted the balance. "You just woke up from the pod back on the ship. Do you remember? The expedition? Going to sleep? Anything?"

She tapped her head to knock the memories loose. She remembered the moon and the trouble they got into with the security there. She remembered her dream— how Huxley held her, but she couldn't remember why.

"Maybe this will help." He tossed a small emblem to her.

She tried to catch it, but it got lost in the fire's light and ended up landing next to her. She felt for it in the darkness and raised it up to see. It was the emblem of Proximata. She recognized it immediately and it brought with it her memories of her ship. She could see the cool silver of the outer hull. And the long bullet-like hibernation pods that sat in the room past the crew quarters. She could still feel her body wrapped in the hibernation gel, like a spoon placed on top of a bowl of thick batter. She remembered the expedition.

She looked back up at the man.

"Did we make it?"

"No."

She looked back down at the emblem. "Where are we then?"

"You were on the way to Proximata, when the ship was attacked by senescents." He lifted a tin canister to his lips and took a sip. "The ship encountered too much damage, and the next jump fell short. The ship crash-landed here."

She rubbed the back of her head and the memory of waking up in the pod with the ships trying to hack their system started to drift back into her mind. "What happened to the crew?"

"Most of the pods were destroyed in the crash and everyone in them." He set his canister down. "You were severely injured, but your pod remained intact."

She went through the list of crew members, in order of rank, one by one, slowly remembering their faces, until she reached her husband's—Huxley!

"Where is Huxley? My husband. What happened to him?"

"Thankfully, this planet has breathable air and ample starlight during the day, and the ship was able to stay powered on. I set your pod to begin regenerating immediately."

"Where is Huxley?" she asked again, straightening.

He paused and looked at her. "You don't remember, do you?"

She shook her head, and she wasn't sure if she was answering his question or shaking her memories loose.

"Where is everyone?"

"When the ship crashed, we were the only two left alive on this planet. And only you barely." He stood. "Let me show you." He walked over to her and reached for her arm, but she flinched away. "Please, you need to see this."

His fingers were covered in gloves, and his face, by the shadow of the brighter moon. When he pulled back her sleeves, he exposed an arm full of scars, as if her skin had been knitted together.

"You have more—most everywhere—but these were the worst. It took a couple months for the pod to regenerate you. I wasn't sure it was gonna work."

She looked down her shirt and found similar scars all over her body. She had been regenerated many times, and never had scars like this. This only happens when a pod was used too many times, or the damage was too great, or worse—when someone was taken out of the pod before their regeneration was complete.

He went back to his stump, sat down, and picked up his canister to take another drink. She looked up at him as he took off his wide hat, uncovering his face from its shadow. A large, bushy beard covered most of his face, and thin white hair shot out his head like dandelion's seeds. Seeing him like this made all the difference. He was the old man from the ship. She remembered him! A memory, which up to that point, had felt like a dream. He must have been there when she woke up after the ship was grounded. He was there, standing over her, along with a young woman—too young. There were a few others too: Huxley! Huxley was there.

She sat up straight.

"No one else survived the crash?" she asked.

"I'm sorry, Maisel—no one else survived."

"Who did you say you were again?"

"Just give yourself time to remember."

"You're one of those senescents that attacked us, aren't you? Boarded our ship before we were able to jump? What the hell happened to my husband?"

He didn't answer, so she asked him again, and he slowly turned his head up and looked at her.

"You know exactly what happened to your husband, and you'll remember, if you give yourself time. After a crash like that, memories come back out of order and don't make sense by themselves. But don't rush it."

"I want you to take me to my ship. Now."

"We will go when you're ready and not before."

"I'm ready now."

"Then tell me where the ship is. What direction?"

She looked around, throwing her hands in the air. "How am I supposed to know?"

"If you don't know, then you're not ready."

"Take me now!" She stood up. She was sure she could take him if she needed to. She was the senior officer of the ship and lead biologist, with a body twice as young as someone his age, and she would not be held captive on an alien planet by a terrorist. She stood up. "Take me directly!" and that's when she felt it. Her legs started twitching. "Now!" She was as serious as she could be, with a left leg that had just gone limp. "I demand to be taken to my ship!" Then the right leg went limp and she collapsed. She tried to catch herself, but her arms wouldn't move.

"What is happening to me?" she yelled as she crashed to the ground. "I can't move my legs."

He walked up to her, kneeled down, and reached for her leg.

"Don't you dare touch me!"

He paused and took a step back. He stood at a distance as she tried to move before going back to his seat where he pulled out his canister and filled it with water from his tin and placed it on a rock near the flames. He walked to the edge of the camp and reached into his bag and pulled out a small bundle. Unraveling the cloth revealed thin gray strips of what looked like dried meat.

He tossed a few into the canister of boiling water and stirred it.

"We need to get you some medicine."

"What medicine?"

"You need cholinesterase inhibitors."

"Cholinesterase?"

"Yeah."

"How is that supposed to help?"

"Your brain had too much damage from the crash and prolonged regeneration—you're suffering memory loss, not just details, but how to do other things: like move your arms, legs, stand... your balance... and if we don't get your memory working again, you're going to be in trouble."

He took the cup off the rock, the steam like smoke rising from it. He blew on it a few times and then touched it with his finger to gauge the temperature before carrying it over to her.

"Here, drink."

"I want nothing to do with your medicine. Take me back to my pod."

"It's broth. It will help. Drink it."

He brought it to her lips, but she closed her mouth, turning her head in protest.

"It's going to help."

She shook her head.

"Look, if I wanted to hurt you, I would have when you were asleep. Or before you got out of the pod. I understand you don't trust me—I wouldn't trust me either. But right now, I'm all you have, so you don't have much of a choice."

Next thing she knew, he was feeding her the broth straight out of the canister. It was warm and soft and made her head feel fuzzy. It sat heavy in her stomach and made her wish she could take a nap. He helped her lie back, and she stared at the sky as it turned from navy to pink to blue, as the nearby star rose over the trees until it shone directly on her, its warmth like a blanket.

***

Maisie woke up with the sun overhead. The fire had died and the stump where the old man had sat was empty. She stood up—the broth must have helped. She looked around and was quickly distracted by the scenery. The landscape was filled with plants she had never seen before, all the brighter in the daylight. Life grew out of every corner and crack and rock, with greens and browns and small splashes of colors. It wasn't Proximata, but it might be better. She had seen their greenhouses, and they were as impressive as they could be for a Class 2 colony, but this place didn't need them. Life grew naturally. The only places she'd seen this much natural growth were in historic photos of Earth.

The most prominent plant stood three times the height of an average person and grew as a thin stalk. At the top, a single, giant leaf grew out of it, like an outstretched wing. There were hundreds of these stalks towering over her, forming a broken canopy of shade. As she scanned the forest of large leaves, she caught a glimpse of the old man pushing through a cluster of green stalks.

She put one foot in front of the other, forcing them to follow him as quickly as she could, hoping he was headed back to the ship. Once she got down the valley, and past a bundle of stalks that grew like a steel rod fence, she could see him in the distance, looking for something—no ship in sight. She continued to follow him, keeping her distance, until he leaned against a tall stalk and sat for a while. She snuck closer, watching where she stepped so as not to make any noise, which was easy, as small plants grew as soft as linen—bright patches of green carpet in long spirals like a python weaving through the thin clusters. She reached for her wristband to capture a few photos of the plants, but her wrist was still empty. So she reached for her back pocket in search of her sketchbook and pencil—out of habit more than anything. She wanted to catalog these moments, but they too were missing.

She hid behind a large leaf and looked down at the old man who crouched a few meters away. He scanned the valley with a wristband. As he scanned, he stopped at a nearby stalk cluster. She followed his gaze to the top of a stalk, where a single leaf held a giant droplet of water. It had to be at least two liters suspended under the leaf. She wondered if this was because of a membrane provided by the leaf or a change in how surface tension worked in this environment. Then the leaf shook, and the droplet released. She followed its trajectory where it hit something, that until that moment, had blended so well into the environment, it was nearly invisible. The impact of the water turned its skin gray against the green surroundings. It was the size of a fully grown grizzly bear and walked on all four—no, on all *six*—legs!

She took a step closer to get a better look.

The water made the creature look gray, but upon closer inspection its skin was translucent, with veins and internal organs all visible, even from this distance. The only color was the large green spot near the center, above its second set of legs, which was the same green as the plants that surrounded it.

The water that fell onto its back didn't splash or fall to the ground. The skin absorbed it like a dry sponge. She watched it happen and couldn't stop watching until it disappeared into its veins. The old man walked towards the creature, pulling out a large knife that he lifted over his head. He was about to kill this creature. She ran to catch him. "Don't hurt it!" But it was too late. The knife went into the creature's flesh, clear liquid shooting out along the edges.

He turned towards her.

"What are you doing here?" he asked, as he pulled the knife out, wiping the blade on his pants.

"Why do you people have to destroy everything?" She walked up to the creature and touched it, running her hand along its back, examining it as she did.

"You people?" he asked.

She ran her hand along its back until reaching its face, and out of its large black eyes, she could see the reflection of the old man behind her, raising his knife. She turned, grabbed his arm, and pulled the knife from his hands. She turned it and pointed it at him.

"I asked you to stop."

He lifted his hands in surrender. "I'm trying to help."

"By stabbing me?" She stopped closer to him, knife out.

"I'm not going to hurt you. But I need to stab this creature. You think I'm cutting this creature 'cause I like destroying things? Are you a fool? I'm doing it to help you."

"How is that going to help me?"

He put his hand down on the creature's back. "When this creature is in shock, it uses cholinesterase inhibitors to keep from losing its memory. They get released, we take them, give them to you, and you get better. I need the knife back—I need to stick this knife into its chest again. It won't kill it, but it will put it into shock to get what we need."

She stopped to think through how this would work and was distracted enough by the theory that she didn't notice him lean in, and grab her wrist with one hand, and the knife with his other. He had it pointed towards her before she could stop him.

"I'm not going to hurt you—and I'm not going to permanently hurt this creature. But I have to finish what I started." He lifted the knife.

"Wait!" She bolted for his arm, but she was too late—his knife went in deep, and the creature curled up into a ball and fell to the ground.

"It's ok! It's ok. Look."

He pointed toward a small organ just above its front leg, visible from the curled-up wrinkles. "It's still beating. It's fine. But the creature is in shock now." As she examined the creature's internal organs, she noticed them slow, but continued to beat. Then the old man uncurled one of the thick, elephant-like legs. "You might not want to watch this part." Using his knife, he cut into the leg.

"What are you doing now?"

"I'm cutting off its leg."

"Why would you do that?"

"This creature," he said in between sawing motions, "is in shock—it can't feel a thing, and it won't feel a thing until his leg grows back. Then when its leg has regrown, it will wake up, and go on its way like nothing happened. I promise."

"How can you be so sure?"

"I've done this many times before."

She stood back.

"How many times?"

He paused, thought for a second, and then went back to sawing the leg.

"How many times have you done it?" She looked at him, but he didn't answer. A little juice shot out of the leg and hit his face. He wiped it off and went back to cutting the flesh.

"We didn't just crash land, did we? We've been here for—how long have you been here?" He didn't answer. He shook his head, focused on the beast's leg. "Who are you? Are you all that's left from the ship that attacked us? Or are there others?"

He tore the remaining flesh from the animal and tossed the leg on the ground. He stuck his knife into the leg and wiped his hands on his pants before picking the knife back up.

"How much do you remember?"

She backed up. "I want to see my ship. Take me there now."

"You can go as soon as you're ready. For now, we cook this." He picked up the leg.

"No. No. No. Take me now."

"Go look for it if you want—get lost on a planet by yourself. But I'm going back to the camp, and if you come with me, I'm going to help you feel better."

"I feel fine. Now tell me where it is."

"You feel fine? Really?" he said, pointing at her with the tip of his knife. She hadn't noticed, but her back was bent, and her legs were shaking. "We need to get back. You shouldn't have come this far from camp." He grabbed her arm, but quickly let go. He looked at his hand and then turned it towards her. There was blood on his gloves. "Check your arms." She pulled back her sleeves. The scars on her arms were bright red, and a few had opened up. She stood there, unable to move, as blood pooled in her open palms.

"Your body is rejecting the regeneration, and a lot quicker than I hoped. We have to get you back to the camp and find some help." He reached for her again. She tried to back up, except her legs felt as thin as stalks. Her arms felt weak too, and after a few steps, she toppled over, turned and before she could fall over, the old man was in front of her, catching her fall.

That night, he bandaged her arms, tucked her into a blanket at the foot of a large boulder, and fed her some kind of soup, which eased her pain and helped her sleep.

Her arms stung, and soon her body started to heat up like the rocks by the fire. She sweated, shaking from chills, and each day he changed her bandages and used a wet cloth to keep her cool. She laid there for a week, waking for only a few minutes each day, often to eat. And each time she woke up, the old man was there, ready to give her something to drink, or adjust her blankets, or stir the fire back to life.

She woke up in the middle of the night once, with him sitting close. He lifted his hand to feel her forehead and smiled through his beard.

"Your fever has broken. This is a good sign. How are you feeling?"

She didn't answer. She pulled the blanket up to her chin.

"I'm feeling better—but tired."

"That's good. Should be able to get up and move around within a day or two."

"Why didn't you put me back in the pod?"

"Too soon since your last cycle—would only have made it worse. You had to heal on your own this time."

She turned to her side, to face away from him. She looked at the plants nearby, and wished she had the energy to study them. She wished she had the energy to get better. She wished she had the energy to do anything. But every part of her was tired.

She thought she might have the strength to sit up, and so she pulled herself up against the bolder behind her. He reached to help, but she stopped him. She wanted to see if she could do it herself, and she did. Her back hurt and her arms were tired, but she could sit up. She looked at the old man, who smiled as if he was witnessing a miracle.

"It's sick, isn't it? That someone with a body as old as you has to take care of someone with a body as young as mine?"

He stopped smiling and then hit his hand against his chest. "My body might look old, but I've taken good care of my body." He smiled again.

"Clearly." He reached behind him for a bowl of broth and offered it to her. She grabbed it and took a drink. "Your kind is illegal where I come from, you know."

"I do."

She looked at her soup as she talked. "And had we met anywhere else, I would have turned you in."

"I have no doubt."

She took a drink of the broth. "We were raised to hate your kind—everyone did. Everyone except my Huxley."

"He sounds like a real decent guy." She looked up at him and laughed.

"One of the best. I could never keep up, you know. Kind of makes you mad after a while." She looked for a place to set the broth down.

"How does that work?" He reached for her cup and set it on the ground for her.

"He was always doing the right thing—made everyone else look bad. Made me look bad. I'm not such a bad person—but next to him, I never had a chance." She turned towards him. "Why are you helping me?" She looked down at her feet. "What I mean is: I'm not sure I would have done the same."

"Of course you would. We're on an undiscovered planet alone—we're all we got." He rose to his feet. "And I'll need you as much as you need me. But that's only possible, if you rest. You should sleep."

∗∗∗

When she woke up, the fire was smoldering and the old man wasn't there. Since her fever had broken in the night, she felt well enough to stand up.

She held her head, and her memories slowly fell back into place. She remembered. She had been in this camp before—a long time ago. She remembered where her ship was.

Hope shot through her legs, and she moved them in the direction of the ship, or at least where she felt it should be, grabbing stalks as she passed to keep her balance. She was able to make it down the small hill without toppling over. When she got to the top of the next, she stopped to catch her breath and that's when she saw it. She could see the tail of her ship sticking out over the stalks on the other side of the valley. She fixed her eyes on it and started to run. When she got down the hill, she lost sight of it, but continued, deviating only once when she ran into a pond, where yellow pads grew inches from the surface. On the other side, she corrected course and reached a thick cluster of green stalks. When she pushed through, she tripped

and tumbled down a small hill and into a large hole, where she smashed into soft
black mud.

She wiped her hands on her pants and stood. The hole had been recently dug, its
walls made of loose dirt. Standing, her shoulders reached the top edge. She followed
the border of the hole to find it was rectangular, three meters long, and a little less
than one meter wide.

She climbed out and looked back at it.

She knew what it was; they still used them on earth for retirement ceremonies.

A grave.

Above the hole lay a stone, and next to it, were a line of stones, each one with a
name engraved on it—names of her crew: Adulx Kilick, Hamilton Forfeit, Sammy
Gight, and Huxley Winslow.

Huxley Winslow carved carefully into a large stone right in front of her.

"Huxley Winslow." She had to say it to believe it.

She sat and stared at his grave trying to put the pieces together—he was alive
when they were attacked. He was alive when she woke up in the pod. He held her.
He was alive. He had to be alive. That's when she noticed something at the corner
of her eye. She could see the final stone lay at the top of the open grave. She didn't
want to turn and look, but she couldn't stop herself: Maisel Winslow etched onto the
stone's surface like all the others; all it lacked was a body laid and covered with silt,
where it would become a part of the mud that fed this planet.

She stepped backward, but she didn't get very far, for standing right behind her
was the old man.

He grabbed her. "You weren't supposed to see that."

"What the hell is that?" she yelled, pushing him away. "What the hell is that?"

"It's nothing. It's—"

"You sick old man! What did you do to Huxley?"

"I didn't do anything to Huxley."

"I remember. He was there when I woke up! He was there. He didn't die in the
crash! What did you do to him?"

"Maisel, I promise, I didn't do anything to him."

"Why do you keep calling me Maisel? No one calls me Maisel," she said. "If you
knew me, if you actually knew me, you'd know that."

She fell to the ground and started to dig into the silt that laid in front of Huxley's
gravestone.

"I know, Maisel. I know. And that's the hardest part about all this: You're not
going to find Huxley down there—not yet." He grabbed her and pulled her off the
grave. She sat back in the dirt, her gloves stained black.

She lifted her face.

"Huxley isn't down there, I'm telling you. Not yet." The old man sat down on a
large rock behind him.

"Then where is he?" she asked.

"Right here," he said, lifting his arms. He didn't smile. He didn't laugh. He wasn't
joking. He looked down at the ground and took in a deep breath, as if ready to explain
something to a child, something he had explained a hundred times before and they
wouldn't listen. "I'm Huxley, and if you come with me, I'll explain everything."

***

Their ship was two-hundred-meters long and capable of long-term space travel, but all that was left of it now was the compartment that held a computer and one hibernation pod. The aluminum shell was overgrown with swirls of green moss and large leaves hung over it, casting shade.

Inside, the old man who called himself Huxley turned on the computer and Maisie sat in the chair.

Her old wristband sat near the edge of the desk and she grabbed it.

"Stopped working cycles ago," he explained.

She turned it in her hands, examining it. It was beaten and dirty, with stains and cracks she couldn't remember giving it, but it was hers, nonetheless.

He grabbed it from her and put it back on the desk. "Don't worry. Everything you had on there has been backed-up on the computer." He gestured to the screen where he opened an application, clicked on a folder, and then held his wristband to synchronize. When it was done, he clicked on a video from the front camera of the ship as it entered the planet's atmosphere. "It happened just as I told you—we got attacked, and barely escaped, jumping to this system. But we took on too much damage to complete the jump. We had to land—which is what we did," he said, gesturing to the ship. "I was the only one awake during the crash, and no one other than you and me survived."

He clicked on a photo of the ship sitting in a patch of dirt and torn leaves. He scrolled to another photo of her asleep in the pod. Then another of him, looking at himself in the shimmer of the outer shell.

"Just like I said, you were severely injured. The pod could regenerate, but it took months, and while I waited—" He scrolled through photos of the camp and pictures of him growing thin. "I wasn't sure you would wake up—but you did."

He clicked on a photo of them standing together outside the outer hull. She was smiling. He clicked again to a photo of them kissing. She watched all of this and tried to remember.

"We had a couple good cycles together. But then you got sick. Your brain stopped remembering how to do some of the basic functions—you started forgetting who I was. The regeneration… it was too much, and your body rejected it—like it is now. Too much damage to your brain, I suppose." He clicked on another photo. "We had to put you back into the pod to recover—and it helped: you got better."

He sat down next to her and continued. "We had a couple good cycles again until you needed the regeneration." He kept scrolling through the photos. "And each time we put you back into the pod, the time we had together got shorter and shorter." He jumped ahead, scrolling past hundreds of photos. He stopped on a photo of them standing next to each other—her young, but him old. "Then you stopped recognizing me."

She turned to him and looked into his aged face—eyes that sat low.

"I don't blame you; I wouldn't recognize me either." He smiled. "But to be honest, those were the hardest cycles—harder than learning to survive." He turned back to the screen, but she kept looking at him as he talked. "A few times I stopped trying to convince you. It seemed to work better to explain things once you've had time to remember on your own. It took a couple weeks—sometimes as long as a month—but it came back. Especially when you saw this."

He pulled out a small sketchbook from his pocket and handed it to her.

"My sketchbook!" she yelled. She turned it in her hands, the binding broken, and the pages held together with twine. She opened it to find her handwriting on every page, from beginning to end, sketches and descriptions of hundreds of plants and animals.

"But this is my handwriting—my drawings. How is that possible?"

She stopped on a page of a sketch of the large, translucent creature, with each organ diagramed and pages of notes on its diet, nutrients, food chain, and habits. She had written in the corner: "An excellent source of cholinesterase inhibitors, this might be the ticket for recovery."

He tapped the page where she was reading. "Over the cycles, you've cataloged every observable species in a hundred miles. But this little discovery helped more than you'll ever realize."

"But I don't remember."

"Well, that's the worst of it, isn't it?" He placed his hands on her shoulder. "The last couple times you were awake, I noticed you were struggling to remember things—more than usual, even after weeks had gone by." He took a deep breath and looked at the floor, and then lifted his face to her. "Maybe I did it too many times. I don't know. But I could tell you weren't remembering anything since before the crash, which is why I took you back to our original camp—I was hoping if you experienced the first of our memories, the rest might follow."

Her head hurt, and her arms stung, and she couldn't breathe. And none of this made sense.

"I'm sorry," he said, "I am. It's a lot to take in—and it's never easy. It's never easy—I—"

She pushed back from the computer and breathed deeply. She couldn't believe any of it. It had to be a lie. Or she was dreaming, a strange hibernation dream, and she needed to wake up. It was just yesterday that they left the station at the moon. Just yesterday they began their journey. This wasn't possible.

"You got to calm down, babe. It will only make it worse. You got to calm down."

"Don't call me babe. I don't know who you are!"

She got up and ran for the exit, just like she had the last time when she woke from the pod, wrapped only in a rope. She turned the corner, but this time her eyes weren't covered in gel, and she could see it for what it was, the blurry shapes now taking form: the corner leading to the outside, stalks growing up over a path lined in stones, and the sun shining through the large leaves. And standing on the path, their shadows stretched to her feet, stood the young girl and next to her, a young Huxley. He stood there, alive and young and perfect. She turned back to the old man, with tears in her eyes. "If you're Huxley, then who's this?"

"You don't remember?" asked the young man. His voice shot through her head like a migraine. His voice wasn't like Huxley's at all. And through her tears, she looked at him. They weren't Huxley's eyes—they were his own.

She fell to her knees, and the young man ran to her, grabbing her. "Mom, it's ok. It's going to be ok. It's all going to be ok."

***

With a cup of broth in one hand, Maisie scrolled through photos of her standing in front of the ship holding a small baby. She clicked again, and it was a similar photo. But there was a small kid standing next to them. Then again, until she stood next to two young kids: a boy and a little girl.

She took a deep breath and then a sip of her broth. She looked at the old man.

"If you're Huxley, why didn't you regenerate?"

140

"I would have—and I tried a couple times. But we only had one pod, and no ship to make sure it ran properly, and each of your cycles got longer than the last. Even if I figured out how to make it work without me, we would have been on opposite cycles—we would have hardly ever seen each other."

"How many cycles has it been?"

"We've spent two dozen cycles on this planet."

"That's too many. That'd make me ancient. I should be preparing for retirement."

"Even without your injuries, you wouldn't have many left. But with them..."

She set the broth down. "How much longer do I have? How much longer do you have?"

"I'm old Maisel. And you are too—you don't look it, but if you give yourself time, you will feel it. We're old and tired. There were just a few things I wanted to do before I'd be ready—and seeing you one more time was one of them." He wiped his eyes. "It's only because of your research," he said while tapping her notebook, "that we were able to stay alive this long. You gave me plenty of amazing cycles, most of them spent with you doing the one thing you love—and that's not a bad life. I'm ready. Our kids are ready to say goodbye too."

"'Our kids.' It's strange to hear you say that." She wasn't sure whether to laugh or cry, so she turned to him hoping for an answer. She looked into his eyes, past the wrinkles and thick eyebrows and she could see him. For the first time since waking up, she could see him: Huxley—her Huxley.

"It is you, isn't it?"

"Yes. Maisel, it's me. I'm so sorry."

Her hands began to shake and he reached for them, and she let him touch her with his thin, skeleton fingers. She let this old man touch her, and she didn't flinch. She grabbed them and held on with all her might.

For the next two days, she sat with her children at the house they built on top of a small hill not far from the crash. It was made of dried and hollow stalks and pieces of her ship. It had a rudimentary plumbing system, and a small fenced-in area not far from the house where a few translucent creatures grazed. When her time came, she retired in the spot chosen for her next to her crew. A few weeks later, Huxley joined her.

Joe Graves is President of the Ohio Writers' Association. Joe began writing back in college when he wrote and produced short films. Over the last six years, he's been focused on completing his first novel, and since 2020, started writing short stories. He's been published in OWA's *Outcasts: An Anthology*, *The Worlds Within*, and *365 Tomorrows*.

Acknowledgments

The Ohio Writers' Association is deeply grateful to the following people who volunteered their time to select pieces for this anthology.

Kaleigh Cox is originally from Defiance, Ohio, but now writes from Nelsonville, Ohio, where she is raising two babies with her husband. She mostly writes creative nonfiction, and when she is not teaching, coaching, or renovating their beloved old house, she is working on writing her first novel.

Adam Doyle was born in Los Angeles and spent part of his childhood there before his family moved to Ohio. He is a graduate of The Ohio State University, where he studied creative writing. He enjoys writing about human relationships, especially family dynamics that have to do with trust and estrangement. Drawing from his life experiences, he also likes to write about the ordinary lives of gay characters.

Kelly Griffiths hikes or bikes as often as the Northeast Ohio weather allows. Her short fiction is published in *Dark Moon Digest*, *The Forge Literary Magazine*, *Reflex Fiction*, and various anthologies. *Gordon Square Review* nominated her flash "Tease" for Best Small Fictions.

Cassandra Martindell is a writer and nonprofit marketing specialist. She is currently working toward publishing her first novel and is a proud member of OWA and the Central Ohio writing community.

Christina Moore works at Ohio State University Libraries in the Bibliographic Initiatives Department. She has a BA in Art History and Anthropology from Oakland University.

Devon Ortega obtained a bachelor's degree from The Ohio State University and a master's degree in creative writing at Ohio University. She was the recipient of the 2011 Gertrude Lucille Robinson Award for poetry. She lives in Pickerington, Ohio with her husband and four children.

George Pallas is a native of Tennessee, growing up in the Nashville area. He moved to Ohio after graduating from Vanderbilt University and started a career in information technology. Now retired, George writes from his home in downtown Columbus where he lives with his wife, Sharon, and t heir dog, Sheldon Cooper.

Madison Pauquette

Chris Reed is a writer and editor who lives in Columbus, Ohio with his wife, two kids, and one truly ancient cat.

Pam Spence has been a writer of many stripes throughout her life: poet, playwright, newspaper editor, reviewer, feature writer, nonfiction book author. While having dabbled in other forms of artistic expression over the years, as expressed in this poem, she is always and forever distracted by the delicious possibility of yet another story.